# Morbid Anniversaries

K.C. Brooks

To all those who have lost someone:
To feel is to be alive, remember to feel it all.

# MORBID ANNIVERSARIES

K.C. BROOKS

# CHAPTER 1

## NORA

D EATH STOOD NEXT TO Nora, at the foot of her brother's bed, as the last of Noah's breath left his dying body. She didn't cry. She didn't plead with Death to let him stay like she had with some of the others. She didn't even say a word. Nora's brother would be the twelfth family member to leave her in as many years.

None of them got easier, she just became more numb.

A curse as real as the immortal beside her.

Nora glanced sidelong at Death, who looked back at her with an indiscernible look. It was sorrow, she realized a touch too late. It was what she should be feeling and as desperate as she was to feel it–to prove that her soul was still alive–it wasn't there. Nothing was there and the emptiness in her chest was oddly painful.

*Existentially* that is.

Death wasn't pained by Noah's passing, but she knew he hated this part–taking someone from her. He would stand as he always did, right next to Nora, so she didn't have to watch her family members' lives slip away all alone, but he wouldn't say anything. He knew she wouldn't want him to. Death would find Nora later, after he delivered him to whatever realm Noah's soul had been condemned to–likely Heaven–and they would get ice cream. Their usual routine.

Vanilla with candy coated chocolate for her, mint chip for him.

"At least you won't be condemned to Hell like him," Noah had said to Nora at their cousin Trent's funeral years ago–Trent had been exceptionally terrible.

"I don't know. I think being sequestered to one singular realm for the rest of time is  condemning in and of itself, regardless of what realm it is," Nora had responded which resulted in Noah looking at her like she had grown a second head. She simply shrugged, it was what she truly thought and the only person who didn't think her insane for it had been Death.

She first met Death when she was seven. Nora had watched her grandfather die in front of her, the life drain out of his eyes, just as she had watched Noah and all the others. When he was finally gone, she had been hysterical. Death settled a hand on her shoulder in a gesture meant in comfort, but she screamed, and she screamed, and she screamed until he assured her he wasn't there to harm her, but to collect her grandfather and show him the way.

He never specified which way, but then again that was privileged information.

Or so she was told.

Death was not as Nora had expected. He wasn't a skeleton with rotten skin stretched over his bones, nor were his eyes sunken holes in his skull. In fact, Death was tall, with hair as black as night and skin so pale she often thought she could see through it to the anatomy it protected. The blue veins running through his body shifted beneath the thin sheen in an unsettling way. His eyes were a soft green that put her oddly at ease, like the fresh green of spring she loved so much, despite the name he bore.

He was always dressed in a tailored black suit, with a gold signet ring on his right hand as if he belonged to some long standing, secret, immortal club.

Everyone has sweet, imaginary friends growing up–the bunnies and teddy bears that talk back in your playroom, who drink imaginary tea and eat imaginary cookies.

Nora's imaginary friend was *Death*.

And he wasn't imaginary nor was he sweet.

He didn't drink tea, or eat cookies with her. They didn't run around in the yard to find magical hidden worlds on the playset.

Death brought her knowledge and played with life.

He was exacting and cruel and rigid in his morality.

He was a third party collector for souls bound for both Heaven and Hell–carrying out divine sentencing for above and below. Someone had to do the dirty work, he had told her once. Souls couldn't be trusted to go on their own or they would linger. They were like leeches in that regard–desperate to cling to what they were leaving.

Over the years Nora had come to learn Death was wildly unbiased, he didn't care who he was collecting or where they were going. He never judged, never asked questions. Death had a job to do.

It was that simple.

In the days after Death took Noah, she buried his body. Nora stood at his grave, surrounded by prominent members of the town, the city council, the board of vultures from the museum, Noah's friends, Nora's only friend, Charlotte, and the caretaker of the Kramer estate, Vincent.

Nora knew she should be mourning her brother, but all she could think about was how she was next–how she was the last one left. It was the only logical next step to the Kramer's doomed lineage. Nora would be in the ground–in roughly a year's time–to the right of her grandfather.

She had to decide if she wanted to wait a year to die or if she wanted to do it on her own terms. However, Nora was exhausted of it all as her will to live was currently being lowered six feet below the ground, waiting to be covered with a pile of dirt.

People began to filter out of the cemetery leaving her behind. Vincent stopped briefly to plant a kiss on her cheek, promising to see her at home.

Charlotte was next. Nora's gorgeous, chestnut haired best friend never failed to show up when Nora needed her. She joined Nora at the edge of Noah's grave and looped an arm through hers. Nora rested her head on Charlotte's shoulder, settling into her warmth.

"You aren't going to jump in there and go with him are you?"

Nora smiled for the first time in days. "No, he's already gone to where he is going."

"And you know this how?" Charlotte asked suspiciously.

"I have a family friend who knows about these things," Nora mused, resisting the urge to turn around and look at Death.

Charlotte scoffed, "Of course you do."

The two of them stood there until everyone but Councilman Sam had left, who lifted a hand in farewell before turning to leave himself.

"God he gives me a weird vibe." Charlotte's body shuddered.

"He is Hell incarnate, Char, he gives everyone a weird vibe."

Sam was a Hell Hound, serving the town's second city council district. He wasn't exactly settling to be around, but Nora had it on good authority the Archangels were worse.

"Do you need anything before I leave?" Charlotte asked, eying Nora knowingly.

"No, head home. Thank you though, you are sweet to ask," Nora assured her.

Charlotte planted a kiss on Nora's forehead. "You are not allowed to leave me, Nora Kramer."

"I won't if I can help it."

"Your undying realism isn't charming, but I love you anyway. " Charlotte shook her head and stepped away.

"I love you too, Char," Nora whispered.

Nora was finally alone, but she couldn't hide from Death any more than she could hide from her own shadow. He sauntered up next to her, waiting until Charlotte was out of earshot.

"I know what you are thinking, little star."

"I very much doubt that, old man," she chided but it was a lie. Nora knew he knew. It was certainly written all over her face like every other emotion she'd ever had. Again, there was no hiding from Death. That included her thoughts.

"You believe this to be the end, just like you did when you were seven." He stood there, in his black suit, with his hands clasped behind his back.

"But it is this time, isn't it? I'm the last one." Tears burned in her eyes as she finally voiced her reality.

Death was quiet for a moment and said, "You are right, you are the last one left, but that does not necessarily mean you are going to die in a year's time."

He could say whatever he wanted to convince her otherwise, but the date of her death was on all thirteen gravestones in front of her. Etched in stone.

"No, because I could just do it whenever I want."

"I will not hear you speak like that, little star," Death warned, malice lacing his tone.

"Then go away," Nora suggested calmly, picking at her thumb nail.

"I am not leaving you alone. Not this time. I don't particularly trust you at the moment."

"Did you ever think that maybe I want to be alone? That being alone doesn't mean I am going to kill myself. That it might just mean that I wanted some quiet?" she asked him, finally turning to look at his face so he could see the pain burning in her eyes. Nora could be cruel if she had to, if it meant he would leave her be.

Death considered her for a moment and nodded. "You have a week to yourself. I will not bother you, but I *will* be keeping an eye on you."

"Fine." She forced her arms to remain glued to her sides, nails biting into her palms.

"Rest, scream, cry. But you will be here when I come back for you."

Nora looked up into green eyes that meant to calm her and only felt worse. The only constant in her life had been Death, as strange as that was. It was never certain that she would live for another year, never certain that she would make it to graduation, have friends, a family again, but Death was unrelentingly there through it all. No matter where she was, no matter what she was feeling, Death was there, watching over her, taking care of her, putting her mind at ease. And now she had a year left with him. A year she didn't know what to do with. A year to pack up her life and leave it behind.

When she didn't respond, he arched a dark brow.

"I will see you in a week."

He reached up to rest a soft palm on her cheek before turning away. Nora watched Death walk through the cemetery, careful not to step on any of the plots, sure and graceful in his stride.

*'It's bad luck to walk on the dead,'* he had always told her. A strange man, Death, but a good one in his own twisted way.

Exactly a year after her grandfather died, her father died and every year after that another person in her family passed away—always on the same day, always on her grandfather's birthday. Both her uncles and all of her cousins, continuing in steady succession until finally, her brother.

Death taught Nora how to deal with people dying. Her grandfather had raised her and Noah, after the harsh realization their parents would rather *not*. Nora's grandfather was the center of her universe, larger than life itself. When he died, her little seven year old brain thought that was the end. That life wasn't meant to go on after that.

In an ironic turn of events, Death showed her *life*. He showed Nora the beauty in the world and what she had to look forward to if only she chose to grow up and go on. She learned rather quickly that *living* would be a fight to the bitter end.

The immortal might have scared the shit out of her, but he had presented himself to Nora because he felt her grief so intensely, citing that it wasn't a usual occurrence for him, blaming a shift in the ether, but she didn't believe him. Nora was not convinced that she was inherently powerful enough to manipulate the makeup of the universe. She was wholly insignificant, just like everyone else.

When Nora got back to the estate, Vincent had cleaned up. The flowers and gift baskets and condolence cards that had cluttered the foyer that morning were gone. Removed from her immediate vision in an attempt to keep her relaxed–an existential state she was far from.

*Relaxed Nora* existed in an alternate universe, a different dimension. Every year, false sympathies would flood in for the family. Then after a while, those sympathies were addressed to her and Noah. Until this year, they arrived with only her name scrawled on the front.

Nora itched to rip them apart, set them all ablaze, smash the vases.

In her mind she did. In her mind she watched as shards of glass and flower petals and cards flew across the room breaking into a million pieces–how it satisfied her to destroy them all with her own hands.

Instead she had stood in the center of the foyer that morning, dressed in her black dress, black tights, black coat and shoes, staring at a stack of cards addressed to '*Miss Nora Kramer,*' drowning in roses and lilies, without moving a muscle. A veritable statue.

Vincent had watched her from the doorway until he couldn't bear it any longer. He took her by the shoulders, walked her out of the house, put her into a car, and sent her to the funeral home. Nora's body was operating wholly outside of her will, a default setting that knew where she needed to be without having to make any real decisions herself.

But now the foyer was as empty as the house. Nora was all that remained. She was utterly and completely alone and for the first time since her brother died she let herself cry.

It came in violent sobs until she doubled over and puked into the sole remaining vase on the table–a blue porcelain one that had been there her entire life. After she was done vomiting everything she hadn't eaten, she slumped to her knees and melted to the floor.

The cold marble bit into Nora's skin, but she was thankful for it. Thankful to at least feel *something*, proving she wasn't completely dead inside. Marble tiles warmed underneath her, the house always adapting itself depending on what she needed, taking care of her as much as Vincent and Death. As much as Noah had. It was forever in tune to her volatile emotions–running hot or cold depending on the source of her ire.

*It is all too much*, she thought as she laid on the floor, fighting the pull of sleep from the warm stone. It was too much to be expected to go on when everyone she had ever loved had left this life already.

Too much loss. Too much pain.

In order for it to not consume her, Nora had to choose not to feel something and choosing not to feel the good was easier, because it didn't allow her to hope.

Charlotte thought her a terrible pessimist, but her friend was everything that was good in this world. But no matter how hard she tried, Charlotte didn't understand because she had never lost anyone before. The thought that in a year's time her best friend would have to grieve her made the pain in her stomach unbearable.

The worst thought of them all flooded her brain–maybe it was supposed to be this way. Maybe she was supposed to outlive them all because she could handle it. Nora decided whoever determined that particular aspect of her fate was an asshole.

But all her pain was temporary anyway. Once she was dead she wouldn't feel anything at all. It was the people who were left alive that death hurt. The fallacy of living was just that–people had to keep living, even after death, and it wasn't enough to hope it didn't cause people pain because it would.

Pain didn't reside in death, it resided in life.

Nora fell asleep, to the gentle hum of the quiet house and the warmth of the floor, too exhausted to fight her own mind any longer.

# CHAPTER 2

## NORA

Nora spent the next week sleeping and drinking enough for a man twice her size. Charlotte brought over food, knowing full well Nora wasn't feeding herself. Only after she ate enough for Charlotte's liking did her friend drag Nora out of the house, against her will, to a bar citing that if she were Hell bent on drinking, she shouldn't do it alone.

She woke up the next morning to violently expel everything from the night before and then some. When she finished retching, her body refused to move, leaving her only option to lay on the bathroom floor shivering.

It became cyclical.

Wake up, vomit, sleep, repeat.

Everything hurt. Her body was sore, her brain was barely functioning, her emotions were in tatters. Nora was a certifiable mess and in no shape to go anywhere. She thanked whatever God was listening that she took online classes for her half-assed degree in art history. One that she wouldn't finish, of course, considering her impending fate, but at least she didn't have to physically be in class.

Her grandfather left the estate to Nora and Noah in a trust, which Noah acquired when he turned eighteen. Until then, her grandfather's caretaker assumed ownership of the property, and of them. Lawyers and financial advisors helped her manage the money, make charitable donations, and allocate funding for many of the town's city council campaigns.

Vincent still lived in the guest house on the estate, looking after Nora for the most part, but letting her live her life without too much input. However, the occasional side eye was thrown Nora's way at her more questionable actions and outbursts. The old man was not the biggest fan of her temper, and in the last few years, she and Noah had been arguing more and more with increasing volatility. Vincent had always scolded her for yelling so harshly at her brother.

Nora would miss his derision now that Noah was gone.

When she finally made it back to her room from the bathroom floor she settled into her window seat and watched the last of the leaves fall from the trees. Nora loved this time of year despite the annual cosmic repossession of her family members.

She loved the way that the trees were bare, unable to hide behind their leaves and flowers, the world finally seeing them for what they were beneath the frill. She loved the way the fire fought to keep homes warm, and the people in them alive until spring.

More than anything, Nora loved the fall because it made the spring all the more sweet. Spring was her favorite season as it was a physical reminder that there is life after death that tricked her brain into believing it too.

Below her window Vincent raked the leaves, a task she had been putting off. There were staff members at the estate, but Nora never wanted a grounds crew. It was more fulfilling to do the work herself.

Vincent looked up to her window as if he could sense her watching him. Nora pressed her palm to the cool window, to which he lifted a hand in return with a sad smile and a nod.

A dark figure emerged at the back of the property, stealing Nora's attention. He was in his usual black, foreboding and omnipresent. Nora knew she should be afraid of Death. His presence should make her tremble, cower, run–deep in her bones screamed a warning she couldn't quite place.

But it did the opposite. It comforted Nora to see him, to have him near. She felt most afraid when he wasn't around. A feeling that surely wasn't *normal*, but then again, she wasn't a normal girl. Nora wasn't sure she ever had been, whether that was good or bad–she didn't have a clue.

Death walked across the grounds towards Vincent, they exchanged a few words and shook hands in their typical uncomfortable, impartial greeting. Vincent knew Death, but didn't enjoy his presence in the way Nora did–a normal reaction, if normal were to be a spectrum.

When she was younger and there were lots of people around, Death could pretend to not exist, knowing someone was taking care of her, regardless of how loose the supervision had been. When she got older and the number of people looking after her dwindled down to just Vincent, Death introduced himself, told him the truth.

The caretaker thought it odd that an immortal was personally looking out for a mortal girl, but he was ultimately happy to not be alone in the task, so he kept quiet.

Death had never been menacing or inappropriate. He knew what Nora needed and helped her where he could–she needed someone to talk to that she wouldn't terrify. Someone who wouldn't run from the dark, depraved thoughts swimming in her brain.

Maybe Nora was borderline nihilistic, but what really was

the point of it all if everyone died anyway? Death was coming for every person one day or the next.

He didn't dispel these thoughts of hers, but rather answered her questions exactly without pandering to an innocence she had long discarded.

They had an understanding, her and Death. He would be truthful with her about life and the universe and she would *attempt* to enjoy it. Nora had for the most part enjoyed it, when she at least had Noah with her.

Noah had been her antithesis–full of light and life. He was the sun and she a distant star, destined to shine at different times, to burn in ways.

By the time Death entered the house, she had changed and made her way down to the drawing room to curl up on a deep green sofa.

"Good to see you still in the land of the living," Death chided.

Nora scoffed, "You should have seen me hours ago, there wasn't much life to be seen then."

Death shook his head and sat down on the settee across from her. The drawing room was full of plush sofas and chairs and cozy blankets. A fire burned in the hearth which the house had lit for her when she settled there to wait for Death.

"Have you calmed down since we last spoke?"

"Of course not," she challenged.

"Perfect, because I have a task for you," he replied, steepling his fingers beneath his chin.

"Oh?" Nora's eyebrows jumped up her forehead. Death never had *tasks* for her, in fact he routinely kept her out of his business.

"I want you to come to work with me today."

Nora made a face. "*Work?* Like to collect souls?"

"Yes," said Death flatly.

"I don't particularly like that you call it *work*." In fact it deeply unsettled her.

"It is my job–what I have been tasked to do. What would you call it if *not* work?"

She considered this for a moment. "I think I am going to call it penance. I can only imagine you did something foul to deserve this."

"I can assure you that is not the case."

"Or maybe someone really has it out for you."

"No one has it—"

Nora cut him off. "Is it God?"

"Nora."

"It's God isn't it."

Death sighed.

"I knew it." Nora shook her head. The movement alone made her stomach twist again.

"Just put your coat and shoes on and come with me. And it's cold out so bring a scarf would you?" Death stood, reaching his full, towering height. He was unnaturally tall and equally as lean, as if someone had overly stretched him out. It only took him three steps to cross the room to the sofa she laid on.

"Ugh," Nora sighed, but let him pull her off the sofa, despite her muscles disapproving of her use of them. She shrugged on her coat *and* scarf, slipped into her sneakers, and met Death by the back door. They exited the house the way he entered, through the grounds, passing Vincent on the way. Nora flashed the caretaker a reassuring smile that he reluctantly returned.

"How are we getting there?" she asked. It was drizzling, barely a mist, but enough to annoy her.

"We are walking." Death looked at her indignantly.

"Walking?" Nora groaned. "Where is this place?"

A hint of a smile flashed over his face. The bastard knew exactly what he was doing to her. "On the other side of town."

Nora suppressed the urge to flip him off, but it didn't take much effort what with her body in active war against her. "I figured your next job would be on another continent or something."

"Other continents are not my domain." He continued his brisk pace with his hands shoved deep in his pockets. The collar of his coat popped up to protect from the wind, which struck Nora as odd considering his immortality shielded him from the changing temperature.

Nora grabbed his arm to stop him. "What do you mean your domain?"

"You are a bright little star. You know what a *domain* means."

She scowled as her mind reeled at this information. The entire time they have been acquainted, Nora assumed she knew him–that he collected souls from everywhere. It never occurred to her that he was not the only *Death* to exist in this world.

"Why didn't you tell me that before?"

Death shrugged. "You never asked."

Nora dropped her hand and they continued over the cobblestone streets. There was a lot she had never asked him about himself. All of her questions had been about life itself and the realms and what Hell was like–she never asked about Heaven as she assumed her crude disposition would hinder her admittance to the realm above.

Nora had never really asked Death about himself and suddenly her selfishness was overwhelming. A million questions flooded her brain, but she didn't know where to start.

"Your other ward. What is he like?" she asked, picking a direction.

Death smiled fully, regarding her. "He is nothing like you." Nora scoffed and backhanded his arm for saying it as if he meant it offensively. "He is your opposite in every way–wholly optimistic, excited about life, loves math and science and is bloody brilliant."

"Not smarter than me though," Nora jested, but she had to make sure.

He laughed, "No, not smarter than you, little star. But he is quite alone as well, so you have that in common."

"He doesn't have any family?" Nora's chest tightened thinking this boy had no one. No one except Death–marking them similar in that regard.

"No immediate family, but he has a few good friends and a distant great aunt who lives far away. She visits when she can." Death's eyes focused on something far in the distance.

"Well it is good he has someone," Nora admitted, understanding coursing through her veins. The confession was as much about this boy as it was about her. It was good *she* had someone–multiple someones.

Death, Charlotte, Vincent.

Death caught her meaning and gave her a tight lipped smile. "It is."

The scarf had been a terrible suggestion as Nora was sweating out every toxin from the last week. Each one burning through her skin with an unrequited vengeance. The warmer she became, the more she wished she would pass out, if only to stop moving for a moment.

They walked down uneven streets, side by side, in comfortable silence–in the metaphysical sense that her brain was comfortable with the silence, however, physically, she couldn't be further from comfort–until they came to a stop in front of a deep blue house with a bright orange door. The color match was odd, Nora thought, but she didn't hate it.

"They won't see or hear you while we are in there–I will mask you. You can talk if you need to," Death murmured, his eyes glued to a propped open upstairs window.

Nora shoved her hands in her pockets and nodded, keeping her own eyes on that strange orange door. They entered quietly into a small home that reeked of death–whoever they were there for had been sick for a long time. It was the way it smelled of chemicals, too, too sterile and rotten at the same time.

The entryway was cramped with a bench on one side and a small round mirror on the other that exposed her languid skin and the mist clinging to her hair and eyelashes. Shoes littered the floor as if discarded in haste. A faded blue runner blanketed the length of the hall.

The house was quiet. The type of quiet that settled on a space when people were waiting for death. A silence where people were afraid to draw breath, too nervous that any sound or movement would spook the person into the next life.

It was a stillness that froze a person when death was near. A gentle nervousness. A motionless tremor.

So still the person could feel the blood rushing through their body to supply their vital organs. Nerve endings prickling from impulses their brain sent to remind them that they were, in fact, *alive*.

Nora followed Death up the stairs into an overwarm bedroom. In the center lay a tiny girl on a small twin bed. She couldn't have been any older than twelve and yet there was no doubt it was her they were there for. Nora's breath caught when she took in the sight of the girl, a shell of her real self.

The girl reminded her of Izzy, her cousin who died when they were both this age. She had been so small, too skinny—all knees and elbows. The cause of her death had been the same as all the others. Sudden cardiac arrest. Each one fell sick in the morning with a fever that lingered until their heart eventually gave out.

Nora had watched them all go. It felt necessary for someone to be with them, so she had taken it upon herself. Call it masochistic, but Nora didn't do it for herself, she did it for them—so they wouldn't be alone.

Noah however, had chosen to stay far away. He didn't need to see them all pass, stating he would see them at the funeral. *Maybe that was how he retained his optimism,* Nora thought.

The air in the room was a mix of warmth and chill as a fire burned in the hearth, but a window on the far side was wedged open, letting in the cool, fall air. The part of her that enjoyed life, small as it may be, warmed thinking the girl's parents left the window open for her soul to exit to its next destination.

It was a common superstition. Nora had done the same until Death had told her souls left with him. Not through the window, but right out the front door. But she chose to appreciate the gesture, knowing it brought these people comfort.

"How long has she been dying?" Nora asked Death quietly, despite knowing the couple couldn't hear her.

"Several years. The family has tried everything, but the sickness has long had her in its clutches." Death looked over the girl fondly, like he had stood at this very spot several times before.

Nora supposed that in a way, Death had to know the dying. That it would be strange if he didn't. How lonely she imagined his job was.

"Where will you take her?" Nora asked, knowing Death wouldn't answer. She decided the girl had to be going to Heaven as there couldn't have been anything in her short life to warrant her entry to Hell. Nora said a silent prayer to Noah, Izzy, and Carter to watch over this girl.

The parents were in chairs on either side of the bed, leaning over their daughter, listening to her breaths, each with a hand stretched across her body to hold onto each other. Their other hand clutching the girl as if it were enough to keep her here.

Nora desperately wished it was.

"It's almost time," Death whispered, never taking his eyes off the girl, but Nora didn't need his confirmation to feel what was happening.

Time slowed as the girl sucked in one final breath through pale, chapped lips, her chest rising fully with it. When her chest fell and the breath left her frail body, the ether shifted, as if the universe was letting them all know the girl was gone.

Then like it never happened at all, the universe's hold on time ceased. A tear slipped silently down Nora's cheek and she had the overwhelming urge to be anywhere else but in that room.

Nora backed out of the door as the mother began to wail and the father slipped from his chair to his knees on the floor. Death reached for Nora, but she put a hand out to stop him.

He shouldn't have brought her there.

Again, it was all too much and Nora didn't know how he stood there and watched people die. She didn't know how he handled it.

Didn't know how she had done it herself for all these years in a row.

Nora fled the house, desperate to fill her lungs with air that wasn't laced with death. She ran down the street, as fast as her aching limbs would let her, needing to put considerable distance between herself and that menacing orange door.

The fresh air did nothing to calm her breathing or soother her nerves or cool her searing skin, but it was better than the air in that horrid room. Nora ripped her scarf from her neck, letting it flutter to the ground as she leaned against the rough brick wall of a house.

She was twelve again, curled up next to Izzy's too warm body. Her breaths were racing through her and Nora was too aware of what was coming.

Death appeared, just as he had for all the others. Nora screamed at him to leave until her throat was raw. He couldn't take Izzy from her–her twin, her sweet cousin, her best friend. *Anyone* but Izzy, she had begged. But Nora's twelve year old will hadn't been enough that day.

He took Izzy anyway and Nora was never the same.

The immortal found her minutes, hours, seconds, later slumped to the ground against the brick house. Sweat dripped down her back, beaded on her forehead, turned her hands clammy. The people walking by probably thought ill of her.

*Let them,* she thought, *they had no idea the true cruelty of this life.*

Nora heard what swirled around the town about her–they all thought her the strange Kramer heiress, too quiet, too stuck up.

Now they'd think she lost her mind.

Maybe she had.

"Come on little star, let's go get some ice cream." Death loomed over her, hand outstretched to help her off the ground.

Nora scoffed as the fire in her chest flared and turned her tear streaked face up to him, forcing on him the dirtiest look she could muster.

"Ice cream?" she yelled as she pushed herself off the ground, swatting at his hand. "You want to take me to get ice cream after *that*?"

A line formed between his brows, the corners of his lips pulled tight. "I thought you would want to stick to what we normally do."

"Oh fuck you," she yelled, slamming her palms into his chest to force him away from her. "What we normally do? None of this is normal. It never has been *normal*."

"Nor—" he started, but never got to finish.

"Why did you bring me here? Did you think this would make me feel better? Did you think you could coerce me into wanting to stay alive?" Nora was crying fully now. She hated him seeing her like this, but she was at her end. Frayed, completely unraveled.

"I thought it would be good for you to see that other people experience loss too."

Nora laughed, "I am not a naïve little girl, Death. I never have been. I am aware other people experience loss. So painfully aware that it threatens to eat me alive, but no matter how hard you try, you cannot manage my pain. It doesn't just go away because you don't want me to feel it. I am not like you. I don't have the luxury of feeling nothing."

By the end, her voice had raised, drawing even more attention from the people hurrying by. Hurt flashed across Death's harsh features, but Nora didn't care about being harsh. She meant what she said.

He opened his mouth to say more, but she cut him off again. There wasn't anything he could say to fix it all, to soothe her burning lungs and she didn't care to hear him try.

"You know what, Death? *Fuck off.* I don't want to see you again until you come back to drag my soul to Hell." Nora snatched her scarf off the ground and left him in the middle of the street. It didn't matter where he went, so long as he didn't follow her home.

# CHAPTER 3

## DEATH

D EATH FOLLOWED NORA HOME–AT a distance of course. He may not be the smartest immortal alive, but he wasn't *that* stupid.

Fighting with her was often inevitable, no matter how much he hated it. She was brilliantly full of anger. An anger he loved, even when she was angry with him. It proved to him that she still had something to feel underneath all that pain. That there were things she loved enough to be angry with. That he hadn't messed her up too badly.

Death knew what was coming for her before he met her–it was why he revealed himself to her in the first place. Death's particular employment came with privileged information and horrific realities. All he had ever done was try to help her through it.

There was a ledger.

It wasn't a good ledger telling him how much money he had or one keeping his social calendar. It was a ledger containing the death dates of every person in his domain.

He hated it and kept it close at the same time.

The dates weren't always final, changing occasionally if the person dying made an ill thought deal with a particularly fiery person. But his ledger was the very reason Death didn't have friends–he knew when they were going to die. It sat heavy on his soul knowing when each person would pass, knowing where he would be taking them.

It was easier to distance himself, easier to not get attached.

A person's end destination would only change if they managed to somehow influence the minds of the divine, which was not common, but not unheard of either. It didn't take much to condemn a person to Hell, as most mortals made inherently terrible decisions, but it took cosmos altering adjustments to change the mind of the unmerciful being above.

Too many souls pleaded with Death to take them to Heaven as he dragged them to Hell. Too many looked forward to meeting loved ones again when Death knew it would never happen.

It was a horrific job, Death's, but one he has done for almost the entirety of his immortal life. Nora assumed he was being punished, but the truth is that he had volunteered. Someone had to do it. He hadn't pissed off God, or the Devil for that matter.

Neither being cared who brought them the souls they were owed.

Death hated being idle and thousands of years with no purpose and nothing to do pushed him into his current predicament. It wasn't terrible at first, but then it became agonizing. Wholly unbearable. The people he knew and many he had loved were on that wretched ledger of his.

It was a blessing and a curse to know. It allowed him to assess how much time he had with a person, to know what he could accomplish with them before they left him.

But the knowing ate at him. Reduced him to a version of himself he didn't recognize–one that lied and pretended reality wasn't as exacting as he knew it to be.

*"I really hate this time of year,"* a lingering soul said from the opposite side of the street. Death was inclined to agree with the dead man, but he made it a habit to ignore the souls who remained in this realm, no matter what they said.

Death decided a long time ago that he wouldn't get attached. That he would mind his own business and keep his head down–e had a job to do–but Death had a soft spot for children. Especially the children of those who had made monstrous deals with the Devil himself. It mattered not what the deal was, just that these children were being left alone because of it.

Death's wretched heart, his undying ability to care, would be the end of him one of these days.

He wasn't exactly caring nor overly kind. In fact it was better if he was blunt–made his job easier. Death's lack of tenderness was for a reason because the last thing he needed were people attaching themselves to him as they left their life. Many colleagues of his have had souls cling to them and in turn haunt their waking hours.

It wasn't an exact science, but a meticulous effort. He refused to allow gross mismanagement to affect him in such a way–despite the menacing council letter burning a hole in his pocket and the building pressure behind his eyes.

Death had been several wards over the millennias of his employment. It had been over a hundred years between his last ward and Nora–then a few years later, Charles. He remembered each of them fondly, but there was something about these two. Something that challenged him. It was not a routine thing for him to look out for children long enough to see them grow into adults.

But again, Nora and Charles were different. The force of

their existences was deafening. Death could feel their movements, their wants and needs. The ether shifted around them in response and the cosmos itself seemed sentient in that regard, blanketing them in concern, alerting Death to their being as though their makeup was that of the universe itself.

Death had told Nora how different she was from Charles, but they weren't. Not really. In personality, they were night and day. Dark and light. The sun and a distant star. Charles burned with optimism, whereas Nora exacted harsh reality. But they were the same for the simple fact they were both strong, resilient, hard headed, and deeply feeling.

He followed Nora until he watched her cross the threshold of the house without a glance in his direction, the heavy door slamming shut behind her. Death was stung by her coldness, but then again he couldn't be more thankful she was alive. He exhaled his relief and the muscles in his shoulders finally loosened.

Death was more worried about her than he had ever been about anyone else. She had always been morose, but it was different this time. The shift in her being was sharper, cutting at him like a knife to his chest trying to excise his heart, as if there was one worth getting to.

Nora always told him she knew he wasn't sweet, but when he took her to get ice cream after the death of her grandfather, she called him exactly that–sweet. It was the first of three times he would be sweet to her in her life.

They were sitting at a table, just the two of them, eating their respective ice cream choices. Nora's vanilla ice cream was topped with enough candied chocolate to rot her teeth. She had been silent for a long time, almost to the dregs of her cup, when she finally looked up at him. The tears had finally stopped, turning her gray eyes to hardened stone.

"This was sweet of you to do." Her voice had been quiet, timid as she wasn't yet sure how to speak to Death in a way that felt normal.

"I am not routinely sweet, little one," Death warned her. He didn't want her to get any ideas about him.

Her eyes lingered on him a moment before she said, "That's okay. Not many people are." Nora forced a tightlipped smile across her porcelain face, returning her attention to the last bite of her ice cream. "And it's 'little star.' He calls me 'little star.'"

*That banker is going to get what is coming to him,* said another soul whose anger radiated off of him in dense waves.

She may be cross with him, but Nora was a hot headed. All wrath and sharp edges. He smirked to himself thinking of someone who was her exact opposite. Someone soft and warm. Someone whose presence would positively infuriate her, sparking an idea in Death's undying conniving brain.

He pulled the letter from the city council out of his pocket and dropped it in the bin on the street corner before heading home to his modest house on the other side of town. A new found lightness in his step.

The second time Death was sweet to Nora, he sent her a friend.

# CHAPTER 4

## CHARLES

"I HAVE A FAVOR to ask of you."

Charles looked curiously at Death from across the table where they sat in his kitchen. The table was small, but it was just Charles in the flat so it was the perfect size. Death had never asked Charles for a favor in the seven years they had known each other, but the immortal had always looked out for him. If there was any way for Charles to repay him, he'd help Death however he could.

"I need you to check in on someone for me," Death stated as though it wasn't atypical for him to have people to check in on. But it *was* strange. Death routinely didn't give a damn about others–it was a shock that he looked after Charles at all–and the immortal definitely didn't have any friends Charles knew about.

"Who is this someone?" Charles asked.

"My other ward."

Charles stumbled over his words. "Your other ward? I thought I was your only one."

Death regarded him for a moment, head tilting to the side. "Well you certainly are special Charles, but no, I have one other." Instead of waiting for Charles's brain to catch up, Death continued. "Her name is Nora and she lives on the west end of town at the Kramer Estate. She is currently quite cross with me so I want you to–you know–go be you."

"Be me?" Death had said it as though Charles were a type *to be.*

"Yes, your overly sunshiney self should do her wonders." Death smirked mischievously. He was plotting something.

"And I am just supposed to do what? Drop by unannounced and say hi? Hang out? Take her to get tea?"

"She prefers caramel lattes, but just do whatever it is that makes you all bright and happy. She could use a touch of it, melancholy as she is," Death grumbled.

Charles's mind was spinning with a million different questions. Death was sending him to his other ward–Nora, who just so happened to be a billionaire heiress–to cheer her up for reasons he was unwilling to elaborate on. Regardless of his endless questions, Death was asking, so Charles would help.

"What is she like, Nora?"

Death took in a deep breath and blew it out slowly, letting his cheeks puff out. "She is blunt. A bit crass. Smart as a whip though, so keep your head on straight or she will run circles around you. She just lost her brother, Noah. They were very close and she hasn't been her normal self since."

Charles watched Death's eyes drift off like they were seeing her in the distance, full of worry and regret. "Okay, I'll do it, I'll go."

"This afternoon," Death cleared his throat, rising from the chair. "Be quick about it and let me know how it goes after."

"Of course." Charles nodded and watched Death stride off, through the front door of his flat.

Nora worried Death and that worried Charles. In all the years of knowing him, Death has been the perfect image of collected. Always put together–his black suit immaculate, not a single worry line on his several thousand year old, unaged face.

But Nora, whoever she was to Death, made his brow furrow, creating a deep crease in the center. It was an odd look for Death. Worry made him fidget, constantly shifting his weight, pulling at his tailored sleeves.

Charles finished breakfast, cleaned up, and rushed to get ready–a quick shower and shave of his day old stubble. He couldn't very well go over to the Kramer Estate looking any- thing less than put together.

The entire town knew of the Kramers. They were a wealthy family of art collectors and philanthropists. Norman Kramer had built up most of the family's wealth himself in the 70's and 80's, buying and selling pieces of art, and auctioning off his own work. When he died in the early 2000's he left his entire estate to two of his grandchildren and if Charles was assuming correctly, Nora was one of those grandchildren.

A stark difference from him and his own family–a mess of drunks and criminals–except for his mum who had been the only family to stick with him when he was sick. Tessa was the best person Charles had ever known to have walked this earth.

Charles shook the memory of his mother from his mind. It only disheartened him to think of her–to remember that he lived in a world without her–and if he was being completely honest, it made him irrationally angry. It was best not to think of her at all.

An hour and a half later, Charles was standing in the drive of the great Kramer Estate dressed in his best navy button down and slacks. He tried to tame his hair, but the only thing that might have done it would have been to shave it all off which

was not a decision he was ever going to make. Running a hand
through the thick locks, he shook off the small drops of rain
that had settled on the walk over and took a deep breath.

The Kramer Estate was one from a storybook. An enormous
gray stone mansion that could easily be a small museum. Stone
steps led up to the massive wooden doors which of course were
the type adorned with iron door knockers the size of his head.
The higher up the stairs he climbed, the more it felt like the
house was swallowing him whole.

It didn't help his nerves that he could feel a hum radiating
from the house, as if it sensed his presence. Charles did *not* enjoy
the feeling that he was being assessed, by a house no less.

*Inanimate objects do not have feelings, Charles, nor do they possess
the ability to carry out action.*

Reminding himself of that fact had little effect on his nerves.
He shook out his hands reaching up to grab the massive iron
before him. Charles hit the knocker on the door twice and the
effort alone felt excessive, the sound rattling through his body.
It felt too loud, rendering him too vulnerable.

Moments later, the door swung open, in slow motion, to
reveal a frail older man in a gray knit sweater and similarly gray
slacks. The man was dwarfed by the massive space looming
behind him.

"How may I help you, sir?" The old man's voice was deep
and grumbly like he didn't use it enough.

"Good afternoon, my name is Charles Riley and I am here
to see Nora," Charles said carefully, trying his best to seem
unassuming. He was after all, a stranger, showing up uninvited
to ask after the young woman who owned this house. It was
mildly improper.

The old man stifled a solemn look and stepped aside. "Please, come in."

"Thank you," Charles muttered as he crossed the threshold into a grand foyer.

The foyer alone was bigger than his entire flat. It was a long oval shaped room with two staircases on either side leading to the second floor. Hallways extended the length of the house to his right and left and the back of the room opened up to another part of the house.

The floors were finely polished, white marble, covered with a deep forest green rug. A thick wooden table was positioned at the center and on it sat a pale blue porcelain vase. Illuminating the entire entryway was a large crystal chandelier that hung from the ceiling. The walls that lined the stairs were a deep brown and covered in works of art that likely cost more money than Charles would ever see in his lifetime.

"Miss Nora, you have a visitor," called the old man.

After a moment, a sweet distant voice from the hallway at the back of the foyer responded, "I am not taking visitors, Vincent."

The old man sighed and shot Charles an apologetic look. "Miss Nora," Vincent said a little more sternly.

"Fine. I'm coming," she shouted, slightly more annoyed this time.

Moments later, in strode a force of a girl, no older than Charles himself. Her blonde hair was pink at the ends and pulled half up with a few pieces loose around her face. Gold necklaces hung from her slim neck and matching earrings shifted as she tilted her head to look at him.

Black jeans stopped just above her ankles, showing off her bare feet. The pale blue jumper she wore tricked his brain into thinking her gray eyes were actually a shade of blue.

Whatever color they really were, they were large and round and knowing.

"You must be Nora. I'm Charles. A *mutual friend* asked me to come by and introduce myself." He extended his hand toward her, but she kept her arms crossed over her chest.

Nora scoffed and looked sidelong at Vincent who stood there with his mouth taught and eyebrows raised. Her eyes rolled back to Charles. When it was clear she wasn't going to shake his hand, he dropped it back to his side.

"Well, Chuck, you can tell our *mutual friend* that I am fine and I don't need his lackey checking in on me." She smiled and turned on her heel to disappear back down the hallway.

Against his better judgment he took off after her. "Excuse me. I understand you are cross with him, but you have never met me and I am not 'his lackey,' by the way," he said with a little more attitude than he had intended to, but her calling him 'Chuck' and outright dismissing him stroked his annoyance in a way he wasn't used to. "He looks after me, just as he looks after you."

That made Nora abandon her retreat, causing Charles to almost run into the back of her. She turned to face him. "I assume you are here because he told you how terribly dispositioned I am?"

*Sarcasm,* Charles noted and he was happy to play along. "He raved about it."

The muscle in her jaw spasmed. "It has been a tense few weeks and it was not my intention to come off initially abrasive. Nonetheless, I do not need a babysitter, so you can go tell Death I'm fine," Nora sighed and the sadness she was masking flickered on her face for just a second.

"I am more than happy to help with whatever it is you

are doing," Charles offered, standing his ground as much as possible.

Nora's eyes narrowed as she crossed her arms back over her chest. It seemed a natural position for them to be in.

"Come on, I am a phenomenal assistant. I'll do all the things you hate doing," Charles pleaded with her. He owed it to Death to try and Charles wasn't known to give up easily.

She stared at him a moment longer, causing him to squirm under her stoney gaze. "Fine. You can help so long as you keep quiet."

"Perfect," he smiled, "just tell me where to start."

Nora opened her mouth to say something, but closed it again without a word inclining her head towards the end of the hall. Charles followed her swift pace into a dusty room filled with boxes. It looked to have been a library at one time, considering the shelves that were built into the walls from floor to ceiling and the piles of books were everywhere. Not a single book remained on any of the shelves.

The ceiling extended to what was certainly the second story. Windows covered the one wall that wasn't littered in book-shelves casting the room in a damp light as the clouds blocked out the sun like usual.

A grand piano sat in one corner by the wall of windows, looking like it hadn't been played in years.

*What it must have been like to grow up with all of these books and a house full of music and people,* Charles thought, smiling to himself. He imagined playing in the garden, just beyond the windows, with siblings he didn't have as his parents, whole and healthy, watched them from inside. Charles was positive he would have never have been bored in a place like this.

How it felt like life thrived within these walls.

He watched Nora as they cleaned in silence. It felt wrong to be packing up all the books, but she was sure in her movements, confident in her actions. If packing up this room pained her in any way, Nora didn't show it.

Death had said she just lost her brother, so he felt it would be best to stay away from that topic of conversation—if he found it in him to break her one rule. Mainly, Charles was curious what brought Death to her—why he had chosen to take care of her.

It had never been a question why Death had come for Charles. He had been dying—or so he thought until Death showed up and took his mother, leaving Charles miraculously healthy. His thirteen year old self had been devastated, forcing him to believe his mother's death would be the end of him.

In a twisted turn of events, it had been Death that showed him it was, in fact, a second chance at life. Tessa had given Charles his life at the expense of her own and he wasn't going to waste it.

Charles decided then and there—there being several weeks after his mother's funeral—that he would have a love for life. He would cherish the gift she had given him.

His drunk of a father had begged off years prior and his great aunt traveled to check in on him when she could, but it was the neighbor across the street from Charles who kept him alive, for the most part. The old man made him dinner every night and breakfast before school and in return, Charles did his house work. It went on that way for several years until the old man's family took him away. But Charles was almost an adult then, capable of looking after himself.

He itched to talk to Nora, to know her, to understand what made her *her*. It wasn't everyday that Charles met another person who knew Death in the way he did. It connected them so horrifically, it was almost beautiful. But Charles had shown up unannounced, which gave off an implicitly *creepy* vibe so in order to respect her wishes, he kept his mouth shut–*against his better judgment he might add*–and helped her pack up the books.

The act of it leaving him melancholic and curious.

*This would be quite the house to move,* Charles thought. He made a mental note to ask where she was moving, because surely there weren't many places large enough to fit all her stuff. It wasn't an answer he needed, but one he wanted.

Unfortunately Charles was about as likely to get a response from Nora as he was to inherit the house he was standing in.

# CHAPTER 5

## NORA

NORA THOUGHT CHARLES INFURIATING for several reasons. The main reason being the boy smiled while he worked for fucksake, forcing her to wonder what thoughts were tumbling around in his brain that kept a grin plastered to his face while stuffing books into boxes.

It was nauseating.

If she hadn't been furious with Death already, her irritation may have been manageable, but it was currently threatening to bubble over and ignite a fire large enough to engulf the entire estate and part of the town.

She didn't *need* friends–a concept which Death should understand, but refused to. Nora had one friend and that was enough. It was already overwhelming knowing the minimal amount of people she allowed to know her, would have to mourn her in a year.

Charles was also infuriatingly handsome. Slim, but not concerningly so with watchful, vibrant, blue eyes she was jealous of. Nora felt self conscious of her gray ones and their drabness when his were so full of life.

Another undying feature of his were his rosy cheeks. At first Nora thought they had been pink because he had walked over, bundled up in a coat that was now discarded atop a box close to him. But it had been long enough now that he should have cooled down, that the rosiness should have receded–it hadn't–leading her to believe they were permanently blushed.

*Maybe he ran warm?* Nora surmised, trying and failing to suppress the other thought that crept into her mind–that if she were to press her palms to his face, she could feel just how warm they were, that maybe they would warm her.

*Get a grip.*

Then there was his hair.

*That fucking hair.*

She wanted to touch it, run her fingers through it, confirm it was as soft as it looked. It didn't have any order, each strand looking as though it had a different direction in which to be.

Maybe she should be thanking Death for sending her something pretty to look at in her final months of this life.

Charles had mostly respected her wishes thus far, making him not as annoying as he could have been. And the feeling that arose in Nora when she looked at him, the one that both revolted and intrigued her, helped his case.

He assisted with the packing in silence until Vincent decided to join them, wherein the two of them mindlessly chatted away, discussing everything from the estate to her grandfather to Charles's own family–which he did not elaborate much on–to his schooling.

Charles took in everything, watching her as she worked. Nora could feel his eyes tracking her movements, surely logging everything to report back to Death.

She should have known that Death wouldn't have left her completely alone after she dismissed him. Nora had hurt him and for that he would cosmically punish her. The smug bastard was probably off somewhere basking in the delight of her discomfort.

It hadn't been her intention to hurt Death, but she had been reduced to a million scattered shards of herself, all sharp and craving blood, wanting nothing more than for him to leave her alone. Nora saw it on Death's typically expressionless face right before she turned to leave.

In his wake was a sunshiny boy with unwavering positivity. He was dressed well, probably thought he needed to dress up coming to the estate, but it was a moot point–there was no one left to impress here and the house, sentient as it was, did not need a bigger ego.

It was funny, *almost*, that Death sent her complete opposite to keep her company. A diabolical move on his part. Charles was warm and smiley where she was cold and angry. He was full of life and she was next on Death's list.

How she envied him.

How she didn't.

*Charlotte would like Charles,* Nora thought. Someone to match her best friend's positive energy. Nora frowned at the returning thought that she would miss her best friend when she left this world. Or rather Charlotte would miss her, Nora realized morbidly, as she wouldn't be doing much *missing* where she was going, which was likely to Hell.

In the world that existed outside her thoughts, Vincent was telling Charles how Nora and her brother used to sit in this room all day and read from the very books they were packing up. Vincent was convinced Noah was going to get through them all, before he died.

"Vincent," Nora warned. The caretaker pressed his lips together. "We aren't talking about Noah."

"Of course, Miss Nora." Vincent returned to his work, lowering a stack of books into the box in front of him.

Charles watched her from his corner of the room, behind a rather unstable stack of books, his smile finally gone. She could see the questions turning in his brain–all of which were bound to be invasive.

"Why are you packing up all the books anyway?"

*There it was.*

Nora stared at him a moment, debating on how she wanted to answer his question. Did she want to shatter his disposition now or later?

Vincent shook his head and left the room. What was left of her heart broke for the caretaker that had helped raise her. He was a sweet old man who had deserved better than to watch everyone in this house die.

"Less than a year left in the house. I am trying to get a head start on the packing," Nora said, shoving the thought away.

"Are you moving?" Charles asked earnestly.

She couldn't do it. Not yet.

"I thought I said no talking."

Nora watched his words die on his tongue as he fought to close his mouth. Charles wasn't fond of her, that was evident, but it was for the best. He would leave here today and not think of her again.

One less person to mourn her.

Nora returned to her pile, putting book after book into a box. She loathed packing up this room–it had always been one of her favorites. Her grandfather would sit and write at a desk that had long since been moved out and Noah would chase her in circles around him.

When they weren't reading in this room, they were doing puzzles, and when they weren't doing puzzles, they were pretending to be pirates.

Charles moved over to one of the bookshelves and she couldn't help but watch as he examined them, running his thin fingers over the wood, dust catching on them in the process. Nora tracked him as he made his way over to her grandfather's grand piano.

Nora's grandfather would play the piano for hours, teaching Nora the chords from where she sat on his knee. She loved playing for him more than anything, but she stopped a few years ago as it had become too depressing playing to an emptying house. Noah hated that she stopped. He would sit and read for hours while she tried and failed to imitate the greats.

The instrument, to her knowledge, had never been moved from its current spot–seemingly bolted to the floor. Charles pressed on a few keys and for the first time in years, music filled the room.

Nora squeezed her eyes shut, the sound was like large bore needles being pushed, without warning, into her bones.

"Chuck, please don't," she begged

"You don't play?" Charles flashed his brilliant smile at her. It was a smile that made her want to do whatever he asked of her despite the pain.

"No I don't and you shouldn't either. Not here." Nora's tone was biting, but it was all the softness she could manage through gritted teeth.

"Oh come on Nora, let me play you a song." Charles sat on her grandfather's bench, letting his fingers dance over the keys, causing her ears to ring.

Nora's brain pounded on the inside of her skull, demanding, begging, pleading for the sound to cease. She stormed over to the piano and pulled his hands from the keys.

"I asked you not to." Charles tried to protest as she placed his hands in his lap, slamming the fallboard down.

Nora was about to scold him further when a part of the bookshelf on the far wall of the library shifted back into the wall and slid to the side. The sight of it freezing her in place.

"Nora?" Charles said distantly, reaching for her hand. His fingers were soft and warm in Nora's cold ones, but she barely registered the feeling as she stared in disbelief at the dark hole where the bookshelf used to be.

Charles, somewhere beyond her consciousness, searched her face as Nora reluctantly pulled her hand from his warmth to walk mindlessly toward the new doorway.

"What is this?" he asked from right behind her, assuming she had the answer.

"I don't—" Nora started but she was at a loss for words. Her grandfather had always told her that his house had its secrets, but she just thought he was being intentionally cryptic.

When she stepped over the threshold, the room illuminated as a fire bloomed in a hearth she didn't know was there and lights on the walls lit themselves. Charles swore under his breath, surprised by the house's ability to act of its own free will. Granted, Nora had just learned of the room itself, leaving her just as bewildered as he was.

Fear settled into her bones the way rot settled into wood, deep and slow with no intent to leave, only to destroy. The room was damp and dusty and filled with things that shouldn't be there. A safe sat in the corner, frames covered in cloth leaned against the wall, boxes of files and loose paper were everywhere–on the desk, the floor, the mantle.

The far wall was set with bookshelves, just like the library behind Nora, however, not a single shelf sat empty. They were lined with more books, small sculpted marble busts of faces she didn't know, and picture frames–all of which were photos of her and Noah and some of her other cousins.

The room felt wrong. Dishonest. Sinful. Every cell in her body screamed in protest, refusing to accept the stimulus her brain was receiving.

Nora walked over to the desk and picked up the file laying in the center. It was crimson and menacing and it had been branded with a seal she had never seen before. A single sheet of paper was tucked inside it.

*By the Order of All That is Unholy…*

A body of words her fear wouldn't let her read.

*Signed in Malice,*
*Lucifer.*

Nora stared at the words on the page until she didn't see anything at all. She wasn't in her body, she was somewhere else, floating meaninglessly toward the void.

A warm hand on her shoulder brought her attention rushing back to her corporeal form, when she turned her head Nora found her vision flooded with dark messy hair and ocean blue eyes she was desperate to drown in.

He was saying her name.

Or at least that was the shape his mouth seemed to be making.

Nora blinked away the white hot pain burning behind her eyes and forced them to focus. She had to get Charles out of there because she didn't know what she would find, but she knew she didn't want him seeing it.

With a hand tight on his arm, she dragged him from the room, out of the library, and back down the hall to the foyer. Charles protested the entire way, but she refused to listen. She yanked the door open to drag him through it, but he planted his feet.

"Nora. Tell me what is going on. Tell me how I can help you." Charles searched her face, frantic for an explanation.

"You cannot help me Chuck. No one can help me. Understand that simple concept and leave."

"Whatever it is that you found in there, I'm sure—" he started, but stopped when he registered the look on her face. Charles quieted, pressing his lips together.

"Tell our *mutual friend,* you did your job and that I am fine," Nora seethed with enough ire for him to get the hint it was time for him to go.

Charles nodded and without further protest, fled the estate.

# CHAPTER 6

## NORA

"WHAT IS ALL OF this Vincent?" Nora said to the old man standing next to her in the doorway of the secret room.

"I have no idea, Miss Nora," Vincent admitted.

"It looks like my grandfather was a criminal."

He said nothing, turning his head to look at her. Worry had settled on his face, his mouth pressed into a thin line. Tension pulled at the back of Nora's neck down to her shoulders. They stared at each other for a moment, looking for a better explanation neither of them had, then got to work.

The two of them sifted through boxes of clothes and works of art and stacks of paper covered in her grandfather's writing for what felt like hours. Nora's head was swimming, her mind a raging storm.

Fear was the first thing to flood through her. It washed through her bones and turned her hands to ice, but the more she read, the more anger burned it all away.

*How could he?*

The singular thought rattled around in her brain as she stood in the center of the room staring at what was unmistakably a Rembrandt that had been "lost to time." Nora's mouth hung open as she processed the painting. She wasn't confident she was breathing or if her heart was even beating.

But then her mind caught up to her body and the panic she had been avoiding took over.

She fell to her knees, clutching her chest, begging her protesting lungs to breathe. Her skin was on fire as her heart threatened to crack a rib with each demanding beat.

A hand landed on her arm and Vincent's face appeared before her, but she couldn't figure out which one of him to focus on–there were too many.

He was shouting her name, but his voice was miles away.

How they got to the drawing room, Nora didn't know, but suddenly Vincent was lowering her into the oversized chair by the fireplace.

It was her favorite.

It had been her grandfather's favorite.

"Breathe, Nora," the caretaker demanded of her. "Breathe."

"Okay," she tried, but the word left her mouth too breathy and disjointed.

Nora inhaled.

The exhale barely made it out.

"Again."

She inhaled again and the air left her lungs a bit easier this time.

Again and again she breathed.

Again and again it got easier.

Nora let her eyes flutter closed for a moment and when she opened them, Vincent was still there, squatting in front of her, watching her intently.

There was only one of him now.

"You're alright, little star," Vincent assured her. He hadn't called her that in years. Her grandfather had given her that nickname. A nickname only Death used now which he started using when they first met because he knew it comforted her. It made Nora feel like a part of her grandfather was still alive. Then she got older and Death refused to give it up. He said that he rather liked the nickname and felt it still suited her, given that she was "full of bright, fiery rage."

"Thank you, Vincent."

He nodded and placed a hand on her cheek. "Stay here a moment while I get you a blanket and some tea." He looked up at the ceiling to tell the house, "Keep her warm."

Fire ignited in the hearth next to her as she tucked herself into the cushions of the chair. Nora's eyes found the window, looking for the sun that had long since set. She forced her mind away from the secret room, but there were too many thoughts in her brain that hurt. Too many memories of people who were no longer there.

Nora decided to focus her mind on her best friend–one she had been horrifically neglecting these last few weeks. She smiled thinking of Charlotte's bright smile, the way she lit up a room. Charlotte was the center of the world. People revolved around her and how Nora reveled in it.

How similar she was to Noah had drawn Nora to her in the first place. In school Charlotte was always assisting the teachers, talking to everyone. Charlotte was a certified popular girl, not a single person disliked her.

They were twelve when they officially met and Nora had just lost Izzy. They were the youngest of the Kramers and were as good as sisters. Izzy's death was different from the rest because it was too close to Nora to make sense of. Everyone who had passed had been older.

Izzy's death made Nora realize Death would indeed be coming for her too.

Nora was reading a book, trying to stay out of the way of the other kids during their outdoor break from class. With Noah in a different building, there wasn't anyone for her to hang out with anyway, but Charlotte appeared out of nowhere, throwing herself down on the bench, causing Nora to jump out of her seat.

"Sorry, I didn't mean to scare you." Charlotte flashed a toothy smile at her, holding her hands up in surrender.

Nora forced a tight lipped smile back and sat down again. "I'm Nora."

"Everyone knows who you are Nora Kramer. I'm Charlotte."

"Yeah, I guess that's true. It is nice to meet you." She flicked the edges of her book, secretly hoping Charlotte would go away.

"You shouldn't think that a bad thing. No one would know me if I didn't make them." A smirk spread across Charlotte's freckled face and despite herself, Nora smiled too.

"It's not always a good thing for people to know who you are, Charlotte," Nora warned.

Charlotte frowned. "I suppose you're right, but surely a few people should really know you, I think. I see you reading all the time and you read the best books. Everytime I see you with a new one I run straight to the library to check it out. They don't have that one though." Charlotte pointed to the book in Nora's lap. It was the second in a six book series, she had eight pages left.

Nora thought about Charlotte's words, that maybe, just maybe, it was important for someone to truly know her that wasn't Noah or Izzy.

That maybe it would be good for her to know someone else

too.

"You can borrow it when I'm done, if you want."

"Oh God, can I really?" Charlotte gaped.

Nora laughed, "Of course. I have the rest of the series at home too."

Charlotte sighed and leaned back against the bench. "I bet you have all kinds of books in your house."

"We have a whole library. You are welcome to come see it if you want." Nora had never invited anyone over to the estate before. It didn't make sense to as the house grew emptier, plus its sentience tended to scare people. She felt she should warn Charlotte beforehand. "The house does sort of have a mind of its own though."

"What does that mean?" Charlotte studied her.

"Just that you can ask it to turn lights on and off, your fires never go out, that sort of thing," Nora tried to explain as casually as possible.

"That is the best thing I have ever heard and yes, obviously, I want to come see your library." Charlotte embraced her before standing to leave. "Oh and Nora? I would be honored to know you."

Nora smiled fully and said, "I would be honored to know you too, Charlotte."

From then on, Charlotte was at the house as often as her parents would let her. She never made Nora answer questions about her own parents or her grandfather or the very real fact that an abnormal amount of her family members had died.

They read and ran around the grounds and talked about seemingly normal topics. Boys, makeup, movies, parties. As they got older they talked about where they would be going to college and what they would study. Nora wanted to study art history. Charlotte wanted to be a reporter.

Nora continued to experience loss year after year causing her to become a shell of herself and Charlotte never left her side–every funeral, every gut wrenching dedication at the museum. She was the first person Nora would call to break the news.

There wasn't enough Nora could do in a normal person's lifetime, let alone her short one, to make up for all Charlotte had done for her, and Nora would feel guilty about it long into the afterlife.

Nora woke up to morning light on her face and the fire burning strong next to her. She had no memory of falling asleep, but at some point Vincent had covered her with a blanket and set a pot of tea next to her–he was asleep on the couch on the other side of the fire.

Nora sighed and straightened her limbs for the first time in hours, her joints were stiff, but eventually her muscles relaxed. She hobbled around like she was ninety, for several moments before they started to work properly. Nora made it over to the window to pull the curtain closed so the light wouldn't bother Vincent. Finally, she poured herself a cup of tea from the pot he had left, silently thanking the house for keeping it warm for her.

Steeling herself with every step, she crossed the hall and entered the library, weaving in and out of piles of books until her bare feet reached the threshold of the secret room.

Nora took a deep breath and a sip of her tea. She decided then and there that she would face it all.

There was no one left to face it for her.

The shock of it had worn off and the bones of it were bound to hurt, but she was strong and she could do hard things. Nora rolled her shoulders back, straightened her spine, and stepped into the room.

# CHAPTER 7

## NORA

NORA SPENT THE NEXT three days sifting her way through the items in her grandfather's hideaway. There was a lot to process, but it all boiled down to her grandfather being an art thief and not the renowned collector and philanthropist the world believed him to be.

What she had believed him to be.

He kept a log of everything. There were newspaper clippings from the stories that detailed his crimes. There were receipts from his transactions. There were journals *full* of notes on the places he was robbing–mostly museums–containing information on everything from the security systems, to the guard rotations, to the vaults and safes.

She couldn't lie, it was impressive. Her grandfather was a brilliantly thorough man and if he hadn't been a criminal, she would have been proud of him.

Norman started in the early 60's with petty crime. Stealing stacks of cash from store registers and ATMs. There was a singular bank robbery and his post score notes mentioned how he would *not* be doing that again. He hadn't liked holding hostages or needing partners. Nora learned he preferred to do things alone, where there was no possibility of anyone besides himself getting hurt.

Which she guessed, was noble.

In the years before he married her grandmother, he had completed nine successful heists and the papers had documented each one. However, not a single investigator thought any of the crimes were connected. Her grandfather had fenced the pieces through international buyers, always during closed auctions.

He had also been working as an artist himself and was a growing name in the art community after the major sale of one of his pieces. The more people started to buy his originals, the more he could hide the money from his crimes.

*'The trick to laundering money,'* he wrote, *'is paying for new additions to buildings, or for the construction of a grand estate, in cash.'*

Nora hated herself for finding it all fascinating. She hated him too, but she also couldn't help but admire him. He was truly brilliant and how he got away with it all, she would never understand.

Unfortunately, Nora had an inkling that the answer resided in the letter on the desk signed by Lucifer. The one she refused to read until she didn't have a choice.

Vincent brought her another cup of tea and joined her to stand in front of the Rembrandt.

"Did you ever think he could do something like this?" Nora asked him quietly as she sipped from the steaming cup.

Vincent shook his head. "Never. I always thought him to be so far beyond reproach."

"Aren't you angry with him?"

He was quiet for a moment. The two of them had yet to take their eyes off the painting. "I should be, but I'm not."

Nora swallowed scalding tea, but it didn't burn. Not when her throat was already on fire. "Well I am."

Vincent smiled solemnly. "I know you are, but this doesn't change the man he was. The man he was in his heart. His soul."

*Hmm,* was her only reply.

"A letter from the city council came today, addressed to you."

Nora's eyes rolled, they wouldn't quit. It was the third letter in as many weeks. The council was desperate to know if she would be making any changes to their funding. "You can throw it away, Vincent."

"Of course, and Miss Charlotte called," he said after a heavy pause.

Nora pursed her lips. The phone had been ringing for days and there was only one person it could be–the one person she was avoiding.

"I can't talk to her, Vincent. I don't know how to tell her about all of this. Tell her that I'll be gone next year." Nora finally looked at the old man.

Vincent frowned at her. "You cannot manage how people love you, Nora. I have lost you all too and I loved you all. Some more than others, however."

He winked at her, she chuckled.

"But unfortunately, there is death at the end of life, whenever that may be," he continued. "None of us can change that, we can only wish to enjoy the life we do live, to be present while we can."

"Have you enjoyed yours?"

He returned his eyes to the painting and the woman staring back. His lips pressed tightly together, the edges pulled down-ward, but he didn't look sad. "Despite its challenges, I have. I have loved and been loved and I have learned a great deal. There is not much else I could have asked for. Aside from more time with you and Noah."

Nora nodded at him—the man who raised her and her brother. In all the years she had known him, her whole life to be exact, she never thought he changed. The same gray hair, the same knowing brown eyes, the same gentleness he had always shown her.

Nora could have sworn Vincent's face hadn't changed, that Time had left him alone, but standing there, in the dim light of the room, she realized he had. Ridges had etched into his cheeks around his mouth, lines burst from the corners of his eyes, the wrinkles in his forehead were more pronounced. His eyes were tired, drooping slightly as the bags under them continued to grow. But he was still the same man she knew him to be.

"These winters are hard on you, Miss Nora. A little company could keep you warm." Vincent planted a kiss on the top of her head before leaving the room.

Nora looked around the room one more time and sighed. Vincent was right. It wouldn't do any good to keep Charlotte at a distance. It would only make Nora feel more guilty than she already did.

She set her tea down on the cluttered desk and headed to the study.

"Nora!" Her best friend exhaled from the other end of the phone. "Thank God."

"Hi Char, I'm really sorry I haven't called…"

"What do you need?"

It was the only question she asked which squeezed her heart in the sweetest way.

Ten minutes later Charlotte was knocking on her front door.

Nora barely got the door open before Charlotte jumped through it and wrapped her arms around Nora's neck, threatening to take her to the ground. Charlotte released her to rest her hands on Nora's cheeks, rotating her face back and forth, her lips pursed and brow furrowed. She only dropped her hands to cross her arms over her chest to look Nora up and down.

"Now that I know you are okay. I am quite cross with you, Nora Kramer."

"I'm sorry, Char, I never meant to worry you. I have just been dealing with a lot."

"Like what?" Her friend immediately softened.

Nora huffed a laugh, "Let me just show you."

Charlotte followed Nora all the way into the secret room. Nora didn't say anything, letting Charlotte look around for herself for a few moments. When she had her fill, she turned to Nora, eyes wide, mouth hanging open.

"Shit, Nora. This means your grandfather was—"

"An art thief? Yes, that is what this all means, unfortunately." Nora frowned.

"How did you find this? When did you find this? Are you okay? What are you going to do?" Charlotte fired off questions in the way she normally did when shocked–in rapid succession with little to no processing time.

"I'm fine now and I am not sure what I am going to do yet. I am still getting through everything. It's like it doesn't end. I found it all three days ago when Death sent his lackey over to the estate to check in on me."

Charlotte gaped at Nora, forcing her to realize what she had said. "Who is Death? Who is his lackey? Are you in trouble?"

Nora sighed, "Charlotte."

"Are you in trouble?"

"No."

Charlotte raised a brow at her.

"I promise, I am not in any kind of trouble."

"Okay, then who is Death?"

"Promise you won't get upset." Charlotte nodded swiftly and gestured for Nora to continue. Nora thought about what to tell her. About what lie to spin so that her friend wouldn't worry, but Nora was done keeping secrets from Charlotte under the guise of protecting her.

It was time Charlotte decided what she could and could not handle for herself. She was stronger than Nora had given her credit for and didn't need protecting from anything.

So Nora told her everything. The whole story. Every last dark and scary detail.

"Then as an attempt to respect my request for space, he sent over his other ward, Charles–who is infuriatingly joyous by the way–just to spy on me. The idiot started playing the piano, I slammed the fallboard down, and it opened up this room."

Charlotte didn't say a word for an unnaturally long time–she always had something to say, always had a retort. Nora had effectively silenced her friend for the first time in the seven years she had known her. It was remarkable and frightening all at the same time.

"Why didn't you tell me any of this before?" Charlotte asked when she was able to speak again.

There it was, the question she knew would be thrown at her, but didn't know how to answer without sounding like a dirty liar.

"At first I didn't tell you because its all a little fucked up and strange. It's hard to meet people and say 'hey I have a guardian angel and his name is Death.' You were my only friend, Char. The only person who talked to me and made me feel semi normal and I didn't want to scare you away. Then we got older and I just didn't want to worry you with it all. You mean more to me than anything and you deserve so much more than that."

A tear slipped from Nora's eye and she swiped it away as quickly as she could. Charlotte on the other hand let her tears fall freely. They were silent, as if the emotion was too raw to have a sound. And then she crossed the room and hugged Nora for a second time that afternoon.

"Oh Nora, I'm sorry too."

"You have nothing—"

Charlotte pulled back and put her hands on Nora's shoulders. "I am sorry that you have gone through all of this alone. I am sorry this is all so terrible. But most of all I am sorry you thought you couldn't tell me, even though it annoys me slightly." She laughed softly.

Nora reached up and wiped a line of tears from Charlotte's cheek. "It's okay. It feels good to tell you now."

Charlotte pursed her lips, letting go of Nora. "I think I have seen Death before."

Fear shivered down Nora's spine. "What do you mean?"

"Black hair? Super tall?"

"Yeah?"

"I've seen him at all of the funerals. I thought he was an uncle," Charlotte laughed and relief flooded Nora.

Nora laughed too. "No, he is certainly not an uncle."

"But now onto more important topics of conversation. Who is *Charles*?" Charlotte said his name the way honey tasted, slow and smooth.

Nora rolled her eyes and sighed, "He is no one."

Her friend's brown eyes narrowed on her wanting details Nora didn't have.

"He has perpetually messy brown hair and blue eyes and I don't know anything else about him other than he is disgustingly cheery because I threw him out the moment I found the letter." Nora paused for a second, finally remembering the folder she refused to open. "I am likely to never see or hear from him again, so there is nothing to know about *Charles*."

"Huh, maybe there should be something to know about Charles." Her friend winked at her and Nora rolled her eyes, but a smile pulled at her lips anyway. "What is this letter?"

Nora exhaled and inclined her head toward the desk and the red folder that sat there.

The girls walked over and stared down at it. Nora wished it didn't exist. She wished that she was a normal girl with a normal family, that she didn't have a grandfather who was an art thief. She wished that her brother were alive.

But her wishes wouldn't change her reality. Nora would only find what she wished for in her dreams and even that was unlikely.

"I can't read it," Nora admitted.

Charlotte nodded and extended her hand. "Together then?"

"Together," Nora whispered, grateful to have a friend to hold onto.

Charlotte gripped her hand firmly as Nora slid the paper from the folder. The letter was shorter than she expected.

*By the Order of All That is Unholy,*

*I hereby ensure the crimes of one, Norman T. Kramer, remain unsolved until the end of time. He shall be free to continue his criminal activity until he reaches the age of seventy, whereupon he will surrender his soul to me and condemn every blood descendant of his to Hell. The terms of this agreement are final and signed in blood by both parties.*

*Signed in Malice,*
*Lucifer*

At the bottom of the page, in his unmistakable scrawl, was her grandfather's name. If not for the words she had just read, the faded red of the signature could have easily been ink.

God how she wished it was ink.

Nora felt a chill slide from her head down her back, continuing down her legs and into the floor, effectively rooting her to the spot. The words, *'and condemn every blood descendant of his to Hell,'* seared into the forefront of her mind like a brand. The realization of their meaning turned her joints to putty.

She gripped the edge of the desk with the remaining strength she had. Charlotte drew her arm across Nora's shoulders and held on tight.

When Nora's breathing returned to normal and it was evident she wasn't going to pass out, Charlotte asked, "What does this mean?"

"It means every one of my family member's souls are in Hell and I am headed there next."

"*Fuck,*" Charlotte whispered. "What do we do?"

"I don't know yet," Nora looked her sternly in the eye, "but I need to speak to Death."

# CHAPTER 8

## DEATH

S EVERAL DAYS AND MULTIPLE trips to different realms later, Death brought Charles coffee. He assumed he owed the boy something after Death sent him to face Nora alone. A similar task to facing down a pack of ravenous wolves.

"How did it go?" Death handed over the coffee slowly.

"That is a certainly loaded question." The boy leveled a stare at him, one eyebrow raised suspiciously.

"Well I knew it wouldn't be easy."

Charles sipped his coffee and huffed a laugh. "That is saying the least."

"How was she?" Death was strangely eager to know. It had been years since he spent this much time away from Nora and it had only been a couple of weeks.

"I imagine Nora was how she always is. She was abrasive, not thrilled that you sent me to check in on her and then I helped her pack up the library. Which I swear we made no progress on. The girl owns too many books." Death's stomach hardened at the thought of her packing up that library. "The old caretaker is cool though. I chatted with him a bit until Nora mentioned moving and he left the room."

*Oh sweet, little, optimistic Charles,* Death thought. How that boy could hear words and never assume there was anything terrible behind them. But Death liked that about Charles, his blindness to the darkness, whereas with Nora, he liked that she never missed the darkness, never shied away from it. It hadn't been moving that Nora meant, whatever her words, he knew she meant her death.

"What happened after that?"

"I tried to play a song on the piano and—"

"Charles, please tell me you didn't." Death pinched the bridge of his nose and squeezed his eyes shut.

"How was I to know I wasn't supposed to? You didn't exactly give me much instruction before sending me over there," Charles seethed.

"What happened after that?" Death asked again.

Charles sighed, but continued, "Nora got pissed, slammed the fallboard down and it opened up a hidden room behind the bookshelf." Death's breath caught in his chest for the first time in over a thousand years.

He had been positive Nora would never find that room, never know what was hidden in those walls. She was afraid of that old piano. Refused to go near it and her fear was enough to convince Death she would never find that room. But he had sent Charles and for as much as he cared for the boy, he had a way of meddling.

"And?" Death pleaded with him to go on. The boy really did not know how to relay important information.

"She seemed a little spooked by it all, rifled through some papers on the desk and threw me out of the house. Told me to tell you that she was fine, by the way." Charles took another long drag from his cup.

*Fuck,* Death thought.

She saw it.

She had to have seen it.

It would have been the only thing to make her upset enough to throw Charles out. Nora was a fiery little star, but she wasn't rude without cause. Death knew she hadn't wanted Charles seeing anything in that room and Charles, God bless him, was probably too concerned about Nora to notice anything else.

Death collected himself. "I'm glad she's fine."

The two of them sat in Charles's flat for a while and chatted about nonsense. Charles liked to talk, always telling Death about the new movies he'd seen or the books he'd read. It allowed Death to relax a bit–he'd never admit it to Charles, but the boy really was calming. A bright spot in all the pain he saw everyday.

He was tired of his job. Dragging souls to Heaven and Hell was getting old, but there wasn't much else for him to do. This was his home and as an immortal, he didn't want for much, just for purpose and this job gave him that–for the most part.

So he sat and let Charles lift his spirits, but it didn't take long before he felt it. A slight pull, a shift in the ether telling him Nora wanted to speak with him. Death avoided the pull for as long as possible because once he gave in, once he went to her, he would have to face his lie.

The lie that he'd kept for thirteen years.

The lie that was the reason her death date was written in his ledger.

He felt like all of those loved ones he watched cling to death beds, pleading with Time to stop, begging to give them more. But Death knew better than anyone that Time was a bastard and he couldn't keep Nora waiting forever.

\*\*\*

Death met Nora at the foot of her grandfather's grave in the town's only cemetery. It was one of those ancient cemeteries where each person had an elaborate headstone or a small mausoleum.

But Norman Kramer's headstone was a simpler one, engraved with all of the necessary elements–name, birthdate, death date, 'beloved father, grandfather, and husband.'

To the left of him was the still fresh plot of Nora's brother Noah and to the right was an open space for Nora. Behind Norman was his wife Roxanne and their sons, Neil, Nora's father, Nathaniel, and Nicholas. The final row was for all of Nora's cousins. Thirteen occupied plots in total.

Nora would make fourteen when she eventually joined them.

Nora and Death stood in silence for a long time–she hadn't even turned to look at him when he came to a stop next to her. Death thought that maybe Nora wasn't going to speak, which she often did when she was worn down or overwhelmed.

"I thought I knew him." Her voice was coarse like she had been screaming. "I thought he was a good man. But he never was, was he, because he is the reason they're all dead." She swung her hand out over the graves.

Then she listed out all the facts, to make sure they were both on the same page. "His image was a lie. He wasn't an art collector, he was a thief and a forger. He stole from people and museums. Art, jewels, sculptures. The greedier he became, the more reckless he became, so he signed a deal with the Devil. One that protected him from the law. One that allowed him to continue with his transgressions and not get caught, happy to condemn us all in the process."

"Little star…"

"But then again, I thought I knew you too." Nora turned to face him, tears lined her burning eyes, but they didn't fall. She was so small, only reaching the center of Death's chest and yet she never stood taller, propped up on all her pain. "But I guess I didn't because you already knew all of that, didn't you?"

There was no sense in denying it so he nodded and watched her eyes close. She was barely breathing.

"All this time I thought you came to me because you were genuinely worried about me. Because I thought you cared, but you were just managing his secret weren't you?" When Death didn't answer she asked again, "Weren't you?" He could have sworn her voice was a knife.

"He asked me too."

Nora laughed.

"When you stood at the foot of his bed and begged for his life, he knew there was nothing he could do. His fate was sealed," Death attempted to explain.

"His and everyone else's," she yelled. Her voice sounded wrong against the quiet of the cemetery.

Death nodded and continued, "He asked me to watch over you and make sure you never found out about the deal. He was scared, Nora. He couldn't figure out how to make it right and he never thought it would come down to losing you or your brother. You two were more precious to him than anything."

Nora looked at him like she hadn't heard a word he said. "Where are they?"

"Where are who?" Death knew what she was asking, but he wanted to hear her say it. Just like her, he valued explicit words. Words that could have no underlying meaning.

Her arm shot out to point at the graves as she screamed, "Where are they?"

Death didn't answer because her question was rhetorical. Nora wanted him to say the words. But he couldn't. He refused to break her shattered heart, though maybe he already had.

"They're all in Hell aren't they, because of his deal?"

Again, Death didn't answer. Nora was too brilliant. Too quick.

"Fuck him," she whispered. Hands covered her face and she exhaled. "Fuck him."

Death watched her drop her hands, just to see the life had drained from her face.

"And you. You let me believe that he loved me. That he loved Noah. You let me believe that you loved me too." Her voice was too quiet.

"Nora, of course–"

She put a hand up to stop him. "I'm done. I will see you when the time comes, but I don't want to see you until then. I don't want to have to pretend that you ever cared for me or that you haven't hurt me. You don't have to pretend to care anymore either or worry about me doing anything rash because I will wait until it's my time and then you can come drag me to Hell. But if there is a way to get my brother out of there, I will do it and you will not stop me."

Before Death could protest, tell Nora more of the truth, she walked out of the cemetery and turned down the street. The wind caught the pink ends of her hair lifting them around her face.

He felt defeated. Like someone had punched him in the gut.

Death wasn't supposed to feel like this, it was why he closed himself off in the first place and now he had to willingly watch one of the two things in his life that he loved, die.

# CHAPTER 9

## CHARLES

A WEEK AND A half after his failed attempt to get to know Nora, Charles walked the five blocks from his flat to his favorite coffee shop, current read in hand. A thin little paperback with worn pages and the spine broken several times over, but he always reread it on his mother's birthday.

The book was her favorite. Charles couldn't count the number of times Tessa had read it to him—a story of warring secret societies who sought to keep magic for themselves.

The coffee shop was everything he was searching for. Warm and cozy and full of comforting smells. It wasn't busy, which was a bonus because it likely meant his preferred back corner table was open.

Charles ordered his coffee and patiently waited at the far end of the counter for them to call his name. When the barista handed the cup over, he thanked her with a smile and went to find his table.

He was disappointed to find that despite the emptiness of the café, his table was occupied. A girl sat in the chair against the wall. A dusty pink knit hat was pulled over her head and a matching scarf hung around her neck. The color was stark against her black jacket and she was huddled over a copy of Homer's *The Odyssey*. A film camera rested next to her coffee.

Charles smiled thinking this was a girl he'd get along well with and was about to set his stuff down at a different table when he caught sight of her pink hair peeking out from under her scarf. He stopped in the middle of the café as storm gray eyes lifted from her book, settling on him.

*Nora.*

Recognition quickly turned her passive expression malicious and she was about to scold him until he put his hands up in surrender, retreating a step.

"I promise I am here of my own volition. I didn't know you'd be here."

Nora sighed, kicking out the chair on the other side of the table, which Charles took as his cue to join her. He deposited his book and coffee on her table and lowered himself into the chair across from her. She watched him over the rim of her latte.

"Any good with that?" Charles asked, pointing to the camera.

"That's subjective. I was out taking photos until it broke." Nora frowned.

"Which piece?"

"I think it's the film rewind shaft. I got through the roll of film, went to wind it back up and the rewind lever just spun in circles." She reached a slim hand out and spun the part of the camera she was talking about.

"Ah," Charles murmured, picking it up. He didn't know a thing about the device and was unlikely to ever learn. He had whatever one would call the opposite of a creative eye.

Nora watched him turn the camera over in his hands. "Know how to fix it?"

Charles met her gaze before setting it back down on the table.

"Definitely not. I know nothing about cameras or photography."

She laughed lightly, picked up her book, and started reading again. When he thought for sure their conversation was over, Charles opened up his own book.

"Have you spoken to Death lately?"

He put his book back down. Her face was expressionless, but Charles got the faint idea Nora was forcing it to remain neutral.

"I have. And you?"

*Mmm.* "Unfortunately," she supplied, returning her attention to *The Odyssey.*

Charles stifled a grin and did the same. He was a page and a half in before she spoke again.

"What are you reading?"

He handed it over to her and watched as she examined it carefully. Nora was overly delicate with it, as if she knew it was special to him without even having to ask.

"Looks interesting. It's well worn," she said with a touch of admiration.

He smiled down at the copy. "It was my mother's favorite. I read it every year on her birthday."

The corner of Nora's mouth curled up. "Is that today?" Charles only nodded, finding it a bit too difficult to form words. "That's very sweet of you. How long has she been gone?"

"Seven years." It came out clipped, but he gathered himself quickly and said, "It was either her or me from what I understand." Nora didn't interrupt. Instead she settled in, letting him talk as much as he needed. "I was ill and dying and the next thing I knew, I was getting better. What I didn't realize was the more I got better, the sicker she became. I didn't catch it until it was too late, until I met Death and he told me how she had bargained to take my place."

Nora reached across the table and slipped her hand into his. Her skin was cold, but soft against his. Charles wrapped his fingers around hers and they started to warm. As soon as Nora felt it, she pulled her hand back to her lap just to pick at her thumb nail.

"That's terrible, Chuck." He looked at her expecting pity, but there was none to be found.

"It isn't so bad, but I miss her so much. I can't decide if I am angry with her for what she did or if I am grateful." Charles's chest loosened as the words left his mouth. A confession that until then had lived in the depths of his mind. But there was something about Nora that calmed him, that made him want to spill secrets he didn't have. Some intrinsic part of himself whispered that she understood these dark parts of his mind.

That she, in fact, had them too.

Nora shrugged. "I think you can be a bit of both. You can be angry with her for what she did and you can be grateful you get to live."

"Doesn't it feel a bit wrong to be angry when her intent was good?" Charles asked the girl across from him that up until now he was convinced only ever felt anger.

"No. It feels good." Nora smiled confidently. "Just because someone loved you doesn't mean they didn't make bad decisions. Death and love do not absolve people of their wrongs, they only make you feel as though you shouldn't care about them. It doesn't change what they've done." She took a deep breath and Charles decided that whatever she had to say, he'd listen–there would not be a day where he'd tire of her words. "Everyone knows that life isn't just black and white. It is full of colors and gray areas, so why do we erase it all when death comes? What is so special about death that we only remember the light when there was darkness too?"

Charles let her words settle in his mind. He felt strangely comforted by her exacting reality, by her ability to acknowledge head on the things people wanted to forget. A smile spread over his face when he looked up to find her gray eyes carefully watching him.

"Have you ever told Death these thoughts of yours?"

"Several times." Nora smirked, making Charles laugh. Of course she had.

"Why are you so cross with him, anyway?" His question erased the smirk from her face and he was immediately sorry he'd asked it. Nora straightened in her seat, quiet for a moment too long.

"Here's the thing, Chuck—I have less than a year left to live," Nora stated as if this wasn't supposed to shock him, as if it didn't phase her in the slightest. But he saw her pause, eyes drifting off as she bit her lip, something he was quickly learning to mean she was thinking. When Nora's eyes met his again, she was as collected as he knew her to be. "Death knows all about it and has been lying to me."

"What do you mean you have less than a year left to live? Are you sick?" Charles knew sick, it was terrible and frightening and lonely and the thought that she might be made him want to fall to his knees and beg someone to make it right.

"No, I'm not sick. Each year, on my grandfather's birthday, a direct blood relative of his dies and I happen to be the last one left."

Charles's mouth fell open, dread filling his bones. He knew what slowly dying was like, but to know when you were going to die, without cause, was wholly different, was infinitely worse.

"Is there any way to prevent it?"

Nora looked at him matter-of-factly. "I am currently trying to figure that out."

"Do you need help?" Charles asked before he could think better of it. Before he could think of what that might entail.

She smiled lightly. "I appreciate the offer, Chuck, but no. I have help and the less people to drag into this mess the better."

He felt strangely stung by that. Part of him hoped she would want his help, that he'd get the chance to spend more time with her, to know more of her. "Let me know if you change your mind."

"I won't, but thank you." Nora picked up her book and Charles did the same. They read in comfortable silence for a while, or rather he stared at the page as his brain was overrun by questions he needed to ask her.

Charles wanted to know about her brother, what he was like. He wanted to know about her grandfather. Where her mother and father were. Did she have any friends? What did she study in school? Did she have a favorite color? Book? Photo she'd taken?

Charles asked every single one and Nora told him every-thing—some in shorter answers than others. Her father was gone and she was happy for it because he was a wicked man with a temper. Her mother was 'God knows where,' having left her father years before his death. Her brother was kind and more brilliant than she was—a statement Charles did not believe—and her grandfather wasn't the man she thought he was, but he had been good to her when he was alive.

Nora had a best friend—Charlotte—who Nora thought Charles would like because they were both "talkative, lively people." She studied art history, though she wasn't very serious about the degree because she struggled to find the point in finishing it if she was going to die before graduation. Her favorite color was blue like the ocean, her favorite book was actually *The Odyssey,* and there was a portrait of Noah she loved.

It was clear Nora was not the type of person to give information freely, but she answered his questions exactly, offering only what was explicitly asked. Charles would have to earn more from her, so he offered up himself to her in the form of knowledge.

He answered all of her questions about his mother and his father and where he went to school and if he had any friends. He told her what he liked to do in his free time. The books he liked and why. The ones he *didn't.*

Why his favorite color was blue—not just any blue, but a deep blue like the far end of the sky, right before the sun slipped from the horizon.

He told her how he liked his coffee black and bitter enough to send chills through his body. The more he shivered, the more he believed it was working.

And the way Nora listened, with her whole body, was intoxicating. As if his words were important to her, as if she were committing parts of him to her memory.

Charles was in awe of her and the way her mind worked. How it leveled with such harsh realities and yet still found wonder in the world—how it craved knowledge. She was angry and sad and she let that be known, but she also had things she loved and enjoyed and he needed to know every last one of them.

Charles would not be finishing his reread of his mother's

favorite book, but he believed Tessa would have been happy knowing he spent her birthday with company.

# CHAPTER 10

## NORA

Nora laid in bed that night and thought of Charles and his messy hair. Of his blue eyes, that if she stared at long enough she was certain to drown in. This *need* to know more of him, despite the limited time she had left, threatened to consume her.

He had told her so much about himself and Nora felt like it wasn't enough. Like Charlotte, he had endless amounts of questions, but in a slower, more relaxed cadence. Each one deeper than the next. Each one begging her to expand on minor details. Each one needing more of her.

They talked until the coffee shop closed–the workers had to politely ask them to leave. It was unlike her talking to a stranger like that. Nora barely talked to the people she trusted and yet there was something about this boy with whom she shared a mutual friend.

Deep in her brain she heard herself screaming that it was a bad idea, but she needed more too.

Before she knew what she was doing, Nora was in the study on the first floor, phone book in hand, dialing his number on the one phone she owned in the entire house.

She was in the process of trying to convince herself to hang up. That no good would come of getting to know Charles further than what she had already allowed. That it would only end in fiery disaster.

But then he picked up.

"This is Charles," grumbled his voice on the other end.

*Shit.*

"I have decided that you can help me. On one condition."

He chuckled, "State your terms."

"You cannot get attached to me, Chuck."

The quiet on the other end of the line unnerved her.

"I agree to your terms, Nora," he murmured, his tone far from convincing.

She cleared the uneasiness from her throat. "Then you have a deal. Come over tomorrow at noon and we can get started."

"I'll see you then." Nora could practically hear him grinning on the other end of the line.

*This is a terrible idea.*

★★★

At exactly noon the next day, Nora's terrible idea knocked on her front door, wearing black jeans, a loose fitting white tee, and a black winter jacket. His hair was the mess she knew it would be.

*How irritating.*

"Punctual," Nora stated, sticking her chin out.

"It should be a crime not to be." Charles smirked. She rolled her eyes and waved him inside, leading him down the same path they took during his first visit.

With each step Nora was grateful Charlotte was already there, that there would be another person between them. As they crossed the threshold of the library, she realized she should have warned Charles.

"Chuck, this is—"

"Charlotte," her friend exclaimed, jumping out from behind a rather tall stack of books. "And you must be Charles. Nora has told me quite a great deal about you."

Charles raised his eyebrows at Nora as heat leapt from her chest up to her cheeks. He swung his eyes back to Charlotte and extended a hand. "It is wonderful to meet you, Charlotte. Nora has told me about you as well."

*Nora* wanted to melt into the floor.

"Well I am just happy to see that Nora has another friend." Charlotte nudged Nora's shoulder, heading into the secret room.

"Ah, well I don't think Nora would call me a friend yet," he said, winking at Nora before following Charlotte.

Nora scoffed, trudging after them. "Well *Nora* is thinking it would be preferable to not have *any* friends, right about now."

The two of them ignored her. Nora let Charles wander through the room and no sooner was his back turned did Charlotte whip her head to Nora.

*"Oh my god!"* she mouthed, shaking her hands.

Nora tried to wave her off to no avail. The part of her that thought Charlotte being there was a good idea, was no longer anywhere to be found.

*"He is so cute."*

*"Stop it,"* Nora snapped silently.

Charlotte's eyes rolled. *"No. He is cute and you know I'm right. Do something about it. Jump his bones."*

Nora gaped, catching the finger Charlotte pointed at her, pulling it out of the air just as Charles turned around and said, "He was certainly a busy man, your grandfather."

Charlotte squirmed under her grip and Nora responded to Charles with a tight lipped nod, hoping he hadn't noticed anything. Only when he turned back around did Nora finally let go of her friend. Charlotte jumped away, putting space between them.

*"I will* not *be doing anything about it." There's no point.* Nora mouthed back.

Charlotte's mouth fell open in a half oval, half smile. *"So you admit he's cute."*

Nora let out a heavy sigh, leaving Charlotte by the desk to join Charles who was staring, open mouthed, at the Rembrandt.

"That's a—" Charles's words were cut off by his bewilderment. He was pointing at the painting lazily, unable to close his mouth. His cheeks were bright red.

"It is," she confirmed.

Charles blinked rapidly as he exhaled. "It's beautiful. I've never seen one in person before."

Nora frowned, recalling the one at the museum across town. "You've never been to the museum?"

He peeled his attention away from the painting, only for his blue eyes to search hers. There were a few freckles on his nose, Nora noted, but his face was otherwise perfectly clear. "No, I have never been, but I imagine you have been enough for the both of us."

It delighted Nora that Charles imagined her spending a lot of time at the museum. Nora could have gone every day of her life and it still wouldn't have been enough. It definitely wouldn't have been enough for him either. Though, with Noah gone, it was unlikely she'd ever find herself there again before she died.

Nora had a feeling the second Charles stepped foot in that

museum, he'd want to spend eternity there. Just because she couldn't stomach it, didn't mean it wasn't worth seeing.

"You have to go for yourself. Not even I can explain how it will make you feel."

Charles smiled brilliantly at her. "You should show me sometime."

Across the room, Charlotte cleared her throat, saving Nora from telling Charles no. "What is this?"

Nora retreated several steps from Charles's side to find her friend holding up a thick journal filled with information Nora hadn't completely deciphered yet. She walked over, Charles close behind her, and took the book from Charlotte.

"I came across this ledger the other day. It's full of every piece of art he stole and from where. There is this bit here that doesn't make sense though. It is likely an indication as to where the pieces went, but knowing him I'm guessing it is in some kind of code." Nora flipped through the pages, pointing to a column in the margin as Charlotte and Charles peered over her shoulders to see what she was talking about. "It's probably a cipher."

The column was a list of numbers. Three numbers, each separated by a period. Three directions, three points, that would tell her the answer–if only she had the key.

"Do you have any idea what the key would be?" Charlotte asked. Charles merely watched her with wide eyes.

"It would likely be a book," Nora started speaking before her brain fully formed the answer. "Books were his usual keys." Her grandfather was always hiding clues for Nora to find in the books she was reading, circling words, underlining letters.

Charles pressed his fingers to his lips, a crease forming between his eyebrows. "Well from what you've said about him, I would bet it's a classic."

Charlotte shot her a knowing look, Nora shook her head in response as Charles's eyes focused on the bookshelf. Nora didn't share details of her life with anyone but Charlotte and her friend was all too aware of that fact.

"Do you have a lot of classics in the house, Nora?" He asked, turning his attention back to her.

"Only the majority of that room out there," she pointed to the library behind her, "and the ones on the shelves in here."

"Well it has to be one in this room. There is no way he would have picked a book out in the library that might get lost," Charlotte said, voicing what they were all thinking.

The three of them searched the shelves in the secret room for a book that would fit the cipher, running through the first several sets of numbers in each book. Nora pulled all of the titles from the shelves she knew had been his favorites, then every edition of each title. Her grandfather owned more copies of the same books than a bookstore likely had in stock at any one time.

Nora found it borderline sociopathic, certainly obsessive in nature, but then again, one would have to be if they were truly a criminal mastermind—which he clearly was. The thought creeped into her mind, sending chills down her spine.

*How could he?*

The question wouldn't evacuate her brain no matter how hard she tried to think about something else. Nora attempted to focus on the nauseatingly quick conversation Charlotte and Charles were having, but she couldn't keep up.

When even that wasn't distracting enough, she screamed.

*In her mind of course.*

One long guttural scream that rattled her bones. She worried briefly that it had been loud enough for Charles and Charlotte to hear, but neither seemed to notice her agony. Nora wondered what they would think if they knew the state of her brain, knew how frayed her thoughts were.

Then she saw it.

The book that stilled her racing mind.

Nora's copy of *The Lion, the Witch, and the Wardrobe* was tucked between Charles Dickens's *Great Expectations* (*boring*) and Herman Melville's *Moby Dick* (*yawn*). She pulled the book from the shelf and examined it.

The copy had been missing for thirteen years, well before her grandfather died. Its cover was worn from greasy fingers, dented from being dropped too many times, and slightly warped from the time she learned reading in the shower was not the best decision.

The title page was marked with her name and a fearsome warning–*Nora's! Do not touch or else!*

It was one of her favorite stories. A magical world inside the wardrobe? *Please.* What child wouldn't love for that to have been their reality.

It was brilliant in theory, having a portal in the back of one's wardrobe, but the physicality of it was rather improbable. Nora grew up and realized that a portal to another world would have to defy the laws of physics which very clearly ruled their existence in the universe.

A portal would prove the existence of wormholes and the multiverse–an ability to travel through space and time without consequence to a person's body. It wasn't possible.

*But then again,* Nora thought, *Death, Archangels, and Hell Hounds existed.* Death traveled to different realms–Heaven and Hell–and he was immortal.

So maybe it wasn't as impossible as she originally thought.

As she returned the book to its spot on the shelf, Nora decided the physicists needed to expand on their research—the six year old in her still longed for a different world to escape to.

"Charles, you must make Nora take you to the museum to see the wing." Charlotte's statement pulled Nora back to reality. A reality in which her family was dead, her grandfather was an art thief who condemned them all to an eternity in Hell, and one where she was going to die come his next birthday.

She made a mental note to check her wardrobe before bed that night.

*Just to be sure.*

"The *wing?*" Charles asked, raising his eyebrows at her.

Nora sighed, "I will not be showing him the wing, Charlotte."

"Oh come on, you have to show him." Charlotte turned back to Charles, her eyes full of light. "It is this gorgeously curated wing of the museum that her grandfather had built and filled with his art."

"I would be delighted to see it," Charles admitted as if Nora were offering to show him to get his approval of the space.

"You'll have to go on your own, Chuck. The next time I'm in that wing will be for my dedication." *Post death,* she didn't add, like all the others before her.

"Miss Nora," Vincent cut in, suddenly appearing in the doorway. "There is someone here for you."

"Who is it, Vincent?" she asked, not taking her eyes off the shelves.

The caretaker sighed and walked over to her to whisper in her ear, "It is Councilman Sam."

Nora's eyes fluttered closed as she let out a slow breath in an attempt to relax herself. "Tell him I am not taking visitors today."

Charles looked to Charlotte for an answer, but Charlotte kept her eyes on Nora, worry pulling her lips into a tight line. Her friend knew exactly who was at the door. The man who for the better part of three years had been vying for Nora's attention despite how inappropriate it was or how little she reciprocated it.

"He is rather insistent," Vincent said, voice returning to a normal volume.

"Fine." Nora gave in. "I can't avoid him forever, unfortunately." She turned on her heel and headed for the foyer.

"Who is *he*?" Charles asked behind her. No one answered him, but they all followed her swift pace to the front of the house.

Sam stood there, back to them, staring up at the painting hung above the door. His coiled, inky hair was cut close to his head, hands tucked neatly into the pockets of his suit pants. He was in his usual navy suit, crisp white shirt, and brown shoes. The tailoring made his legs look miles longer than they were. No coat, Nora noted, but he ran warm, like all the other Hell Hounds.

The winter chill was a mortal issue.

"I've always liked this one." The *one* he was referring to happened to be a depiction of the Earth with Heaven and Hell painted seamlessly into the canvas as if the realms were woven into one another rather than separate entities.

"You could not have come at a worse time," Nora said as if he hadn't spoken a word.

"Oh how I have missed you, sunshine." Sam faced her, a smile plastered on his perfect face, his movements too smooth. His deep brown, blemish free skin shone in a way that filled her with envy. What she would give to have clear skin like that–however he was immortal, which explained everything it needed to about his youthful glow, and *that* she would never be jealous of.

"What do you want, Sam?" Nora crossed her arms over her chest.

"The council wants to see you." He pouted, following it with the shrug of one shoulder. "I wanted to see you."

"I'm sorry, who is this?" Charles asked with a sharpness Nora didn't need at the present moment.

"Shh," Charlotte scolded him.

"Well, you've seen me. Now you can tell the council to go fuck itself. You are included in that." Nora smiled sweetly at him.

Sam grinned back, he had never been deterred by her ire–in fact he routinely voiced how he thought it was *cute*. He glided over to where she stood to plant a kiss on her cheek, his lips overly warm. "Do come by. There are things we need to discuss about your grandfather's estate."

Nora forced her face to remain neutral, as if the request didn't rattle her, but neutral turned into a scowl. She didn't respond, giving him the faintest of nods. Sam knew she wouldn't refuse, knew she *couldn't,* when it came to her grandfather. It only made the pit in her stomach widen to a chasm.

He touched her shoulder lightly before returning his hand to his pocket and retreating towards the door. "It is always a pleasure, sunshine."

Charlotte and Charles walked over to flank her, watching with her as the door swung shut. When Sam was finally gone Charles cleared his throat.

"At the risk of sounding redundant, who was that?"

"City councilor and an old friend of Noah's," Nora answered him without looking away from the door.

"He's a dick," Charlotte supplied. Charles scoffed his agreement. "What did he want, Nora?"

Nora finally met their worried eyes. "The council apparently wants to discuss my grandfather's estate."

Charles watched her carefully as Charlotte asked, "What are you going to do?"

She shook her head slightly. Nora was exasperated and overwhelmed and she didn't want to talk anymore. "I have my impending death to deal with, so nothing for now."

Charlotte's face hardened. Nora knew her friend did not appreciate the continued reminder of her ever approaching death. Nora wasn't happy about it either, but someone had to remain realistic in a room full of optimists.

"Regardless of us finding the key to the cipher, there has to be a way to make sure you don't die, Nora," Charlotte said.

Nora knew of one person who could potentially give her the answers she needed to save herself, to get her brother's soul out of Hell–Isabel and Carter's too. However, the person she needed to talk to was the same person whose name was signed in malice at the bottom of the contract in the red folder.

"I have an idea," Nora mused, meeting Charles and Charlotte's respective blue and brown eyes, "but neither of you are going to like it."

The house shuddered around them.

# CHAPTER 11

## CHARLES

L UCIFER WASN'T NECESSARILY A hard person–*person?, being?, entity?,* Charles didn't know–to track down. It involved talking to Death who was reluctant to give up the information to a still wrathful Nora.

Death also insisted on joining them on their venture. *'Since you need me to get there and all, I will be going. It is non-negotiable.'* The last part had been said directly to Nora, in a rather acerbic tone.

Charlotte wouldn't be joining them, another of Death's conditions and she was rather put out by it, but Charles thought the less people who descended into Hell, the better.

It was late in the afternoon when Death led Charles and Nora to the far end of the cemetery. Just at the edge stood two large, marble mausoleums, both identical in structure, the only differences were the carvings.

Each structure was well worn, with vines crawling up the sides, dirt littering the steps, and years of acid rain dripped green streaks from the roof to match the gravestones behind them.

The mausoleum on the right was carved to look like the tree of life–the door was the trunk and the space around it was covered in carved branches and leaves. A censer hung from a post on the wall next to the door, old incense lingered in the bottom.

Death stood in front of the mausoleum to the left which was much less intricate than its divine counterpart, and by much less, Charles noted there were no carvings on in the marble–no need to sugarcoat Hell, apparently.

Death turned slowly to address both Nora and Charles.

"You two remember my rules?"

Nora, whose arms were folded across her chest narrowed her eyes at Death. The scarf she had wrapped several times around her neck, to shield her from the wind, covered her whole face except for her eyes.

*However,* Charles thought, *those gray eyes were enough to convey exactly how she felt without a word.*

"Yes, we remember," Charles answered for them both. His hands were shoved deep in the pockets of his thick wool coat which was zipped and buttoned up to his chin, but he was still shivering like a nervous ankle-biting dog.

Death raised an eyebrow, leveling his own murderous stare at Nora. Charles was quickly becoming less and less worried of the realm looming beyond that marble slab than he was of the two people standing next to him.

"There will be no talking unless he asks you a direct question. Keep your eyes on the ground. Do not wander. Stay alert," he paused for added emphasis, "and absolutely no attitude."

Nora seemed to look straight through Death.

She didn't utter a word.

Death turned and laid a hand on the door. At his touch, the marble slab shifted backwards into the mausoleum. It shuttered to a halt before sliding to the left and out of the way.

Hot, sticky air flooded from the vault, threatening to suf-focate Charles. It took several deep breaths before he had recovered enough to breathe properly again. On his right, Nora was unwrapping her scarf, sweat shining on her forehead.

"There will be hooks just inside for your coats," Death informed them, shedding his own as he stepped across the threshold.

Nora and Charles exchanged a look before they silently stepped through the door, following Death to Hell. The world and the cemetery faded away behind them as the heavy marble door slid back into place.

Only the dead knew where they were now and they wouldn't tell a soul.

Dim orange light spilled into the room from a staircase on the other end of the vault. The interior was completely bare, no tomb, no sarcophagus raised from the center of the floor. With the door closed, the room was damp from the thick air, moisture slipping down the walls in dense rivulets.

Charles had never been in a sauna, but he assumed it was much the same.

He took Nora's coat and mindlessly hung it next to his, keeping his eyes glued to the top of the stairwell. There was nothing to give Charles the impression something would ascend those stairs and emerge from the ominous source of light, but he wouldn't take any chances.

Death crossed the room and casually descended the stairs to the pit, like he was comfortably at home.

Charles stood frozen next to Nora despite the heat. The two of them were barely breathing. He couldn't hear her inhale or exhale, but he could feel the rigidity of her body next to his. He knew her stillness intimately as if it were his own while she too kept her eyes on the top of the stairwell.

"Charles?" Nora breathed. Her voice was barely a whisper

and he might not have heard her had she not shifted next to him.

It registered belatedly that she had used his *full* name. She hadn't called him '*Chuck*' like she had since the first time they met.

Nora had used his full name and that alone caused him to forget the omnipresent threat at the end of the room and shift his focus to her. She was already looking at him, lips slightly parted, eyes round, crease forming between her eyebrows. Tawny light gilded her face, making her pale skin golden and gray eyes amber.

"Nora." An answer to her question.

Charles reached up to brush his thumb over her chin, the pad skimming the pouted edge of her lip. The sensation sent fire down his arm, racing back to his brain screaming, '*Holy fuck, I need more of that,*' but they were standing at the entrance to Hell.

He needed to get it together.

*Fucking cool it, Charles.*

The heat was suffocating.

Nora let out a shaky breath. "Are you with me?"

"Of course I am." There was no question to whether he was with her or not.

Charles knew for fact there wasn't much she could ask of him that he wouldn't do.

Except for murder. He'd draw the line at murder.

*Maybe.*

Charles dropped his hand from her face reluctantly–he had been touching her entirely too long, but yelling at himself to stop had little to no influence on his actions. Nora immediately slipped her hand into his, pulling him with her towards the stairs.

Death was long gone, likely at the bottom of the stairs that seemed to never end. Charles walked next to Nora at a steady pace, the temperature increasing with each step. They were wide enough for several people to descend side by side, but Nora was tiny and Charles, who was not overly large himself, giving them ample room.

After what felt like forever, the two of them reached a landing and caught up to Death who was waiting for them at the center of the platform.

"Took you both long enough," Death seethed.

Neither of them responded, but Charles felt Nora's hand tighten in his. Wrought iron gates sat closed as flames licked the bars, extending from the top in a fiery blaze. Smoke drifted up to catch under a nonexistent ceiling before falling down what should be walls and pooling on the floor.

In the grand scheme of things, what he was seeing made sense despite his rapidly declining brain function.

Charles looked from side to side, taking in the red-orange, smoke filled nothingness of this new realm. He felt it should make sense there were no walls, that they were in fact at the entrance to another realm which by all intents and purposes meant the normal laws of reality didn't apply.

Even time felt different here, as if it moved slower–that was, if it moved at all.

Unanswerable existential questions about time and space aside, a steady pounding under his feet reminded Charles of his physical form. The gates snapped apart like two strong magnets that required significant force to separate.

The world beyond came into view as they slowly slid open. It was similarly desolate terrain to the platform they stood on, aside from the roar of life—or what would be life if anything was truly alive beyond the gates of Hell.

The *crowd* was a mass of smoky, person-shaped blobs, for lack of a better term. Charles's mind was functioning at the level of a toddler, unable to fully comprehend what he was seeing, as if his brain was saying *'surely that is not correct'* and his eyes were screaming back, *'would we lie?'*

After a moment, the smoke started to swirl around a singular figure making its way through. He was a tall being, definitely person-shaped, and was concerningly lanky, even more so than Death. The man was dressed in a deep crimson suit, black patent leather shoes, and no dress shirt. It took a certain kind of person—*being?*—to pull off the no shirt, suit jacket look.

But Charles thought if anyone could pull it off, it would be Lucifer.

Lucifer's hair was a blond not naturally achievable in the mortal world and his skin was almost see-through, with a golden sheen to it. His features seemed to shift the longer Charles looked at him, as if molding themselves to Charles's version of perfect.

It was wholly unsettling.

"Death," Lucifer hissed, "as lovely as it is to see you, I don't believe we had a meeting scheduled, but you brought friends. Are they mine?"

Death fidgeted, Nora was a statue, Charles was somewhere in between. "They are not for you, Lucifer. We had a few questions about the deal you made with Norman T. Kramer."

Lucifer smiled eerily. "Ah, Norman. One of my more lucrative deals might I say. That big family of his has really increased my capital."

"Of course you'd think that," Nora snapped.

Death pinched the bridge of his nose, Charles pulled at her hand, and Lucifer turned his attention to her, raising an eyebrow. "And who might you be, sweet thing?"

"I'm Norman's granddaughter, Nora." There was no hesitation in her voice, but Charles silently begged her to *shut up.* "I want to know how to amend his deal."

"His little star." Lucifer licked his lips. "There is not much you can do. That deal was signed a long time ago."

Nora radiated heat despite the ungodly temperature it already was around them. Her muscles were so tight she was shaking.

"There must be something."

"Christ, Nora," Death warned.

"Death," Lucifer chided, "if you are going to take anyone's name in vain, take mine."

Death threw his hands up. "Fucking Hell, then."

"Better." Lucifer winked, turning his attention back to Nora. "I did not say you were without options, dear one. I am benevolent after all." Lucifer's lips curled away from his teeth in what was surely the most terrifying look Charles had ever seen.

"What would those options be?" Nora asked.

"There is only one, unfortunately for you. You can right all of the wrongs Norman created, undo what he did, and I'll let you keep your little life."

Nora watched him for a moment. "It is that simple."

*Let it be that simple, Nora,* Charles silently pleaded. He was there for moral support, which made an interjection from him unnecessary–plus he intended to follow Death's rules, even if she did not–rendering him helpless when all he wanted to do was shake her and yell, *'take his solution and run!'*

"It is that simple, dear."

Nora dropped Charles's hand and stepped forward. His palm

felt cold without hers in it. "What about my brother's soul?"

"Ah," Lucifer rolled his eyes, "you are certainly welcome to exchange your soul for his. I would be happy to let it go as I do not hold on so tightly to my things as *someone else* does. Yours must be given willingly of course."

"What happens if I complete your little project, could you not release him then?"

Lucifer frowned. "No, I wouldn't do that. My kindness only extends so far."

"But—"

He raised a hand to stop her. "Those are my terms. Take them or leave them, but I surmise I will see you either way."

Lucifer ended their conversation and strode back through the gates to the pit he emerged from. Charles glanced at Nora, whose fury was burning from her skin in thick waves. Her bloodshot eyes bore into the back of Lucifer's head, but the Devil didn't spare her a second glance. Death, like Charles, was watching Nora. They were all in a bit of shock, but unpredictability glinted in her eyes.

Not a second later, something shifted across Nora's face and she took off running towards the gates of Hell, towards Lucifer, towards her brother. Charles caught Nora around the middle and dragged her back to the stairs—it wasn't an easy feat with rage backing her fight. Death threw himself between them and the gates as they slammed shut with a crashing boom.

Nora thrashed in Charles's arms, kicked her legs in every direction, desperate to make contact with something. She pleaded with Charles to put her down. Screamed at him to let her go. He could hear the gut wrenching agony in her voice as her need became more desperate, felt it in her chest as her body struggled to contain her sobs.

Charles managed to get her to the stairs and when it was apparent she wasn't going to stop in order to walk up them, he picked her up and draped her over his shoulder. If he had to, he would force Nora's return to the land of the living.

Well, to the cemetery which would technically be the land of the dead but the semantics were unimportant. Death climbed the stairs behind them, pleading with her to calm herself.

"Please, little star...please."

"Fuck you."

"Just get upstairs and we will talk."

"Put me down, Charles."

"I can't do that, Nora."

"Fuck you."

Charles could take her ire. She could fight him and scream at him and tell him to fuck off all she wanted, but he would save her life from stupid, ill thought decisions.

Nora wanted to get to her brother–Charles could understand that–but in order to get to him, she would have to willingly enter Hell herself, effectively condemning her soul to an eternity there.

And damn it all if he let that happen. Lucifer had given Nora the information to fix this mess, to save herself and the little ball of fire almost threw it all away.

He wanted to thwart her.

About halfway up the stairs, Nora relaxed. Charles was putting that lightly because her limbs may have stopped flailing in every direction and she may have stopped begging him to put her down, but tension lined her body–Nora's muscles were tight under his hands where he held on to her. At that point, Death surpassed them on the stairs to open the door that would take them back to the cemetery.

When Charles reached the top of the stairs he was sweating, his legs burning from use. Climbing the stairs was one thing, but carrying Nora had doubled the effort.

He didn't set her down until they were out of the mausoleum and back on the gravel walkway with the door closed behind them. The second her feet touched the ground, she retreated several steps ready to fight again.

Charles took his coat from Death and slipped it on. The cold air would take a moment to settle back into his body, but he wanted to be prepared.

Death offered Nora's coat and scarf to her, but she didn't take it. Instead she stared at Death as though she was imagining all of the ways she could free his head from his body.

"Nora," Death begged.

She scoffed before snatching them from his hand, taking off in the opposite direction. Charles started to follow her, but was stopped by Death's arm in front of him.

"Give her a minute. She won't go far," Death said defeatedly as the two of them watched her charge off. About halfway through the cemetery, she stopped at a grave and fell to her knees, covering her face with her hands. Charles's chest tightened, his eyes burning from the smoke and Nora's pain. He could feel it clawing its way into his chest through his ribs, desperate to get to his heart.

"What do we do?" Charles asked.

"*We* aren't going to do anything. She won't speak to me for sometime and I can live with that, but you can help her." Death placed a hand on Charles's shoulder.

"I'm not sure I know how."

"You just have to be there, Charles. Nora needs people, despite her attempt to convince us otherwise. Help her with what she needs until she comes to the right decision."

"To save herself," Charles stated. It wasn't a question of what the 'right' decision was–there was only one option.

When Death didn't respond to his redundancy, he added, "Do you think she'll do it?"

"I do. She is angry now, but her anger will quickly turn into action. It always does. Nora is too stubborn to not solve a problem." Death was confident and sure in his words–his little star would do the right thing. He started off toward the exit of the cemetery, leaving Charles alone in the gravel.

"Wait," Charles called after him. Death stopped, looking back over his shoulder. "You aren't going to stay?"

Death, with his hands deep in his pockets, smiled at the ground. When he looked back up his eyes were full of feeling. "No, but you stay, Charlie boy. Make sure she gets home."

Charles nodded and Death turned again to leave the cemetery–Charles turned back to face Nora. She was still kneeling there in the grass in front of a rounded headstone, face buried in her hands, shoulders shaking.

He wanted to be cross with her, to walk over and scold her for being so *goddamn* reckless, for almost throwing her life away, but he couldn't because he understood. If it wasn't for the promise he'd made to his mother, to live the life she sacrificed herself for, Charles would have gladly burned himself to get to her too.

# CHAPTER 12

## NORA

NORA COULDN'T CONTROL HER breathing, was sure her chest was caving in. It was as if it had been cleaved in two and the only thing holding it together was her fraying will.

*Noah Jackson Kramer.*

The name stared back at her, attempting to excise her heart from her already open chest. Beneath his name, etched in stone, were the dates of his birth and death. His barely twenty one years were brandished there for eternity, or at least until acid rain ate the stone, rendering the years of his life illegible.

Death had left the cemetery. Nora had felt him go like the pressure of an airplane cabin dissipating before deplaning, but Charles remained, waiting by the mausoleum for the right moment to come over.

She could feel his presence too, similar to how she felt Death, but whereas Death settled over her like a blanket, Charles pulled at her very being.

She felt him deep in her soul.

Nora willed herself to hate Charles for dragging her up those stairs, but she couldn't find any anger left for him. A small part of her was grateful–the part of her that was desperate to live.

She remained kneeling in the dirt of Noah's grave until Charles's brown leather boots filled her vision. The winter air had settled deep into her muscles, intent on never allowing her to be warm again. Charles bent over to scoop her coat and scarf from the grass where she had discarded them and offered her a hand.

Nora took it, letting him pull her off the ground. He was warm and she wanted him to wrap her in his arms and tell her it was okay, that he was confident they'd figure it out. She wanted him to thaw her frozen, battered heart.

But Charles couldn't fix her reality and Nora was still intent on keeping him at a distance.

Charles wordlessly helped her into her coat and she buttoned it up to her chin before wrapping her scarf around her neck. His blue eyes were soft when she finally allowed herself to look into them. There was no pity there, if anything, she saw understanding and that alone was enough to stitch her chest back up, to keep her heart where it belonged.

And then it registered, far too late, that his mother would be down there too, having made a deal herself to save the life of her only son.

Nora and Charles's loved ones were all in Hell.

What morbid solidarity.

"Coffee?" he asked as if the sun wasn't setting.

"Yes, coffee," she answered as if the stars weren't dotting the far side of the sky.

They walked in silence to the coffee shop. It was something she liked about Charles–his acceptance of her silence. He never forced her to talk when she didn't want to, granted, when she was up for talking he had a million and a half questions, but he never demanded she answer any of them. Charles seemed content to let her be, happy to be present for her quiet.

Nora liked a lot of things about Charles, but most of all she liked his ability to talk her out of her own head—when she was up for it. She lived in her thoughts, was often consumed by them, whereas Charles was ever present in his reality.

The way he talked about life fascinated her. He spoke with an air of levity that was enviable, like he had never seen anything terrible in his twenty years. But Nora knew that was a lie, making her enjoy it that much more.

Charles had suffered a sickness that had almost taken his life and then was forced to watch his mother die slowly as he got better. Nora imagined it to have been some version of Hell itself, and still he smiled.

"I'm sorry today was so difficult," he said, pulling her out of her head once again.

"Oh don't apologize, Chuck. But I do wish it hadn't sucked *so* badly." Nora feigned a laugh to lighten the mood.

He smiled softly at her, blue eyes simmering. "So you aren't cross with me for dragging you up those stairs?"

Nora looked down at her latte. She was angry, just not at him. Her anger resided where it always had, with death. Not Death himself, but in the act of dying. It was the leaving she couldn't quite get over.

For the second time that evening, she searched for enough anger to assign to Charles and came up empty. When she looked up again, he was watching her as though he'd wait a lifetime for her to reply.

"Of course not. Contrary to popular belief, Chuck, I actually want to live, most days."

"Oh," he startled, clearly not expecting her to answer that

way. "Then what do we do?"

"We fix what my grandfather broke." She looked him in the eye as sternly as she could before she fled the coffee shop.

By the time Nora returned home it was almost midnight. The coffee shop wasn't far from the estate, but she wandered around town, lingering in the park for longer than she should have. Only heading home when even her coat wasn't enough to fight the cold.

Vincent had stayed up, waiting for her to get back. When he finally saw her and rested his hands on her face, the tension seeped out of him. He ushered her upstairs and only left her to go to bed when she promised him she would shower and get in her own.

The shower was one of the best Nora had ever had. It finally warmed her up to the temperature an alive person was supposed to be and better yet, it rid her of the burnt, smoky smell that lingered in her hair.

Her mind was strangely quiet. Debriefing with Charles helped settle her. He listened to all she had to say and didn't balk once, both unnerving and comforting her.

Once Nora finished washing away the remnants of Hell, she dried off, donned her coziest pajamas, and turned to look at her bed. She knew the second she laid down, her mind would race again, it would refuse to settle and the demons that lingered in its depths would be out for blood.

Sleep pulled at her muscles and joints, begging to be obeyed, but instead of giving in, Nora left her room. Next door was Izzy's old room, where Charlotte was sleeping. Her friend hadn't been allowed to join them today, but promised Nora she would wait at the house.

Charlotte was fast asleep, her dark hair fanned out on the

white pillowcase. Nora tiptoed her way over to the other side of the bed and slipped under the covers. Nora laid on her side, watching as her friend stirred and rolled to face her.

"Nora," Charlotte whispered half asleep, her eyes still closed.

"Don't wake up Char, I'm fine." Nora smoothed her hair down, brushing it out of her face.

Charlotte reached a hand towards Nora, her last movement before sleep claimed her again. Nora slipped her hand into Charlotte's and let sleep take her too. The storm of her thoughts dissipated before it could do any damage. The demons never came.

The following morning, Nora got dressed to meet with the city council, deciding that she would rather cross off the rather trauma-inducing tasks on her to-do list as quickly as possible. Even if that meant a twenty four hour turn around.

Charlotte, like always, had a million questions about the previous day and Nora did her best to answer them in a way that wouldn't overwhelm her friend with worry. Neither Vincent nor Charlotte believed Nora when she uttered the words, '*I'm fine,*' to the point where Nora herself was skeptical. She felt fine, all things considered, but maybe she wasn't.

Maybe she shouldn't be.

Any normal person wouldn't be, but Nora had been through this before. The events of her life were cyclical like the seasons. A never ending loop of the same trauma. Someone dies, winter freezes her in melancholy, the spring washes away her pain, the summer warms her back up, the fall strips her down to an all-consuming dread, someone dies, and around it goes.

Nora had her grief down to a science, going about her life as normally as possible, albeit forcing herself to keep moving. Nora had things to do and they wouldn't wait just because she was mildly depressed–thus her decision to visit the council, despite her having just been to Hell.

Nora had little respect for the group of immortals who had been "elected" freely and fairly by the citizens of the town. Election tampering and voter intimidation notwithstanding. Not to mention the mysterious lack of opponents they seemed to have for their seats.

The council consisted of two co-chairs, a Hell Hound and an Archangel. Each party was awarded five additional seats to oversee the ten districts and one at-large seat remained up for grabs every four years. The at-large seat was currently held by the Archangel Mike, giving the Archangels a seven to six simple majority over the Hell Hounds.

People in town proclaimed it was because "good" always prevailed over "evil," but Nora thought it all a bunch of bullshit, election tampering *withstanding*. It was not lost on her that the Hell Hounds had the only woman elected to the council–Lily, whom Nora could actually tolerate–but that was an issue to be discussed at a later date.

The council chamber was tiered, two seats at the top, eleven total in the second, curving around her in a semicircle. All elevated to loom over the witness who was meant to sit at the table in the center of the floor.

Nora didn't sit, but rather stood in front of the table, leaning against the edge. Enough of her grandfather's money was allocated each year to fund their elections and the town, decorum be damned. They relied on *her* and she would be happy to withhold whatever she needed to.

Council Co-chairs, Jude and Gabe sat at the top. Directly below them was the at-large councilor, Mike. To his right, the rest of the Archangels, to his left, the Hell Hounds. Sam was in his usual seat next to Mike smirking down at her.

"Good to see you, Lily." Nora smiled at the green eyed brunette sitting next to Sam. "You all requested to see me?"

Gabe smiled at her, his unnaturally perfect features were unsettling. Nora braced herself. "We know that Sam told you we wanted to discuss your grandfather's estate, but we would actually like to talk about Death."

Nora shot Sam a dirty look, he had played her–lied to get her there. The coward kept his eyes on his hands in his lap.

"What about him?" she demanded. The council knew the nature of her and Death's relationship, they did not however, know she wasn't speaking to him at present.

"It seems there is an issue with his job performance," Gabe continued.

"Which would be?" Nora was growing impatient.

Jude sighed, "He hasn't been delivering souls to their realms." *That was incorrect.*

"Yes he has, he's always busy," Nora defended Death.

"He hasn't," Jude stated bluntly. His long deep brown hair brushed his shoulders as he looked down his pointed nose at Nora. "There are a great many souls lingering in this realm, where they shouldn't be. Had Death done his job, they would be resting."

Nora's mind struggled to keep up with what the Hell Hound was saying. Death was always off working, unless he was with Nora or Charles. What was it to her if he was terrible at his job? It didn't affect her life.

"And you wanted to talk to me about this because—"

"Because he refuses to come in and the veils between the realms are becoming unstable. Souls are meant to move on, when they linger, they cause rifts. Enough rifts will cause the veils to collapse." Mike explained this to Nora in a threatening tone like she was a child who had yet to learn the consequences of her actions.

She looked around the room at the tense council members. They were all on edge, even Sam. "Why can't you all fix this?" It seemed like an obvious question to ask, the answer to which she assumed was laziness on their part.

Jude shifted in his seat. "We are not allowed to interject in afterlife affairs which is why Death was assigned this job in the first place. All we need you to do is speak to him and report back to us about his movements."

Nora may be cross with Death to the point of keeping her distance from him, but she would not betray his trust. If they needed her to report on his movements, they didn't know where he was. She could only imagine what they would do once they found him–Death would die, which was poetic in a way.

There had to be a way to fix this issue without handing Death over to the barbarous council before her. The idea that sparked in Nora's mind was certifiably insane, but it would have to do for now.

"Okay."

Sam's eyes narrowed on her as the rest of the council let out a collective sigh. Unfortunately Sam knew her–Nora never agreed to anything this easily. But his skepticism wasn't a bad thing because she would need him for part of her plan.

"We appreciate your willingness to cooperate with us, Miss Kramer." Mike flashed his perfectly white teeth.

Nora smiled back. "Oh of course. In the meantime I will review the council funding for next year. It is clear there are several functions of this council that have been grossly miscalculated, as it is evident you do not have as much power as you claim."

Protests rippled through the council members, Sam shook his head trying to suppress a smile, and Lily grinned, waving her goodbye.

"Sam." She beckoned him with a tilt of her head towards the door. Nora left the chamber without a second glance, knowing his curiosity would force him to follow.

The Hell Hound indeed followed her out of the council chamber and down the hall to a private meeting room. Nora shut the door once he was through and leaned against it.

Sam looked at her in a way that made her skin crawl. It always had. It was as if he was picking apart her very being, choosing only to focus on the parts he liked, discarding the ones he didn't.

He would show up at the house with Noah entirely too often and taunt her, telling her all the things he thought beautiful about her. Her blonde hair. How funny she was. Her freckles. The shape of her mouth.

Everything Sam *liked* about her were all superficial aspects of her being, all things she didn't care about–she did like that people found her attractive, if she was being honest–but Nora cared more about the person that she was, about the things she was interested in.

The Hell Hound was superficial himself in a way–always concerned about his appearance as if he were preemptively covering up blemishes that would never appear.

"What's up, sunshine?" Sam tilted his head.

"I'll do what the council asks," Nora blurted.

He frowned. "You told them as much, without protest, which is wholly unlike you."

"I want to help Death fix this."

"And just how do you plan to do that?"

Nora shrugged. "There must be a way for me to do so without turning Death over to slaughter."

Sam looked at her as if to argue that Death wouldn't be killed, but he knew better. "There might be a way, but you'd need permission."

"So grant it to me," Nora pressed.

"Do you even know what it would entail?" Sam crossed his arms, his brows pulling together.

"Obviously not, but it couldn't be that hard."

He sighed at the ceiling. "You, yourself, would have to drag each soul to the realm it is meant to be in, which is not an easy task."

Nora imagined as much. Death had always told her souls were sticky. They longed to stay, to be with their loved ones, for their life to not end. Most of them would do just about anything to stay.

"That doesn't mean I can't do it." She stood her ground against him. Sam would not talk her out of this. The loss of Death wouldn't just be inconvenient for Nora, it would hurt Charles and that alone was enough to drive her to this solution.

It was easier to think about it in that manner–helping Charles, not Death. Part of her wanted to let Death deal with his mess himself, but that meant his end and she refused to let him do that to the boy whose happiness seemed shatter proof.

"If anyone has the tenacity to do this, it is you, sunshine," Sam conceded.

Nora was getting impatient. "So grant me permission or whatever you need to do and let's get on with it."

"How are you doing, by the way. I never see you anymore,"

Sam pouted, ignoring her request.

"I'm fine," she tried to dismiss him.

"Nora, I may be several hundred years old, but that does not mean I don't know a thing or two about death. Or grief for that matter."

She supposed he was right, a person's mortality status did not shield them from feeling. "I'm alive, Sam. That's all I have at the moment."

He nodded, as he crossed the room to her. Sam rested his unnaturally warm palms on her cheeks and pressed his lips to her forehead. "I miss him too, sunshine," he whispered against her skin. Nora nodded, fighting back tears, as sparks fluttered over her skin, radiating out from where his lips had been to the tips of her extremities.

Sam pulled away, but didn't drop his hands. "You now have the ability to locate the souls bound for Hell and enter the realm. In order to do so, you must lure them to the gate itself, how you do it is up to you. However, you will need the blessing of an Archangel to get into Heaven."

Nora backed away from him, desperate for space between them, only to run into the door. "There must be one of them you trust." Sam scoffed. "Okay, then one you can tolerate."

He contemplated her request with pursed lips. "There may be one."

It would have to do.

Nora followed Sam out the door and back down the hall to an office on the other side of the building. It took a bit of coaxing and slight groveling on Sam's part, but eventually the Archangel Rami gave in, blessing Nora in a similar manner Sam had.

She left them both to argue about the integrity of their

respective parties and the fallacies of their individual ideals. She could only handle a certain amount of existentialism and her own took precedence.

On her walk home that evening, Nora saw them.

So many of them.

Souls floating through the air, in the same shape they had been when they were alive except now they were transparent, devoid of color and mass. The ones marked for Hell were charcoal, those marked for Heaven were almost white, as if they were simply clusters of mist.

Pressure formed behind her eyes the longer she walked. Some of the souls were screaming for their loved ones, others verbally assaulting anything they could. One old man was chastising a plant for its audacity to be alive in his presence—he unsurprisingly was charcoal gray.

A heaviness settled over Nora, an overwhelming feeling of being lost. She realized it wasn't a feeling that belonged to her, it was theirs. Nora could feel their desire, their inherent needs as if they were her own.

It was debilitating.

It was fascinating.

*Oh, Death. What have you done?*

# CHAPTER 13

## CHARLES

C HARLES'S BOOTS TREADED THROUGH the slush of slowly melting snow and ice. The late winter sun was trying its best to rid the earth of the cold, but it would be a few more weeks before the cold relented. He had just finished his only in person class and was headed to meet Death for lunch.

It had been over a week since they had seen one another because Death had been busier than usual lately. The rate at which people died did not follow any sort of trend which meant Death was busy at random times.

It felt good to check in with him and see how he was doing, especially with how much Death had looked over Charles. Over the years of their acquaintance, Charles never knew Death to have any friends–aside from Nora and himself. That was if Death considered either of them a friend. Charles hated the idea that Death didn't have anyone to turn to.

The two of them ate slowly, in a crowded sandwich shop, talking about whatever thought popped into Charles's mind. He always liked that about himself–his ability to talk to anyone about anything.

When he was younger, his teachers were constantly scolding him for being too talkative. His mother on the other hand encouraged Charles's sunny disposition, always egging him on.

Often making ridiculously grand gestures just to see him smile.

During one of his stays in the hospital, Charles's mother decorated his room in streamers and photos of his favorite band. The band was having a concert and despite his pleading and *light* begging, he hadn't been able to go.

He was devastated.

That particular stay in the hospital had been unexpected, his doctors determined he needed surgery–it would be his fourth–and the outcome didn't look great, but the doctors were hopeful.

The doctors told Charles and his mother how the disease had become aggressive, but there was a new procedure that was showing promising results in other patients like him. Neither Charles nor his mother felt confident in that solution, but there wasn't much else they could do.

Tessa would never let Charles see how upset she was and she certainly wouldn't let him dwell on it either–always helping him to see the good.

The day of the concert, Charles was scheduled to undergo a scan and some tests, keeping him from his room most of the day. When the nurses wheeled him back in, they were grinning, unable to pretend any longer that nothing was going on. The band's music played through a speaker loud enough it could have been the concert itself, making him forget he was missing it at all.

A giant grin broke out over his face when he saw the photos of the band plastered all over the walls of his hospital room. His mother was giddy as she pulled him from the wheelchair to his feet.

"Dance with me," Tessa had said, tugging on his arms to move his body back and forth. The two of them sang and danced for as long as he could before he tired. Tessa laid with him in the hospital bed for hours after, running her fingers through his hair as they listened to the music.

Nurses came and went, his doctor checked in on him periodically. The music played on and on.

It was after that surgery he started to get better.

It was after that surgery his mother started to get sick.

Charles forced his mind back to the present, as nostalgia turned to anger. It was a happy memory and yet every time he thought of it, his chest tightened and his stomach bottomed out. This feeling turned his thoughts to sinister ones, which was exactly why he chose not to think of that part of his life–the part that stole his mother.

"How is she?" Death finally asked before they parted ways. Charles knew the question had been eating at Death from the moment he joined Charles at the table.

"You really haven't spoken to her?"

Death shook his head. "I promised her space. Nora will let me know when she's ready."

"She's good." The lie slid off Charles's tongue too easily, but he didn't feel comfortable sharing about Nora. She wasn't speaking to Death for a reason and he would respect her decision, regardless of his inability to understand the feud. The last thing Charles needed was for her to shut him out too, especially when Charles was lying about how she really was.

Nora was not *good*.

She hadn't been good for the last few months if he thought about it properly. She was distant, different from her normal–Nora was always in her head, always thinking, but never distracted. She had headaches more often than not and she was always tired. Going to bed early, sleeping in late.

Charles arrived at the estate at noon on the days he went over there, unless he had class, and several times she was just getting out of bed. Until recently, Charles knew Nora to be a morning person. It had become increasingly worrisome, but he wouldn't burden Death with that. Charles didn't want to add to his stress over her.

"Good, good," Death muttered idly.

"I'm headed over there now, I'll tell her you say hello."

Death looked at Charles like he meant to protest, but his face softened. "You're a good lad, Charles."

Charles gave Death a quick hug and made his way across town to the estate. The last few months hadn't produced any progress in their attempts to decode the cipher, but they had learned a great deal about her grandfather's crimes. Norman was truly a brilliant man, that was if you didn't take into account how morally corrupt and clearly selfish he was.

He and Charlotte spent as much time as they could with Nora. Charlotte was desperate to fix it all, desperate for Nora to live and Charles found himself becoming more and more desperate too. The more he learned about Nora–there was always something to learn–the more infatuated with her he became.

Of course he thought her beautiful, but she was vastly complex. She didn't hide a single part of herself to please others because she didn't care to be falsely liked. It was fascinating and refreshing.

To Charles's detriment, and seemingly to Nora's, Sam started showing up occasionally. Typically in the evening when Charles and Charlotte were getting ready to leave. Sam was always 'just checking in,' but Charles wasn't convinced it was as innocent as the Hell Hound claimed.

Charles submitted to his ritualistic arrival and pounded the giant iron knocker twice on the door. The action no longer feeling wholly absurd. Vincent answered with his usual smile.

"Hello, Mr. Charles." Vincent was in a green sweater, a deviation from his usual gray.

"Good afternoon, Vincent. I love the choice of color today." Charles smiled back, crossing the threshold of the house, feeling its hum of a greeting beneath his feet. He shrugged out of his jacket and handed it to the caretaker.

"Thank you, young man. Nora is in the drawing room."

"Thank you." Charles thought that was a good sign–Nora was already up and downstairs. Already busy. He made his way down the hall to find her pacing in front of the fire, chewing on a nail, sheets of paper in hand.

"There you are," he said joyfully when he laid eyes on her.

"Hi Chuck," Nora said without looking up at him.

Charles walked over to stand in front of the hearth, grateful for its warmth. "What do you have there?"

She stopped pacing to thrust the papers out to him. "Apparently the museum wants to loan out a few of my grandfather's original paintings as some kind of rotating exhibit."

It was all there in the letter. A curator had visited the Kramer Wing several weeks ago, liked Norman's original works, and brought the idea to the curator at the museum here, a *Mr. Blake.*

"This is good isn't it? Other museums showing an interest in his work?"

Nora looked at him like he had grown a second head. "No," she exclaimed, "his work is to stay in the wing. Right where he wanted it to be. They don't get to just loan his work out because they like the idea."

"Well certainly what you say goes if they are writing to you for your permission," Charles suggested.

"You make a good point, Chuck. It is my decision." Nora stormed out of the drawing room and down the hall. Charles struggled to keep up with her swift pace to the study.

It was just like the rest of the rooms in the house, paneled walls, painted a deep green, and bookshelves–always bookshelves–built into the wall behind the desk. A thick, dark mahogany desk, which matched the gothic style of the house perfectly sat just in front of the shelves with a plush, brown leather chair pushed in neatly behind it. Charles imagined himself getting a lot of important work done at that desk.

Nora picked up the phone and started to dial when a drop of something hit the wood.

"Shit," Nora cursed, dropping the phone to pinch the bridge of her nose.

It was blood.

Her nose was bleeding–a lot.

Charles rushed over to her and coaxed her into the chair. *Coaxed* wasn't completely accurate as he half asked, half pushed her down. He swiped the box of tissues off a nearby shelf and handed her a wad of them. Nora leaned forward, resting her elbows on her knees, and replaced her hand with the tissues.

Blood dripped down her hand to her wrist, quickly approaching the pushed up sleeves of her sweater. Charles knelt in front of her to wipe the blood from her hands and forearms while Nora continued to pinch her nose.

"Nora, what's going on," he demanded.

"I'm fine, Chuck." Her stoney gray eyes begged him to stop asking.

He wouldn't.

"Try again."

"I haven't been sleeping well. I'm just tired. That's all."

It wasn't a complete lie. Charles could see how tired she was, from the bags under eyes to the redness that lined their edges. However, not sleeping wasn't the sole cause of her deterioration.

"You can talk to me, you know. About anything," Charles reminded her. They talked about a lot of things, but there was clearly something she was keeping to herself.

Nora nodded. "I know."

"Death says hello, by the way," he said, offering her a smile and changing the subject, choosing to let her keep her secret.

For now.

*Hmm,* was her only response, but Charles could see the sadness in her eyes as they watched the floor. Nora would never admit as much, but she missed Death as much as Death missed her.

"Let me see," Charles whispered, gently pulling her bloodied hands away from her face. He took Nora's chin in his hand and moved her head from side to side, examining it.

Dried blood covered her nose and around her mouth, but the bleeding had thankfully stopped. Charles could count her freckles from this distance. They littered the bridge of her nose, fanning out over the tops of her cheeks. Nora's gray eyes settled on his, undying determination blazing in her irises. She was beautiful, even covered in blood. "Do you have a headache today?"

"No, Charles, I'm fine." Her eyes narrowed.

"I almost believe you," he chided and dropped his hand. The corner of her mouth quirked. "I have an idea for today."

"Oh do tell."

"What if we ditched the life saving crusade for the day and

just watched a movie. Like normal people." Charles arched a brow at her, challenging her to say yes.

Nora laughed and the sound was like music in his ears. "You and I are not normal people, Chuck."

He smiled back at her. "No, but we can pretend can't we?"

"We can certainly try," she conceded.

"Good, now go wash your face. You look like you've been in a fight." Charles pushed off the floor to straighten himself as she stood from the chair.

"Who says I haven't been?" Nora winked before leaving the room and Charles thought that maybe she actually had. Not a physical fight of course, but a mental one. Maybe with herself. Maybe with Sam. Or the museum. Or the council. Regardless, Nora was wearing herself down and Charles was at a loss for how to help her.

Twenty minutes later, Nora joined him in yet another room of the house–the living room. He was only calling it that because it was the one room with a TV.

The lack of technology the Kramers possessed was shocking. One phone, one TV, a record player, several film cameras, a typewriter. Charles had always assumed rich people owned the latest *everything*, but this house looked as though it stopped aging decades ago.

Nora sat herself down on the couch next to him, face and hands free of crimson stains, and pulled her knees to her chest. Charles found a movie, but not long after it started, he looked over to find Nora asleep, her dark eyelashes resting softly on her cheeks.

He grabbed a blanket to drape over her, tugging it up to her chin and around her shoulders. The sun was long set and Charles was on his third movie by the time she finally stirred from her "nap."

Nora's face contorted as she stretched her limbs for the first time in hours. "How long was I out?" She asked, voice groggy, eyes still closed.

"A few hours," Charles answered, underselling her reality.

Nora opened her eyes to glace out the dark window, her eyebrows pulling together. "You didn't have to stay, Chuck. I didn't think I'd fall asleep."

"You clearly needed it. It's no worry at all." Charles was just happy she got some rest. Happy she was comfortable enough around him to do so. He didn't have anywhere to be anyway.

"Thank you for helping me today." Nora reached a hand out from under the blanket and slipped it into his. She had a habit of touching him when she wanted Charles to know she well and truly meant something.

Similar to her use of his full name, it demanded his attention. Forced him to hear her words–not that he wasn't already listening. Her fingers were cold in his, despite them having been under the blanket. Charles tightened his grip around hers, willing his body heat to warm her.

"Always, Nora. You never need to ask. I'm happy to help." Charles said, hoping she heard him.

Nora had insisted he go home to rest himself, that she didn't feel like moving to her room to go back to sleep. Charles bid her goodnight and headed to the coffee shop nearby that was always open late. He ordered a hot chocolate and not his usual black coffee because he didn't need the caffeine at the current hour. Charles was merely desperate for something warm to hold onto for the rest of his walk home.

As soon as he exited the coffee shop and turned the corner, he saw her. She was bundled up against the cold in her wool coat, pink scarf wrapped around her neck. Nora was headed some-where with a purpose, muttering to herself. Concern slammed Charles in the chest.

It was late and she was supposed to be resting.

Was this why she wasn't getting any sleep? Because she was walking around town late into the night?

Where was she headed?

Who was she going to see?

Thousands of questions swirled in Charles's brain as an un-familiar feeling pooled in his stomach. He felt overly warm, despite the chill, as he fought the urge to walk right up to her and demand she tell him everything.

It wasn't a difficult decision to follow her. Part of Charles was uncomfortable with the act of following her. It felt invasive, it felt wrong, but light stalking for the purpose of looking after her well-being certainly couldn't be a bad thing, he decided.

*Even if it was positively creepy.*

*Even if it was technically a criminal offense.*

Charles discarded his uncomfortability like an old coat and followed her into the night, all the way to the back of the cemetery.

# CHAPTER 14

## DEATH

C HARLES WAS LYING TO him.

Part of Death was okay with it–the part that was happy someone was there for Nora.

Part of Death was *not* okay with it–the part who knew Nora could be a shifty little brat.

*He meant that as lovingly as possible.*

But Nora was not okay.

Death knew it, Charles knew it, and he had no doubt Nora knew as well. Death had been watching, from a distance and never for very long, for proof of life. She was leaving the house late at night and spending time with the cantankerous Councilman Sam. The Hell Hound made Death's unbeating heart burn with rage.

Nora tolerated Sam solely because he had been a friend of Noah's, but Death had always been skeptical. Here is where he would make ill assumptions about Hell Hounds all having bad intentions, but that thought could not be reserved for their party alone–the Archangels were equally as abhorrent, if not more so. Self righteous bastards that they were.

Aside from the occasional lunch with Charles, Death truthfully had been busy. There were a lot of people dying these days and with his attention strained between his two wards, he had little to no time to think about the dead and where he was taking them.

Death told everyone he was a third party collector who kept his head down and did his job without question. Unfortunately that was a lie.

*How shocking.*

Death had opinions!

He had a moral compass!

There were a number of souls who didn't deserve the realm they had been condemned to and he would agree with Nora that an eternity in a singular place was condemnation in and of itself. Death didn't need to subject them to either eternity, especially when their condemnation wasn't warranted.

The powers at be weren't all knowing. They shouldn't have the right to officiate morality as if it were some kind of game when they were morally ambiguous themselves. However, that was an existential crisis for a different time, a different millennia.

It didn't mean Death was any better, but that he could recognize flaws in the universe, having lived in it. The issue at hand was Death's active defiance of the ledger, the council, and the beings that oversaw them all.

*It was a hefty mess.*

Death hadn't always been like this. His morality came and went like the tide until too many years had passed for him to remain complacent. Life had a way of shaping one's morality—and the semantics of Death's *life* were questionable at best.

Was it a life if his heart didn't beat or he lacked warm blood flowing through his veins? But wasn't it just that if he was wholly conscious? If he *evolved* just like the rest of the world?

The more a person saw, the more they had to choose between right and wrong, had to differentiate between good and evil. Every being, functional heart or no, had to make concessions which drove their moral compass, and Death, despite his best efforts, was no exception to that rule.

Over the past however many thousands of years of his life—Death didn't keep track, as was his prerogative being an immortal—he had been *accidentally* forgetting to drag certain souls to their intended realms. He had been rather diligent with his work, until he wasn't. At first there were a few he truly did forget about—a particularly antagonistic old man, a woman who never stopped wailing, and a quiet little boy.

Death expected consequences for his forgetfulness. He was on edge for weeks only for nothing to happen. The veils remained intact. No higher power showed up to smite him.

From then on he was intentional about who he "forgot." Mostly it consisted of people who were inherently terrible and somehow made it into Heaven. Or those who had made a deal with Lucifer in order to do something good, thus condemning them to Hell.

He never offered to let Norman stay, the man was a criminal after all. However, he did offer to let Charles's mother, Tessa, stay, but she turned him down. Tessa wanted to rest and didn't want to potentially burden Charles.

It was hard work being Death. It wasn't easy deciding who he left behind and who he drug to their eternal resting place. The art of dragging a soul to its intended realm was simple. It took a little coaxing, something for the soul to connect with, to feel seen and safe. Death could provide that comfort, which was the main point to his job. It wasn't exactly difficult when their most prominent desires radiated off of them like waves from the ocean, lapping over him in pure understanding.

But souls lingered.

This fact has always been true. They routinely did not like to move on and the town was full of them as he made his way home. Souls floated through each other, through the walls of buildings, through those still living–the living remaining blissfully unaware.

The more souls that lingered, the harder it was for Death to pretend they didn't exist. Their screaming never stopped. Their desire never dissipated. And only he could hear them all.

*"Please sir, help me find my way back to my house."*

It wasn't enough to just turn his mind off.

*"Mark my words! When I catch that bitch, she's dead!"*

The stress Nora caused him was pulling his mind in too many different directions to be useful any longer.

*"Noooooo! Please, someone please!"*

Death knew a lot of the blame rested on his shoulders. The lies. The deceit. The trust he betrayed by not telling her the truth.

*"Sir, do you happen to know where my mummy is?"*

Nora valued truth above all else. She craved it. Her constant need to know information drove her and Death could understand that.

*"I can hear her… My baby. Where is she?"*

People had either lied or been cruel to Nora most of her life. Her father was the scum of the Earth and was lucky he had never laid a hand on Nora or Death himself would have taken Nathaniel from this realm well before his scheduled departure.

*"I have an idea–if you would just listen–if you could just tell my Margie I love her, I will go and never bother you again. Please, sir!"*

Nora's mother was no saint herself. She wasn't cruel, but

rather completely detached, which Death considered to be cruel in its own way.

*"THESE FUCKING PLANTS!"*

He knew Norman's betrayal would hurt the worst, which was the exact reason Death had never said anything. Death, like Norman, had assumed there was nothing to be done, plus he had made the mistake once before of telling his ward the truth–his first ward, James.

*"How sweet it would be to feel the sun on my face."*

James had similarly volatile parents to Nora, except his hit him just as much as each other. His mother was having a long standing affair with a local businessman when she became pregnant with James, but those were the days where divorce was unheard of and adultery was dealt with by force.

James's father was not his father by blood and thus resented James for his mother's actions. Death started watching over James when his mother died from consumption, leaving James alone to contend with his father.

The boy was fifteen.

It wasn't until years later when his father killed James's real father, the business man, that James had questions. He wanted to know why. To know what drove his father to such an unspeakable act.

Death thought it best to tell the boy, he thought it would help him. But in the end, James hated Death just as much as he hated his father and left the continent, leaving them both behind to rot.

So when Norman asked Death to watch over Nora, he decided he would do things differently. He wouldn't repeat his past mistakes.

He wouldn't lose Nora too.

Unfortunately that decision backfired as well. Death's only saving grace was that Nora hadn't left yet. No matter how difficult she was, she stood her ground, never ran from a fight. It may not have been the right choice to lie to her, but it hadn't been a complete waste either.

*"Children these days are so spoiled."*

Death needed to get home. His sanity was on the verge of breaking and if he didn't close his eyes soon, he was going to find a negative outlet for it all. However, the negative outlet would result in him punching a wall or a person.

If he punched a wall, he'd definitely break his hand, however, if he punched a person, there was a high probability of said person fighting back resulting in a broken face. Death was too vain to consider that option and despite his sanity teetering toward masochism, he appreciated not having broken bones–face, hand, or otherwise.

*"Does anyone have the time!"*

*"Or the date, I would settle for the date."*

*"Yes, I would love to know what year it is."*

*Is there not a paper around anywhere?"*

Pressure continued to build behind Death's eyes, the beginning of a headache that hasn't plagued him in a millennia.

*"Why doesn't anyone know the date?"*

*"How about the town? What is this town called?"*

*"Does it matter?"*

*"Fuck off."*

*"That's it. I am uprooting every last one of these fucking plants."*

"EVERYONE SHUT THE FUCK UP!" Death screamed, coming to a stop in the middle of the street, his hands shaking, vision blurring slightly.

He shocked even himself with his outburst, but it worked.

The world around him went quiet. Time itself stilled a moment and Death felt more at ease than he had in years.

A woman, who was very much alive, gaped at him across the street.

*Right,* Death thought, *how the living still exist. Silly me.*

If Death wasn't *Death,* he would have known all too well the street had been quiet–that the insufferable noise was indeed coming from the dead.

He inclined his head at the woman. "Respectfully, of course."

She scoffed, pulled her coat tight around her before fleeing. The other people who had been staring, continued on their way and Death turned down the street to his home. The souls resumed their normal activity, having stopped momentarily to gawk at him as well.

Thankfully, his walk home was not a long one. From the center of town it was only a few blocks away. The cobblestone streets were forever uneven, but Death loved them, leading him to where his house sat alone at the end of the road.

It was quaint. A simple white house with a red door. Nothing grand, but he didn't need grand, he needed it to stand, needed it to be quiet.

Death had moved many times over his countless years and loved this place more than any of the others. A single bedroom home just for him, a small kitchen, a reading room, and a back porch. He didn't own many things to fill it aside from a few books and his photos–mostly of Nora and Charles–and his journals.

When he laid his head down on his pillow that evening he thought of his two wards. They brought him peace despite their ability to frustrate him.

In all the wrong he had done in his life, in all of the questionable acts, if there was any good, it was because of them.

# CHAPTER 15

## NORA

I T WAS WELL AFTER midnight and Nora was in search of her third and final soul to take to Heaven. Months ago, when she started this task, the first few souls had been cooperative and easy to convince to go with her.

The first had been a young girl. Nora talked to her about dolls and horses, because most of all, the little girl missed her toys. She missed her parents too, but her *toys*. The little girl went quietly with her to the gates of Heaven, which were Hell's opposite in every way.

Structurally, Heaven was the same as Hell, but that's where the similarities ended. The stairs ascended, which made sense to Nora's brain, and once she was at the top, she was overwhelmed with the smell of roses instead of smoke.

Nora hated roses.

They reminded her of death–littering every funeral in copious amounts to mask the scent of embalming and decay.

The platform was covered in a mist and everything was gilded with white light instead of a smoky orange haze. Nora found herself squinting against the brightness of everything to see around the space. The gates were solid gold and clouds swirled around the rungs, constantly shifting as if there was a steady flow of air Nora couldn't feel.

Nora stood there, taking in everything that was meant to make her feel at peace–the blinding white of the atmosphere, the stillness of the perfectly chilled air, the intense flower smell–but she felt more unnerved than ever, her muscles tightening with each breath she took. When the gates opened, they did so with ease. Gliding gently over the ground without a sound or disturbance to the space around them.

More clouds flooded from the open gates, and floating atop them was the most gorgeous woman Nora had ever seen. Chestnut brown hair flowed down her back and around her shoulders to her waist. She was dressed in a long, white dress that shimmered with each movement.

The woman reminded Nora of Charlotte. Dark bushy eyebrows adorned her face over brown eyes which drifted over Nora before settling on the young girl.

"You must be Kendall," said the most overpoweringly ethereal voice Nora had ever heard. The sound of her voice came from every direction, echoing around Nora as if it had come from inside her head, making her feel even more unsettled. "We have been waiting for you."

The woman smiled and stretched out her hand to Kendall who asked, "What is this place?"

"This is Heaven," the woman said in her all-encompassing voice.

"Are you God?" Asked Kendall, her mouth hanging open.

The woman nodded, the movement too smooth. "I am."

"You're a woman," Nora cut in, frowning slightly.

"I am." The woman–*God*–shifted her gaze to Nora. Nora's muscles tensed again, as she found it suddenly difficult to breathe. She wasn't sure how she felt about being looked upon by God. Or how she felt about God being a woman compared to the antiquated male version Nora had always envisioned.

Her mind was reeling.

"I look differently to everyone," God said as if Nora's thoughts were not her own.

Nora loosed a breath, "Oh." Words were far from her brain, her ability to form thought was rapidly declining.

"Thank you for bringing this little one to us, we have been waiting a long time to greet her." God's deeply tanned skin glittered golden in the white light.

"Of course, but I should be going." Nora's uneasiness settled into her bones, hardening her spine.

"Of course," God said, smiling brilliantly at her again, but the way she said the words insinuated that if Nora wanted to stay, she would be welcome.

Nora backed away as Kendall slipped her tiny hand into God's outstretched one and walked with her through the open golden gates of Heaven. They closed behind them as carefully as they had opened–without a sound.

Once Nora was out of the mausoleum, she stood in place for a moment. Her mind taking a while to catch up to her corporeal form. Relaxation washed over Nora with the fresh air, loosening her muscle the second the mausoleum sealed itself shut behind her. Then she smelled the roses clinging to her and her stomach churned.

The smell never got better after months of bringing souls up to Heaven. It never became more bearable. Nora made a mental note to make sure there were no roses at her own funeral in the fall. If Nora found out someone covered her grave and casket with roses, there would be Hell to pay and he would haunt every last one of them.

Later that evening while walking through downtown, past a

particularly pungent house, she added lilies to the list of banned flowers at her funeral.

The soul of an older man sat on a bench in the center of the park near the fountain. Nora assessed him like all the others, letting his desires wash over her. Nora's chest tightened, her throat constricted and after a moment, her eyes started to sting.

He was miserable. Consumingly so.

Nora walked over to the bench he was on and sat down beside him.

"I love this fountain in the height of summer," Nora stated.

He sucked in a sharp breath. "You can see me?"

Nora smiled at him and watched him deflate with relief and the pressure in her chest lightened. The old man had been waiting to be seen.

"It has been so long since I have had a conversation with anyone." Nora let him continue, "This is one of my favorite spots in the whole town. I would come here with my family every day the sun was out. After I died, I came back to wait for my wife to visit. After months of waiting I gave up believing I'd see her, until she finally showed up." His glassy eyes lingered on the waterless fountain. "My Penny brought our kids and grandkids with her.

"I sat in this spot all afternoon watching them play, watching Penny and my kids talk for hours, until the sun went down. They were so beautiful." He turned his face back to Nora. "All of them were beautiful. Penny, my god, she was as beautiful as the day I married her. She never changed for me. She grew with me, but I swear I was the only one who aged while she remained her youthful, joyous self."

Nora's lip shook as a tear slipped down her face. "Did they come back often?"

"For a while." His eyes lowered to the ground and his lips pulled taught. "But Penny got sick. Our kids brought her until they didn't anymore. I felt her leave this Earth, you know." The old man put a hand over his heart. "Right here in my chest, I felt it. It was as if someone had excised a part of my soul and I was thankful in that moment for not being alive because her death would have surely stopped my heart."

"Where do you think she is now?" Nora asked, desperately trying to keep her voice even.

The old man looked at Nora fully and smiled. "I know she's in Heaven. There is no other place for her to be."

The night air bit at her cheeks, threatening to freeze the tracks of her tears on her face. He glowed silver in the moonlight next to her, how obvious it was he should be in Heaven too, with his Penny.

*What have you done, Death?* Nora asked herself for what felt like the thousandth time since the council meeting a few months ago.

"Do you want to join her?"

His face fell, leaving his mouth slightly open. His hope was overwhelming. "Is that possible?"

"I can take you there."

"I would love nothing more," his voice cracked and if this version of him could cry, Nora believed he would.

"I'm Nora, by the way." She stood, gesturing for him to follow.

He nodded. "Nora, I'm Richard."

They moved slowly out of the park and across town to the cemetery. Her muscles ached and the thought of ascending those wicked stairs for a third time that night made her want to lay down right there in the park grass, but this old man deserved to see his wife again.

He deserved to rest.

"How old are you, Nora?"

"I'm almost twenty," she answered flatly.

"Oh to be young again," Richard sang. "You don't seem very excited about the prospect of getting older."

Nora laughed lightly. "Not really. I haven't enjoyed my birthday for a while."

"You are too young to not enjoy your life, Nora." Richard looked at her sidelong, she could feel his eyes on her, but she refused to meet them.

"All my family is gone, so there isn't really anyone to celebrate with anymore."

Richard nodded in understanding, and Nora thought if anyone did, it would likely be him—this old man whom she hadn't known existed before this evening. "I am very sorry to hear that. Surely you have friends who would love to celebrate you."

The corners of her mouth curled. "I have a good friend, Charlotte."

"What about boys?" he teased. "A pretty girl like you surely has a boyfriend."

"Not a boyfriend," she laughed.

Richard raised his eyebrows. "But there is a young man."

Nora rolled her eyes, but gave in all the same. There was no harm in giving this man what he wanted in his final moments when there was no one for him to share her secrets with. "His name is Charles."

"Tell me about Charles." It was a demand, one she was surprisingly happy to oblige.

So Nora did.

She told Richard about his hair that drove her insane, his

enviable blue eyes, how he smiled at her as if she were more than just a measly, distant star. Most of all, she told Richard how he listened to her.

Charles had a way of paying attention that made her feel more seen than anyone ever had. He knew she was having headaches, knew something was off, but he was gentle enough to not push her either. Nora never felt like he was making her talk, making her do something she didn't want to.

Most importantly, he didn't shy away from the dark corners of her mind. Nora was comfortable around him and she wasn't sure if that was due to their mutual friend or if it was just *Charles.*

Nora suspected it was just Charles.

She also told Richard how Charles terrified her. How his happiness was so foreign to her and how she worried about corrupting him, making him dark like her. He was like Noah in that regard–*the sun*–an eternal bright spot in her life. Charles shone with a brightness that threatened to set her on fire if she wasn't careful.

And despite it all, Nora wanted desperately to let him.

Richard murmured how sorry he was that she wouldn't get to live a long, wonderful life, and she assured him it was alright, that she didn't mind.

They both knew she was lying, but neither of them said anything.

The old man listened to her talk the entire way to the mausoleum and up the stairs to the rose smelling platform.

"I'm sorry I talked so much," Nora admitted, but she was lying again because she wasn't sorry in the slightest. Her chest felt lighter, and despite the growing fatigue in her muscles, a true wave of calmness washed over her for the first time in a long time.

"I am honored you shared it all with me." Richard was looking at her solemnly, his lips pulled across his face, but the smile only half met his eyes.

"I'm happy I found you tonight, that I could reunite you with your Penny."

Richard let out a heavy breath. "Thank you for this, I will remember it for the rest of my existence."

Nora nodded and turned to head down the stairs, but Richard cleared his throat, pulling her attention back to him.

"No matter how long you have left on this earth, sweet girl, you need people and I am here telling you that it's okay to need. That your pain won't ruin other people, but they may, in fact, heal you. The point of life is to know other people, to let them teach you about yourself. And the beauty of life are the connections we make when we're alive, the love we feel." Richard looked at her sternly and she nodded, tears welling in her eyes. "Hold your people close, Nora. Hold your Charles close, because the fear you feel now is worth it. It is worth knowing."

With one last reassuring look, Richard turned to head off toward the gates with a God that looked too much like Charlotte. A single tear fell down Nora's face as she made a silent promise to the old man she helped find his way home.

*She would try, God, how she would try.*

When she finally made it back down the stairs her legs were wobbling and the pressure behind her eyes was unbearable. It was the only time she thought her mortality a hindrance. Every time she ascended the stairs to Heaven, it rendered her exhausted, barely able to stand.

Nora loved her mortality, the finality of her life. She loved knowing there was an ending, that everything she lived through, everything she did, was worth it because there was an end. But she was tired and a momentary lapse in judgment found her wishing she was immortal–for the sole purpose of not feeling fatigue.

Death certainly didn't have this problem. In all the years she's known him, he hadn't had a headache once. He didn't look any different. His nose never bled. He was never tired.

Nora on the other hand was at Death's door–metaphorically that is because she didn't actually know where he lived or if he even owned a home.

She was able to make it out the door and down the mausoleum steps before her legs gave out. Nora's knees hit the gravel hard, the tiny stones biting her skin through her jeans and cutting the palms of her hands. She lowered herself the rest of the way to the ground, too tired to focus on the dull stinging of her broken skin.

*Might as well lay here for a bit,* she thought.

And she did.

Nora laid in the gravel, letting the lingering winter chill blanket her. Heaven wasn't scalding hot like Hell so there had been no need to take her coat off which turned out to be rather lucky.

In the last three months of this life draining task, Nora had only taken souls to Heaven. She did as many as she could each night until she was on the verge of passing out–unashamed to admit that she laid in this exact position several times, having lost count of the total.

Taking souls to Heaven wasn't easy, obvious by her current state, but they were easier than the souls bound for Hell. An assumption Nora made due to her having not taken a single one down there and her blatant avoidance of all the charcoal gray figures in town.

But Nora didn't exactly trust herself to enter Hell again. She was mature enough to admit that. The temptation to walk through those gates and never look back was still too great.

Nora turned her head, the gravel shifting beneath her skull, to look at the door to Hell. Her brother was somewhere down there.

A place he didn't deserve to be.

"You going to lay there all night?" Asked an overly smooth voice.

"It's more comfortable than you think," Nora answered keeping her gaze pinned on the marble slab.

Brown dress shoes entered her field of vision, perfectly hemmed blue suit pants stopping just above them. His ankles were bare, showing off his deeply browned skin. When she finally looked up at him, his hands were outstretched to help her off the ground.

"Up you go, sunshine."

Sam pulled her to her feet and held her upright until they were both confident her legs would do the job.

"How did you find me?" she seethed. Nora had hoped he'd leave her alone after he'd granted her permission to enter Hell, but she should have known better. That wasn't who Sam was. He could never just let her be. He'd been showing up to the estate more frequently, he was bound to turn up in the cemetery eventually.

Sam tilted his head. "You really have to ask me that?" When she didn't respond, he continued, "I was worried about you. You haven't been yourself lately."

Nora scoffed, brushing herself off. "You don't know me,

Sam. How are you supposed to know I haven't been myself?"

"For starters, that was your first dig at me in weeks and it was half-assed," his mouth twisted and one of his eyebrows raised mockingly, "and secondly, you look like shit, Nora."

"Ouch." She pretended to be hurt by his comment, but ultimately she couldn't argue. Nora *had* looked better, that was for sure, less sullen and sickly. She was always pale, but never *this* pale. Her nose bleed that afternoon had not helped her case.

"When are you going to admit you need help, sunshine?" Sam asked, reaching up to brush her cheek. She batted his hand away.

"I have help."

"Who? Charlotte and pretty boy?"

Nora rolled her eyes and turned on a heel to exit the cemetery. "His name is Charles."

"Huh, must have slipped my mind," Sam muttered, falling into step beside her.

"I'm sure it did." She picked up her pace. Sleep was settling into her bones and Nora desperately wanted to wash off the smell of roses clinging to her before she fell into bed.

"I don't know what you see in him. He is too cheery for you."

Nora laughed and the pressure in her head jumped. "Charles is rather cheery, isn't he?" It was a quality she enjoyed about him —is undying state of bliss.

It was foreign to her.

She envied it.

They rounded the corner to the estate, stopping at the entrance. Nora pinched the bridge of her nose and squeezed her eyes shut, willing the pain behind her eyes to dissipate.

"Are you having headaches?" Sam asked, rounding to face

her.

Nora groaned her response. It was becoming debilitating, the pain. She stood there for a moment breathing through it when his hot hands settled on her face. Sam's thumbs pressed lightly together between her eyebrows moving outward over her forehead. He repeated the motion several times, the pain lessening with each pass.

Nora's muscles loosened and the sensation of it was so arousing it threatened to melt her into the ground. But then she remembered they were Sam's hands and the feeling was gone in an instant, her joints stiffened, her hands balled into fists. He repeated the motion one last time and the pressure behind her eyes was completely gone.

When Nora finally opened her eyes again, he was smiling softly down at her.

"Thank you," she murmured shyly.

Sam's eyes lifted to something behind her, something from the way they came. "You need only ask, sunshine. I'm happy to ease any pain you have."

When his eyes found hers again, they were burning with lust. Nora rolled hers, tempting her headache to return. "You are delusional."

He chuckled, leaning down to press a kiss to her cheek, "Good night, Nora."

"Good night, Sam."

Nora left him on the sidewalk to stare at whatever only he could see down the street.

# CHAPTER 16

## CHARLES

C HARLES WATCHED FROM THE end of the street as Sam kissed Nora on the cheek and bid her goodnight. An insidious heat crawled its way up his spine to lick his cheeks as his hand tightened around his paper cup. He had forgotten it existed–the hot chocolate that had been meant to keep him warm on his walk home was hours old, not a sip of it gone. Charles had been following Nora all night, staying far enough away to watch, but not be noticed.

The night had gotten colder and the usual fog that descended upon the town was beginning to settle on the streets. Charles was ready for spring, for the warming sun, the rain, the fresh smell of new life. He loved the spring air. It made him feel new and whole again, giving him the energy to conquer the world.

*He wouldn't, he just liked the feeling that bloomed in his chest.*

When Nora and Sam stopped in front of the estate, Sam noticed him lingering at the end of the street. The Hell Hound's stare felt like a hand wrapping around Charles's throat. Sam waited until Nora was firmly inside the house before walking down the street to greet Charles. He was in his usual blue tailored suit with no coat to shield him against the cold.

"Chris, right?" Sam asked with a devious smirk.

His jaw clenched. "It's Charles."

"Ah, right. Charles," said the Hell Hound with a touch of disdain. "What are you doing out here at such an hour?"

"I could ask you the same question," Charles shot back.

Sam shifted his weight, slipping his hands into his pants pockets. "Just seeing my sunshine home safely."

Charles scoffed, "*Your* sunshine."

"Well she certainly isn't yours, Chris. Or am I missing something?"

"Not missing anything, Samuel."

"It's 'Councilman,'" Sam corrected.

"Whatever you are making her do, *Samuel,* stop. It's killing her. Or have you not noticed?" Charles seethed. He felt his anger taking over, unsure if his fingers were going numb from the cool temperature or his rage.

Sam's smug expression faltered for a brief second. He was worried about Nora too, but he wouldn't admit it, at least not to Charles. "The things she does are her own choices, surely you know she doesn't do anything unless she wants to."

He was deflecting, but he also had a point–Nora never did *anything* she didn't want to. If Charles knew one thing about her, it was that.

"Tell me."

"No."

Charles gaped at Sam. "I can't help her if I don't know what is going on."

Sam frowned. "Well if she won't tell you, then it looks like you are out of luck." He clapped Charles on the shoulder and started down the street, footsteps echoing in the still air around them.

"Then why is it you aren't helping her, or are you okay with her killing herself for whatever this task is that she's doing?"

Charles followed Sam's quick pace. He knew poking at Sam's worry for Nora would get him to talk sooner than simply begging the Hell Hound to give up the information. Sam cared for Nora, maybe even believed he loved her and Charles could work with that.

Could understand that.

"If it were up to me, Nora wouldn't be involved in this at all, but my hands are tied. There is nothing I can do to help other than check in on her and ease her pain." Sam's tone was calm, but Charles could see the tension in his jaw, the stiffness in his movements.

"Look, you don't have to like me, we don't even have to speak after this, but if you can't help her, tell me there is something I can do."

Sam stopped his desperate pursuit to leave Charles behind and turned around. "She is dragging souls to Heaven and Hell to help out the council. Turns out Death is quite terrible at his job, or has been intentionally selective. Whatever the case, there are too many souls that haven't moved on and it is causing a rift in the veils."

"What?" Charles's lungs stopped taking in air.

"Exactly what I said Chris."

Charles grappled with the information he was just given, his mind swimming in a thousand different directions, struggling with which emotion, thought, or feeling to focus on first.

"She is taking souls to *Hell*?" Charles's words choked out of him. The thought of her descending into Hell made his stomach bottom out.

"No, just Heaven. We gave her access to both realms, but so far she has only been entering Heaven, though I have no idea why." Sam grimaced, shifting his weight again and examining

Charles.

"What." Charles really couldn't breathe.

Sam choked out a laugh. "Have you lost all comprehension ability? I said she hasn't gone to Hell."

Charles knew exactly why Nora wasn't going down into Hell–she didn't trust herself with the temptation of staying–but he wouldn't be sharing that particular piece of information with Sam. Regardless, his lungs were working again. Barely.

"Let me take care of Hell," Charles blurted without thinking. He needed a task. He couldn't sit any longer and watch as Nora withered away, fighting her desire to free her brother's soul. Plus he needed a distraction from the rage boiling in the pit of his stomach with Death's name on it.

Nora was doing this, despite her continued animosity with Death and the immortal either didn't care, or had no idea. Unfortunately, Charles would have to deal with that later.

"No," Sam said without an invitation to argue.

But Charles would be arguing. He looked into the dark eyes of the Hell Hound, taking in his flawless brown skin and hard set mouth. This was a man who thought he knew Nora, but didn't. A man who thought he knew what was best for her. Maybe Charles didn't know what was best for her either, but he knew enough to try.

"Yes, because even I know you don't want her going into Hell. It might be the only thing you and I can agree on when it comes to her, and it still needs to be fixed, so let me deal with it."

Sam looked at Charles for a long moment, as though he was imagining a thousand different ways to remove Charles's skin. "Fine, but I have one condition."

"Name it," Charles said a little too eagerly.

"You never mention this to Nora. She doesn't need to know that I let you into Hell."

"Deal."

Sam sighed heavily, pursing his lips. He removed his hands from his pockets and placed them on Charles's face. They were unnaturally hot–if Charles wasn't already uncomfortable with Sam touching him, he'd have been concerned about their warmth, but then Sam brought his lips to Charles's forehead and the feeling doubled.

A tingling sensation spread over the top of his head and down his body, all the way to his toes. Goosebumps formed on Charles's skin in its wake. He shook off the sensation and Sam's hands, putting space between them.

"Was that necessary?" Charles asked.

"It was if you want access to Hell." Sam raised an eyebrow.

"How does that work?"

"You now have permission to enter the realm of Hell and the ability to see souls bound to it. How you get them there is up to you." Sam grumbled and began to walk away, looking defeated, but Charles had one last question.

"Why do you call her 'sunshine' when her nickname is 'little star?'" It had bugged Charles from their first encounter at the estate.

Sam turned back around, annoyed. "Because she is more than a measly 'little star' Chris, she is the sun. I thought that obvious."

"But she's not the sun." Charles didn't mean that in a bad way, but it was the truth. Nora was not bright and wholly optimistic like the moniker, "sunshine," implied. She didn't burn like the sun, but she was radiant all on her own, just a little colder and a bit darker.

It didn't make her any less beautiful and brilliant, but it was clear Sam didn't see these parts of her or he simply refused to.

Charles did.

He saw it all.

The light, the dark, the beauty of them both. Nora's anger drove her in a way that Charles might not understand, but one he could respect. She didn't need to be the sun, she just needed to be *her*.

"Whatever, pretty boy," Sam said, shaking his head and leaving Charles for good this time.

On the walk back to his flat, Charles began to see them–the souls that belonged to Hell. They were the same menacing gray as the smoke that engulfed the realm.

He could see their faces, hear their voices, feel their longing. All of it sitting on his chest like a boulder. Charles avoided them the best he could on his walk home, keeping his head down, but no matter how hard he tried, he felt it all–their emotion–as if it were his own.

When he finally laid down in his bed he thought of Nora doing this alone and the tightness returned to his chest. How could she keep this from him, or more appropriately, *why*? Why was Death not fixing this mess? Who did she think she was protecting by keeping this to herself?

A million questions raced through his mind, too fast to focus on just one.

The only solace he found in it all was the resounding fact she hadn't gone to Hell. That she seemed, by all accounts, to be avoiding it. However, the thought only calmed him long enough before he remembered she still had unfettered access to the realm.

Charles took a deep breath, in an attempt to steady himself.

His mind was a mess, his heart was racing, and he surely wouldn't be sleeping that night.

Charles wasn't due back at the estate for a few days which gave him time to determine the best way to get these souls to their intended realm. It was evident they all wanted something–most of which was revenge on the people who had wronged them. Their collective fury blanketed Charles in oppressive heat.

An incredible amount of souls lingered in their realm, begging Charles to wonder why Death had left them behind.

*Surely he had a good reason.*

If Charles knew anything about Death, he was intentional with his actions. If he left these souls here, he surely believed it to be the right thing to do. Death was exact in that manner–never doing anything without explicit reason.

Regardless, Charles chose to help Death in order to help Nora, and the first few souls Charles managed to get into Hell weren't overly difficult. All he had to do was lie and tell them he knew where to help them find the people they were looking for.

One was looking to smite a brother, another was looking for her husband, a third, his dad.

A few he passed by longed to return to their loved ones, no murderous rage to be found, leaving Charles to question why they were marked for Hell in the first place.

Down in Hell, Lucifer hardly acknowledged him, which Charles could hardly complain about. The first soul he brought awarded Charles a single smirk from the Devil himself. With the second, he didn't look in Charles's direction at all.

Each time, the soul he tricked screamed, cursed at him, threatened his life. Charles didn't take it personally as he'd probably feel the same way if he realized he was being drug to Hell for the rest of eternity.

He officially understood Nora's headaches. The pressure behind his eyes blurred his vision, making it hard to keep upright at times, but it didn't last forever. After the second day, Charles took a break. He needed to be thoroughly rested before he showed up to Nora's as he couldn't risk her finding out what he was doing—at least not yet.

Charles would find a way to tell her eventually, which would likely result in him confronting her about her own actions and inadvertently confessing his in the process. He wasn't known to be able to keep information to himself for very long. A trait he thankfully hadn't blurted out when Sam asked him to keep their little secret. The Hell Hound never would have given him permission if he had known Charles's true nature.

When Charles finally showed back up to the estate, Nora was nowhere to be found. Vincent let him in to find Charlotte alone in the library.

"What's going on?" Charles asked as he joined her by the wall of windows to look out over the grounds.

"Hi Charles," Charlotte said, a touch too melancholic for her usual tone. "Nora is gardening."

When Charles finally spotted her, she was kneeling in the dirt, wearing a ratty sweatshirt and jeans, with her hair gathered on the top of her head. The sight of it pulled the corners of his mouth down. In the months he had known her, he never would have imagined her doing yard work. But there she was doing a seemingly mundane, relaxing task, except her movements were stiff and forceful. She drove a trowel into the ground with such force the handle and her fist buried themselves in the dirt along with it.

"Isn't it a bit early to be planting anything?" March was fast ending, but it was likely to frost again before spring truly arrived.

"Oh it is." Charlotte's tone fluttered over him, sending a chill into his bones.

"What is it Charlotte?"

"Nora won't be joining us today, Charles." Charlotte frowned at him.

His brows pulled together. "Why not?"

Charlotte sighed, "Her birthday is coming up. She gets like this every year."

"How soon?"

"Next week."

He gaped. "Next week? Why didn't I know this?" Charles felt like he had been left behind somewhere, unsure how to get back.

Charlotte placed a hand on his shoulder. "Oh Charlie boy, Nora hates her birthday."

"Nora can't stand a lot of things, but surely everyone likes their birthday."

"Not Nora," she stated simply, without explanation, as if that was just the way of things.

As if Nora herself were explanation enough.

"Then we have to do *something* for it."

"You are entering dangerous territory, Charles," Charlotte warned.

That may be so, but he had been to Hell too many times than he'd care to admit. Charles was confident in his abilities to handle just about anything. "Help me plan something then. It doesn't have to be anything elaborate."

"She'll absolutely hate it," Charlotte said, a grin slowly

stretching across her face. "I'm in."

# CHAPTER 17

## CHARLES

A week later, while Nora was out, Charles and Charlotte decorated the drawing room. Nora had told him, during one of his first visits, it was her favorite room in the house. "There are no bad memories associated with the room, only good ones," she had said.

Charlotte had been in charge of decorations while Charles got cards and flowers–zinnias seemed to fit Nora best. He may have picked up a gift for her too, but he was keeping that from Charlotte. It was for Nora's eyes only, safely tucked in the pocket of his coat to give to her later.

Vincent worked with the in-house chef, a new revelation to Charles, to make a cake, and once it was done, the room was ready. They were just waiting for Nora to arrive.

Nora had been out of the house most of the day–Vincent wasn't sure where as she hadn't told him, but Charles was certain she was in the cemetery, spending the day with Noah. Charles's heart squeezed in his chest at the thought of her sitting out there alone and then he realized how long it had been since he had visited his mother.

It had been years.

Guilt lingered around his heart, but the act of going to visit a dead person, even his own mother, unnerved him.

Charles hadn't heard the door open, but he felt Nora arrive in the house with a familiar hum in his bones. Vincent's voice carried down the hall, letting Nora know Charles and Charlotte were in the drawing room. She protested, but her footsteps approached them regardless.

"Happy birthday!" Charlotte yelled the moment Nora walked into the room.

Charles couldn't help but grin as Nora's wind kissed cheeks blushed further and she bit down on her lip, desperately trying to suppress a smile.

Charlotte rushed across the room and picked Nora up off the ground, resulting in the two of them laughing to the point of almost falling over. Vincent and Charles watched from opposite sides, the caretaker shook his head, laughing to himself.

Once back on her feet, Nora shook her head. "I am quite cross with you, Charlotte Hayes. And you," she leveled a stare at Charles over Charlotte's shoulder before turning her head to eye Vincent in the doorway, "and you too old man."

Nora's words were infinitely more menacing than the smirk she was fighting. Vincent merely shrugged, wholly unfazed.

"You are not," Charlotte cooed.

Nora's teeth flashed as she took Charlotte's face in her hands. "Fine, you caught me. You are too sweet to be mad at."

Charles's chest warmed watching the two of them–the relationship he had been lucky enough to be around these past months. His mind drifted for a moment to what life would be like without Nora in it. How Charlotte would change without her best friend. How Charles himself would change.

He blinked the thought away as quickly as it had come. Nora was there. She was alive. Why would he dwell on her death if she was perfectly alive and in front of him? To which Nora would surely say, "why not be prepared anyway?"

"Oh shit, we need plates." Charlotte released Nora completely and fled the room, pulling Vincent with her. The girl was not as clever as she thought she was as Charles caught a devious glint in her brown eyes.

Nora settled her attention on Charles, her face softening before closing the distance to wrap her arms around his neck. Surprise caught Charles as he snaked his arms around her back and held her tightly to him.

"Happy birthday," he whispered into her hair. She smelled sweetly of pears–like always–and light rain. It was becoming his favorite scent.

Nora kept to herself, didn't like to be touched, really, which made these rare moments all the more precious. His eyes stung as he realized, holding her, how much he craved a hug.

It felt so simple. So insignificant. But he'd needed it.

Living alone, being alone, for the better part of seven years, Charles rarely thought about touch as it was easy to forget about something you didn't have. So he held on to Nora as much as she was holding onto him and they stood there, content in the quiet.

"Thank you, Chuck. You are sweet for indulging her. You don't have to, you know," Nora murmured, her gray eyes shining as she stepped back.

Charles shrugged. "It was for a good cause." He looked down at her muddy shoes, then up slightly to the wet knees of her black jeans. "How was Noah?"

Nora started as if she was going to protest, but she shook it away and said, "He was good."

"I'm glad."

She laughed, "Your hair is a mess today, Chuck."

"Ah well, by now you ought to know it has a mind of its own." He ran a hand self-consciously through the thick brown mop on his head.

Nora tilted her head slightly, watching him. "I like it a mess."

Charles stilled, feeling his cheeks warm. Thankfully, he was saved from further embarrassment of his blushing as Charlotte rushed back into the room with plates in her hands and Vincent in tow. Nora turned away from Charles quickly, the pink strands of her hair lifting off her back with the movement.

The four of them ate cake and chatted well into the night, the fire in the hearth never dimming in the hours they sat in the drawing room. Vincent left them at a reasonable hour to get some sleep, muttering that *someone had to take care of the house.*

Charlotte told Charles embarrassing stories about Nora, Nora told stories about Charlotte. He listened and laughed and allowed himself to enjoy being around these two girls who could not be more opposite of each other.

Charles missed his friends. He *did* have them, he just didn't see them often. Andrew, Marty, and Dylan had all gone to the same school as him, the four of them grew up together. They stayed friends through Charles's illness, his mother's death, Andrew's dad's passing, and Dylan moving to a different town. Dylan ended up coming back for university, but Marty had moved away.

Now Charles only saw Dylan and Andrew when none of them had class, which was rare they were off at the same time, or when Marty was home for a break. He hadn't been able to come back this year for winter break and Charles hadn't seen Dylan or Andrew since before the holiday. Charles had been busy, of course, but he made a mental note to make time to check in with them more often.

The clock on the wall chimed, indicating to the three of them it was midnight. Charles stood and went to grab his coat from where it hung over the back of a chair.

"I should be going," he said to Nora and Charlotte, reluctant to leave the cozy warmth of the drawing room to venture home.

"It's late, Chuck. Just sleep here," Nora responded, watching him from where she was curled up into Charlotte's side.

Charles shook his head. "Oh I couldn't impose. Plus it's not a far walk."

"Oh Charlie boy." Charlotte shook her head, collecting their plates from the coffee table.

"Charles," Nora rolled her eyes, "there are sixteen rooms upstairs of which only two are currently occupied. I think we can spare you one."

He laughed and raised his hands in surrender. "Fine, lead the way."

"Leave the mess, Char. I'll get it in the morning. Off to bed you go too," Nora instructed her friend.

"I'm going. I'm going," Charlotte conceded and exited the drawing room, but not before kissing Nora on the cheek and whispering something that made Nora's cheeks blush. When she left, the fire in the room receded slightly, waiting to go out fully until Charles and Nora followed. The house effectively was shutting up the drawing room all on its own.

Charles trailed Nora up the grand staircase and down the hallway to the east end of the house. Rooms lined both sides of the hallway. Each door was firmly closed, keeping the secrets of their previous occupants. Nora stopped in front of the second to last door on the right.

"You can stay in here," she said, turning the knob slowly to uncover a room filled with buildable sets and posters of cars and a navy blue bedspread.

"Whose room was this?" Charles asked.

"This was Carter's room," Nora supplied, answering his question exactly–only offering the information necessary like she always did. Her tone suggested she didn't mind being pushed on the subject as the corner of her mouth curled slightly.

"When did he pass?"

Nora's gaze lifted to him. "Almost ten years ago now. He was only eleven."

Charles nodded. "Is your room close?" His curiosity craved to see her space, but even more, his hands itched to touch her, and she was so close. Charles could feel her breath on his skin causing heat to bloom over his chest and creep up towards his neck.

*Be cool, Charles. Be cool.*

Her eyes widened slightly. "Just across the hall." Nora pointed over her shoulder to the last door on the other side. "Charlotte is just next door to me, in Izzy's old room, should you need either of us."

"Of course. Thank you for letting me stay." Charles said, all the while his mind was screaming, '*I need you. I desperately need you.*'

Nora left him in the doorway to Carter's room to slip quietly behind her own door. The room was different shades of blue, from the carpet to the curtains to the chair in the corner. The moment he entered and closed the door, a fire bloomed in the hearth, lamps lit themselves on twin bed-side tables.

Charles silently thanked the house, reserving his more bewildered comments for the depths of his brain. Months in this
house and he was still not used to its meddling.

He walked across the room, discarding his coat on the bed
before heading to the chair to take his shoes off. The room
was warming nicely to a comfortable temperature from its
previously chill. If Charles was right and the rooms were never
used, they should be covered in dust. But the layer of grime was
noticeably absent from every surface.

He shook his head, becoming more impressed with the house
at each new revelation. When he grabbed his coat off the bed
to hang it on the hook by the door, the small box of Nora's
present rattled inside the pocket.

"*Shit.*"

Charles pulled the small package from his coat and flung the
door open to pad as lightly as he could over to the door Nora
had disappeared behind. He listened for a moment, but heard
nothing.

"Nora," he whispered, knocking lightly.

"Come in," she responded just as quiet.

He eased the door open to find her seated on a bench built
into the wall below the far window. Charles meant to hand her
the gift and leave, but the way her eyes didn't exactly meet his,
made him pause.

"Do you need anything?" Nora asked.

"No, I–are you okay?"

"I'm fine," she assured him, but her words were a touch too
quiet, even for a whisper.

"Nora," Charles said tentatively, slipping the gift into his
back pocket before crossing the room to sit with her on the
bench. She hadn't asked him to join her, but she hadn't told

him to leave either.

She sighed and pulled her knees into her chest. "Today typically isn't the best of days. I guess I'm a bit melancholic about it all."

Charles offered her a smile. "Why don't you like your birthday?"

Nora took a deep breath and turned her face towards the window. The moonlight kissed her face, sharpening her delicate features. "That is a complicated question, Chuck." He kept quiet—Charles knew Nora would answer him, she just needed a moment to gather her words. Every word she spoke was well thought and meticulous and he would wait as long as she needed him to.

"Our birthdays were always special. My grandfather made such a huge deal of them bringing in whatever it was we wanted. My cousin Trent asked for a circus one year and my grandfather had tents and booths set up on the back lawn. There was even a tiger, Chuck." The way Nora rolled her eyes to him made him laugh.

"But then my grandfather died—on *his* birthday no less and none of us had parents who cared enough to put in the effort to keep it going, so the excitement of it all went with him. After the first few years, the number of people who were left to celebrate my birthday dwindled. And then I became less and less worried about who was around and more worried if it was going to be my last."

"That's terrible, Nora." Charles said instead of apologizing because 'sorry' wouldn't be enough and she wouldn't want his pity.

She shrugged and looked down to her fingers resting on her knees. Charles didn't know how she could get smaller, but with her knees pulled into her chest, she became a shell of herself–as if keeping herself close would inhibit its desire to fall apart.

"Today was wonderful, but I can't stop thinking about how it's likely to be my last. How everything I do until my grandfather's birthday will be my *last* experiences." Nora picked at her thumbnail, a nervous habit she had.

"I think whether this is your last birthday or not, it is important to enjoy it."

She kept her eyes on her fidgeting fingers. "It feels wrong to celebrate it, when it's all going to end anyway, don't you think?"

Charles let her words sit with him. Maybe it was a moot point to celebrate life when you were facing death. But he had faced death and not a day went by where his mother didn't celebrate his life. Where she didn't put a smile on his face.

Charles reached out and grabbed Nora's hand to stop her from pulling off her entire nail–to distract her from the dark corners of her mind he knew she was falling into.

"I don't know, I think it is important that we still celebrate life–that we enjoy it. I know for a fact that if my mother were here, and this were my birthday, we would be dancing until our legs gave out. The house would be covered in streamers and confetti and music would be blaring. Just because we are dying, Nora, doesn't mean our life isn't worth living."

Nora rested her chin on her knees, her eyes focused on something beyond the window, their hands clasped between them. Charles felt her cold fingers begin to warm in his. It was odd, he thought, her constant state of chill, but odder still that her touch never made him cold. Never dulled his heat. Like she was keeping it from him in a way.

"You are too wise for your own good, Chuck. You may

make me an optimist yet," Nora whispered, the corner of her mouth curling upwards.

Charles brushed his thumb over her knuckles. They were as soft as the skin of a peach. "You've found me out, Nora. Making you an optimist is the central plot of my diabolical plan."

She laughed wholly, covering her face with her free hand. "You having a diabolical plan is not something I would expect from you."

"I am a man of mystery," he said, leveling his best conspiratorial stare at her.

Nora met his eyes at long last, forcing the air to rush from his lungs. Their gray glowed silver in the moonlight. "That I certainly believe."

They stared at each other for a moment, both of them still aside from the soothing motion of his thumb. The air warmed around them and Charles thought time irrelevant. It didn't matter if the world was continuing on without them, just as long as Nora was looking at him.

He was expecting her to pull her hand from his, as she always did, but Nora lingered. Her stormy eyes bore into him like she could see directly to his thoughts and he wanted to give them all to her without a care for what she would do with them.

Charles had tried his best to not let himself develop feelings for her—or so he told himself—because Nora had asked him not to. Maybe it was believable because he chose not to actively think about what he knew was there, but it was in these little moments that he couldn't stop. His mind flooded with thoughts of her, his heart pounding against his ribs.

Charles remained sitting there with his hand in hers, but in his imagination ran away from him. He would leaned in and pressed his lips to Nora's as he sunk his fingers into her hair. He would pull her onto his lap, snaking an arm around her waist to hold her against him.

In his imagination, Nora relaxed into him as he ran his hands across the smooth skin of her cheeks to her neck. He'd peel off the silk sleep shirt and shorts she wore and carry her to the bed where he'd do all sorts of unspeakable things to her.

Charles cleared his throat and his mind. "I should let you get to bed."

*Alone.*

"Right. It is late." Nora nodded, eyes fluttering as she slipped her hand from his and rose to her feet, putting an infuriating amount of distance between them.

Reluctantly he did the same and headed for her door. Charles needed to get out of her room before he combusted, destroying her and her room in the process.

Nora followed him to the door. "Thank you for helping Charlotte today. It really was the best birthday I've had in a long time."

That hand closed around Charles's throat again. "Of course. Get some sleep, Nora."

She nodded and turned the door knob as Charles's hand brushed his back pocket.

He had almost forgotten.

*Again.*

"Wait, I have something for you."

# CHAPTER 18

## NORA

C HARLES PULLED A SMALL box from his pants pocket as she pulled her door open to let him out. He handed it over to Nora and shoved his hands deep into his pockets like he was forcing them to still. Charles had already gotten her zinnias, somehow picking up on her aversion to roses–Charlotte likely told him.

There was no need for him to have gotten Nora anything and yet he went out of his way twice. She turned the small box over in her hands.

"Sorry it's not much, but I noticed you haven't taken any photos lately—"

Nora carefully freed the box from its paper wrapping.

"And it got me thinking that—"

Sitting in her hands was a new part for her film camera.

"Maybe you hadn't gotten yours fixed yet—"

The very part that had been broken for months.

"So hopefully this works."

Nora's eyes jumped between the tiny camera part in her hands to his face. Charles was looking down at her with wide, nervous eyes, chewing on the inside of his cheek.

"You remembered," she muttered. Nora hadn't thought he was even paying attention to her that day in the coffee shop when she told him about the broken part. It had been an awkward, idle conversation in order to break the ice from their disastrous first encounter where she had scolded him and thrown him out of the house.

"Of course I remembered," Charles said as if it were audacious to assume otherwise.

Nora's chest constricted, suddenly finding it hard to swallow. His ocean eyes clung to hers, demanding her to be seen, to be known, and she didn't know what to do with so much pressure. Didn't know how to properly thank him.

She clutched the piece to her chest and raised up on her toes. Nora pressed a hand to his chest to steady herself, his heartbeat pounded on the other side of his ribs beneath her palm, and planted a kiss on his cheek. She let her lips linger a moment longer than necessary, savoring the warmth of his skin beneath them.

Charles's hand settled on her waist, pulling her flush to him. Nora breathed the light vanilla scent of him deep into her lungs. The smell warmed her chest and spread down her limbs, mingling with the searing heat of Charles's hand on her waist.

When Nora stepped away, his cheeks were flushed with the same heat crawling up her own neck. "Thank you, Charles."

He returned his hand to his pocket, taking his heat with him, as she stepped back out of his space. She didn't want to overwhelm him, didn't know if touching him was a good idea, despite her body's desperate need for it.

"Happy birthday, Nora," Charles whispered before walking back across the hall, shutting himself in Carter's room. Nora shut her own door and let out an unstable breath.

"Get it together," she scolded herself.

Nothing good would come from the feelings pooling beneath her ribs. She needed to get rid of them. Nora had not been doing a good job at keeping a distance from Charles despite these thoughts tumbling around in her brain.

It was his fault really–his hair was distracting and his eyes were always on her. His constant need to put a smile on her face. His ability to see her for who she was.

She needed to focus her thoughts on something other than his lips. She needed a cold shower.

Nora deposited the gift on her desk and threw herself onto her bed. The gift made her want to cry. Made her want to scream. Made her want to barge into the room across the hall and surrender to Charles's warmth. The gift made her want to run in the opposite direction.

The demons of her anxiety didn't find her that night, but she had nightmares all the same. Ones where Charles told her he loved her. Ones where she laughed with him. Ones where he slept next to her in her bed and she whispered how she felt about him too. They all ended with him standing at her grave heartbroken and angry with her for tricking him into feeling anything for her.

Hours passed and all she managed to do was toss and turn in her bed. Nora was itching to move–thankfully she had work to do. She jumped from bed, changed into warm clothes and headed out into the early morning darkness to distract herself from the unwanted thoughts.

Nora took two souls up to the golden gates before she found herself exiting the cemetery, headed in another direction entirely.

The town was eerily quiet before dawn. Even the souls seemed to be resting this early in the morning. Fog hung low over the ground, blowing out the light from the street lamps in a hazy aura.

Nora loved this town–the beauty of it, the continuity of style, the people who took pride in living here. It was an old town, forever stuck centuries behind, but Nora didn't mind because she loved the history of it, the ghosts that made it what it was today.

Fifteen minutes later, Nora found herself standing in front of the museum's glass doors, pressure building behind her eyes. Her breathing shallowed in her chest at the sight and the muscles in her legs refused to obey her command to move any further.

The last time Nora was on the other side of those doors was a year and a half ago for her cousin Tonya's dedication.

Noah had insisted she go–forced her was more accurate–but in the end she went simply because he'd asked her to.

The dedication was the worst part of each of their deaths. A permanent memorialization of each of their lives. It was a sick nod to their bitter end. Adorning their terrible deaths in art and wonder. Each of their lives had been cut short–for what Nora now knew as her grandfather's doing–all to be commemorated inside those walls.

She hated it.

As the service was wrapping up, Noah leaned in and whispered, "Thank you for today, Nor."

Nora nodded, but didn't respond. Didn't have the words to express how she felt that wouldn't upset Noah. They were fighting enough as it was those days. When it ended and people started to clear out of Tonya's room, Noah grabbed her hand and pulled her down the hall, and into his own room.

It was full of light, it was full of him. On the ceiling was a vibrant orange sun whose rays extended to the edges. The walls were white and covered in his favorite artwork—all of which were beautiful, brightly colored paintings. The only dark one in the room was that of a night sky, shining with stars, painted by her grandfather, that hung directly next to the portrait of Noah's smiley, nine year old self.

The plaque under the painting read, "*The sun is nothing without its stars.*"

"What is it, Noah?" Nora had asked as she watched him fidget. He never fidgeted, that was *her* nervous habit.

"I think it's me next," Noah said, not meeting her gaze.

Nora shook her head, refusing to hear him. "No. I am not having this conversation with you."

"We have to have this conversation, Nora. We have to," he pleaded with a strained voice. Nora stood there with her arms crossed, staring daggers at her brother. "We both know one of us is next and I want it to be me."

Nora's hands went numb as tears formed in her eyes. She willed herself to not shake, but it was no use. "How dare you."

"I need it to be me Nora. Because maybe it will end with me. Maybe I'll be the last one and you will survive us all." Noah's lip quivered.

Her own did the same. "What am I supposed to do without you? There is no way you'll die and it will just end. Whatever *this* is, it's taking all of us, Noah."

"What if there was a way to stop it?"

Nora scoffed, "Come on, if there was, we probably would have found it by now."

Noah crossed the room and grabbed her shoulders, leaning down to look directly into her eyes. "Promise me, Nora. Promise me you will at least look for a way to live, that you won't just roll over and let death take you."

She didn't want to promise Noah. She didn't want to commit to living when she was certain there would be nothing left for her once he was gone. She wanted to scream at him, but this was her brother, the sun she had been orbiting all her life. The only person, living or dead, Nora would do anything for.

"I promise," she muttered because she had no choice.

"And promise me, you won't have one of these god-awful ceremonies for me when I am gone."

The two of them laughed as tears broke free from her eyes. "Don't worry, *that* I can definitely do."

Noah pulled her into his arms and they stood for several minutes, simply hugging each other, in the center of the physical embodiment of his soul. The two of them walked around the wing for several hours after everyone cleared out.

They visited each of the rooms, laughing over memories of their cousins, passing quietly through their father and uncle's rooms, venturing down the hall of the grandmother they never knew.

Finally making their way to Nora's room where Noah teased her for her portrait. How tiny she was. How innocent. How full of joy. He walked around, looking at each painting in turn, committing them to his memory.

The two of them ended their tour of the wing in their grandfather's room.

Norman's room was the first room in the wing, the one that granted entry to the rest of the space. Visitors had to go through him to get to all of the others–an access point, a buffer.

The entombment of him included paintings that were full of life, of family and togetherness. They were light and dark, busy and lonely. Her grandfather, like the works that adorned his space, was larger than life, all consuming, omnipotent.

From the captivating still life of a singular orange to the chaos of children running around a kitchen table. Norman was significant on his own and yet nothing without his family.

Nora and Noah stood next to each other, taking in their grandfather's portrait. He shared Noah's brown hair and wide, unabashed smile, but Nora had his eyes and the freckles that kissed his cheeks.

"I miss him," Noah admitted softly.

"Me too," she sighed. "Let's go home."

It was the last time she had been to the museum, and the one promise to Noah she'd kept. Nora refused to have a dedication for him after his death.

The museum curator called repeatedly to set something up–all of which she avoided until she finally answered one afternoon, informing him that it would not be happening in a rather acerbic tone. He stopped after that.

But there she was, standing there for the first time in over a year, feeling just as lost as she had five months ago when Noah died. Time was dwindling as it always did and she still had no idea how to save her own life.

Guilt washed over Nora when she realized she hadn't exactly made an effort to find a way to live like the other promise she'd made to Noah. It hadn't been intentional, but rather felt like a moot point.

She looked one last time at the museum doors as the sun began its ascent into the sky.

"I'm trying Noah. I really am trying," she whispered into the ether, hoping that he heard her.

Nora turned on her heel and headed home with the drive to make an effort and to wash the smell of roses from her skin.

# CHAPTER 19

## DEATH

DEATH HAD HAD ENOUGH. He was going over to the estate to see Nora whether she wanted him there or not. Her wrath was nothing to him.

He was immortal!

He wasn't afraid of some mortal girl!

*He wasn't.*

Death wasn't sure who he was convincing–himself or the ether, because surely no one else was listening to his thoughts, nor cared. He had been away too long. Left her alone for too long. Nora was spending her time with Councilman Sam when she was meant to be spending time with Charles. He was supposed to be a good influence for her.

On second thought, maybe he needed to have a chat with the boy.

*There's an idea.*

The walk over was quick. Death went straight from the cemetery which was only a few blocks from the estate. He thanked the cosmos, no one was screaming at him because he was in the mood to scream right back.

Death hadn't gotten Nora a gift for her birthday, but he never did. He thought for a second that he should have, that it would help to ease the tension, but thought better of it. He stopped a block away, waiting for his mind to make a decision.

*Yes.*

He turned to head off in the opposite direction to find her something. He had no idea what. A sharp knife? It would certainly make her attempt at eviscerating him easier.

*This is stupid.*

He strode back towards the house.

*You're stupid.*

Death changed direction again.

*No. I'm not getting her anything.*

Who was he even arguing with?

Water dripped from the stones of the house as spring fully took over. The yard was returning to its usual vibrant green and bulbs formed on the trees that in a few weeks would make Death's nose and eyes itch.

*Fucking spring.*

He walked up the steps to the massive front doors and pounded on them with his fist, refusing to use the obscene door knocker that hung there. Usually, Death would just walk onto the grounds at the back of the estate, but he was trying to be respectful, to go through the usual channels.

*Like a mortal,* he groaned, eyes rolling with the absurdity of it all.

The old caretaker answered the door with his usual air of contempt reserved specifically for Death. Vincent ushered Death into the foyer before calling down the hall.

"Miss Nora! You have a visitor."

"Charles is already here, Vincent," she called back.

"Mr. Charles has a visitor as well."

Unintelligible bickering filtered down the hallway. A conversation that Death was imagining going something like:

*Nora: "I don't want to see him."*
*Charles: "But he wants to see you."*
*Nora: "Then you go see him."*
*Charles: "Just come with me."*
*Nora: "I'll go but I'm not going to be nice."*
*Charles: "Are you ever?"*

In Death's imagination, Charles had a bit of an attitude–something the boy would never possess in his lifetime which made the act of giving him an attitude in a noncorporeal state all the more amusing.

Death was feeling a tad manic.

His two wards approached the foyer, one willingly, one begrudgingly.

"Hi, Death." Charles shot him a tight lipped smile.

Death smiled back. "Good morning, Charles."

"Death," Nora stated as if his name was acid on her tongue.

"Nora," he shot back with equal ire.

"What brings you by?" she asked.

"Well for one, I wanted to tell you happy birthday. So, felicitations and all that. Second, I wanted to see how you are doing. As I see you are alive and well, I can rest easy."

The two of them stared at each other from across the room. Nora was forcing her face to remain neutral in the way she always did when she felt any emotion she was desperately trying to contain–sort of slack jawed with unfocused eyes. Charles on the other hand could not have been more uncomfortable. Death willed himself to not laugh at the poor boy whose eyes were glued to the marble floor, pursed lips, rocking back and forth on his heels.

"Been busy, have you?" Nora crossed her arms, narrowing her eyes on him.

Suddenly his skin started to tingle, if he was a being whose body temperature changed based on feeling, or a being who really had any feelings at all, he would have gone cold under her stare. Nora's dark blonde eyebrows were pulled together, deeply creased in the middle, one slightly raised. Her jaw was set, pulling her mouth in a tight line.

If he was being completely honest with himself, it was terrifying. It was as if she was looking straight through his chest to his unbeating heart, just to say '*how utterly disappointing. I thought it would do more.*'

But to reiterate, he wasn't afraid of some mortal girl!

"Of course I've been busy. I'm always busy."

Nora slowly nodded her head, Charles was biting his lip, and Death was just hoping the boy's eyes wouldn't pop out of his head from how much they were bulging.

"Ah, I guess *busy* looks different on everybody, but who am I to judge?" Nora shrugged one shoulder, frowning.

"What is that supposed to mean?" Death challenged.

She didn't answer his question. "Sam's been looking for you."

This would be another instance where Death's blood would run cold. Where fear would take over and his limbs would go numb. Instead his chest tightened slightly. He knew the council was looking for him because he was actively avoiding that very council.

The worry that settled into his thousands of years old body was from the chance that the council may have told her *why* they wanted to see him–which he would have known too, had he not thrown all of their letters into the bin before reading them.

Hindsight or something.

"Tell Sam he shouldn't be bothering you. That Hell Hound needs to leave you alone," Death seethed. Charles, who was still watching the floor, nodded in agreement. "Charles mentioned he has been coming by."

The boy snapped his head up to Death, gaping at him. Nora turned her murderous gaze on Charles and cocked an eyebrow.

"Nora—" he started.

"Save it."

"Little star, all I wanted to do was to check in and wish you a happy birthday." Death held his hands up in surrender. "I didn't come to fight."

Nora scoffed, making Death's body tense further. "There is no need for you to check in with me when you have your little lap dog to tell you anything you want to know."

"Nora," Charles bit off.

Her head swiveled between the two of them, lip curled. "Oh don't lie to me now, Chuck. That's why he sent you here in the first place isn't it?"

The truth boiled like molten iron in Death's throat so he nodded, unable to feign ignorance.

Not even for Charles's sake.

"Yeah," she sneered. "Have a terrible day, Death."

Nora turned on her heel and walked off in a swift exit back down the hall. Death looked to Charles who merely shrugged and bit his lip. The two of them stared at one another for a long moment.

Charles was torn between his loyalty to Nora and his desire to speak to Death, but Death couldn't very well blame the boy for getting close to her. After all, Death *had* sent him here with the purpose of befriending Nora the in hope that Charles might thaw her slightly and that Nora might teach Charles it was okay to be upset with the world.

Charles had taken it upon himself to be nothing but happy after his mother died, effectively forcing himself not to feel half of his emotions. Nora had done the opposite.

There was joy in Nora and anger in Charles and if Death knew anything it was the two of them would find it in the other. Find the acceptance of it.

For that reason alone, Death wasn't upset at Charles for being torn, in fact the corners of his mouth tightened as he nodded at the boy reassuring him. Charles smiled back, pink cheeks brightening, and headed off after his little star.

Defeat weighed Death's shoulders down, but Nora was upright and breathing which was all that truly mattered at the end of the day.

Death could have sworn he heard the sound of the piano as he was leaving the estate.

# CHAPTER 20

## CHARLES

C HARLES FOUND NORA IN the library, where he knew she'd run off to, but was surprised to find her sitting at the very piano she scolded him for playing not five months ago. Her lip was caught in her teeth as she stared at the keys, brows pulled together, hands clasped in her lap so tight her knuckles were turning white.

He crossed the room quietly to sit on the bench next to her.

"I know this house has a mind of its own, but the piano won't play itself."

A languid hum was Nora's only response.

Charles leaned his shoulder into hers slightly. "I have never told him anything about you by the way. I only mentioned Sam because he asked about him during lunch one day."

Nora turned to him, gray eyes narrowing. "You haven't?"

"Of course not." Charles shook his head. "It didn't seem like my place. He asked me after the first time I had met you, when I thought I'd never see you again, so I told him you seemed fine. That your disagreeable disposition was likely your normal state. He assured me it was."

Nora's face softened into a smile right before she burst out laughing and the sound was music itself. It was a full body laugh that finally loosened her hands from their tight grip only to cover her face.

"He was the reason we all played." By *he,* she meant her grandfather. Nora sighed and rested her delicate fingers on the keys. "Me more than others."

"What did you play?" Charles asked quietly.

Nora looked fondly at the instrument and pressed down on a key. The sound made her body go rigid. "Mozart, Beethoven, Chopin. *'Anything but the greats is beneath you, little star,'*" she mocked her grandfather.

Charles silently agreed with the man. Anything less would surely not be worthy of her time.

He reached up and pressed a key, mirroring her movement. "Play me something?"

She turned her head to look at him, pursing her lips, mischief dancing in her eyes.

"Listen well, Charles Riley, I may never play again," Nora taunted, splaying her fingers out across the keys.

And he did.

Charles didn't just listen, he felt it in his bones, in the way it changed the physical makeup of his soul. The song she played was heartbreaking and beautiful and it was every bit of her.

A mix of opposing ideals.

A war of feeling.

Charles's eyes burned at the edges. He desperately wanted to slide from the bench and let the music drain the life force from his body. He would do anything, give *anything*, just for her to keep playing.

Nora's body remained rigid, face pulled tight, the muscle in her jaw pulsed with strain. The only relaxed part of her body were her hands, exacting magic from her fingertips, kissing each key at precisely the right moment.

He committed the song to his memory and stored it safely next to his soul where it would live forever. If she never played again, he wanted to remember this moment. If she died and left this world and took her music with her, he wanted to be able to hear it, wanted it to break him all over again.

A single tear fell down his cheek, but he didn't bother to wipe it away, there was no use.

More would follow.

Nora continued playing for several minutes and from the corner of his eye, Charles caught Vincent standing in the doorway. He imagined the caretaker overflowing with pride for the girl that quietly owned this house–the girl he had helped raise.

In the short time Charles had known Nora, he knew for fact the universe spun around her. He wasn't sure how he had lived over twenty years of his life without knowing her.

Nora didn't want him to know her, would have preferred he didn't at all, but now that he did, he would never be free of her. Charles would submit to his hedonistic tendencies to understand more of her–condemning his soul to the corruption of desire in order to change his physical makeup to *her*. Nora believed she was destined for Hell and he would follow her willingly into the fire, in every lifetime.

When Nora finished playing, her hands stilled over the keys like her fingers were in disbelief of what they had just done. Slowly she returned her hands to her lap. Charles couldn't speak, not that he knew what to say anyway.

Vincent was long gone and the house was positively humming around them as the two of them sat in comfortable silence for what could have been an eternity.

"I hate that I can be so mean sometimes," Nora finally whispered without looking at him.

Charles regained the use of his limbs and reached up to brush the curtain of blonde-pink hair over her shoulder so he could see her face better. "You can be mean to me, I can take it."

Nora turned her head, searching his eyes. They were wide and shining with unshed tears. "But you shouldn't have to. I'm angry all the time and I don't even know about what anymore—just that I am. I feel so consumed by it that I have no room for anything else, no room to be happy. I am all sharp edges and violent words and I only hurt the people I care about."

"I don't think that is true." Nora frowned, but Charles continued, "If it were, people wouldn't keep showing up for you. Charlotte and Vincent and even *Death,* wouldn't bother to take the time to care about you in the way they do."

"And you?" Her words were barely a whisper.

Charles tilted his head. "Your sharp edges are not as sharp as you think, Nora. I get it. Your anger, that is. I was that way for a long time after my mother died." Charles let out a heavy sigh, "How selfish I thought her, to have thought only of *her* want to not lose me, because what of my desire to not lose her? How could she do that to me? And when I thought of my father, I was blind with rage. I wanted to find him and scream at him until my throat went raw. To tell him how horrible I thought him to be—not because he left me, but because he left her. Because the burden of me fell to her alone and *how could he*?"

Nora watched him, listening to his every word. "But you aren't angry now."

It wasn't a question.

Charles forced a smile that he knew didn't meet his eyes and said, "No. I have no use for it when I have a second chance to live. How can I be angry with my mother when she gave me my life? So it is for her that I am grateful, that I look at life a little more joyously–or try to at least."

"I can only imagine she is proud of the person you are." Nora smiled at him.

"I think the same of your grandfather about you." Charles slipped his hand into hers. It was cold, but he let his warmth settle over her as her fingers tightened around his. Nora let out a breath and leaned her head down to rest on his shoulder.

They leaned into each other quietly until she said, "And Charles," she used his full name, demanding attention she already had, "loving someone, despite their need for help does not make them a burden. It makes them irreplaceable."

Charles left the estate early that day to head back to his flat. On the walk home his mind lingered on Nora and all of her anger. Deep down he understood it, like he'd told her, but it was as foreign to him as a language he couldn't read.

It had been years since he acknowledged his own, preferring to pretend it didn't exist at all. Anger made him uncomfortable because he was angry with his mother for leaving him the way she did, for taking his sickness for herself. Angry with his father for leaving them both without a second thought. Both of them leaving *him* to feel guilty for it all.

But he pushed it down and forgot about it because the feeling felt useless and misplaced. What his mother did stemmed solely from her love for him. Being angry with his father wasn't worth it if he'd never see him again.

They were both gone.

If the people he was cross with weren't around for him to direct his anger toward, then what was the point? It was better to forget about it rather than place it somewhere else, on someone else.

By the time Charles got home he was back to his normal self, the fire in his stomach had subsided. He was glad to be home, to be surrounded by the comfort and love that lingered there, even without his mother to physically grace the halls.

He hadn't been home five minutes before the phone on the wall rang. It was Nora's voice on the other end–calm and commanding.

"I want to show you something."

Charles laughed. She was never one for introductions, always straight to the point. "And what, Nora, would that be?"

He heard her take a deep breath before she said, "The museum."

"Okay," Charles said immediately, without hesitation. If Nora wanted to show him the moon, he would meet her there without a thought to the equipment he would need or how he would get there. But this was a place that was precious to her and so he would be there, everyday if she wanted.

"Tomorrow then?"

"At noon?" Charles asked despite already knowing the answer.

Nora laughed, "Yes, Chuck, at noon sharp. I expect your usual punctuality."

"If I'm not, you can have me arrested."

"Don't tempt me," she teased before hanging up.

# CHAPTER 21

## CHARLES

A T EXACTLY five minutes before noon, Charles stood in front of the museum, coffee in each hand. One was bitterly black and the other was a caramel latte, just the way she preferred it–entirely too sweet for his liking, which he only knew because he had tried it. The sugar lingered on his teeth.

Charles had gotten there early in anticipation of her arriving early, but Nora was always exactly where she said she would be at the exact time. He wasn't surprised to see her walking toward him when he looked up from his watch.

The cool April air kissed her cheeks pink, a shade lighter than the ends of her hair. Nora wasn't wearing a coat despite the lingering chill. He suppressed a smile recalling her words from a few days ago. *"Why would I wear a jacket and pretend it's still winter when the sun is shining, Chuck?"*

"For you," Charles said, holding out the cup containing her latte when she came to a stop in front of him.

Nora took the cup, eyeing him skeptically. After taking a sip, she pursed her lips and inclined her head towards the museum doors. Charles had never met someone who didn't need a single word to convey their directness.

He would never tire of it.

He followed her to the ticketing desk where they were

greeted by a quiet, old man. Nora was in the process of asking the man for two tickets when a second emerged from a side room, rushing over to meet them.

"Miss Kramer," he called and Nora went rigid next to Charles, forcing a smile to her face that didn't meet her eyes.

"Mr. Blake."

"You should have called, Miss Kramer, we would have prepared for your visit." He extended his hand to her. Nora took it, but her movements were stiff, her shoulders pulled tight into herself. Charles stepped closer to her as discomfort radiated off of her in dense waves. He felt Nora lean into him slightly, just enough for her shoulder to rest against his chest.

"Please, call me Nora, and there is no need, Mr. Blake. I just came by to show my friend Charles here the wing."

Mr. Blake placed a hand on Nora's back and ushered her away from the counter leaving the man behind it without another thought. "By all means make yourself at home, and you know you needn't pay here. Do let me know if you need anything, Miss Kramer."

Charles answered for her, sternly, "Thank you, Mr. Blake."

The bespeckled man looked at Charles as though he had just registered his presence and nodded curtly. Mr. Blake dropped his hand from Nora's back and Charles took the opportunity to step between them. The curator scurried back in the direction he came and Charles turned his head just in time to see Nora roll her shoulders back and head into the first gallery.

Nora led Charles through several galleries until she stopped to stand in front of Johannes Vermeer's *The Astronomer*. It was a gorgeously dark painting where the shadows forced the viewer's eyes to pay attention to the subject, hiding secrets in its dark corners.

"What is this one?" Charles asked, eliciting an incredulous look from Nora. He sipped his coffee, offering her an innocent shrug of his shoulders.

She knew he knew what it was.

She knew he was asking her an abhorrent question.

But *he* knew she didn't want to talk about the curator from the lobby.

Charles tilted his head, looked at her sidelong, and pleaded, "Tell me about it."

Nora narrowed her eyes at him for the second time that day, a smirk tugging at the corner of her mouth. After a long moment, she indulged him. "*The Astronomer* is one of Vermeer's more famous works. He was a Flemish portrait artist who produced art during the height of the Northern Renaissance, known for his oil on canvas portraits. This particular painting is said to be in close relation to another of his paintings, *The Geographer*.

"It was bought and sold to collectors all over Amsterdam for years until eventually it was sold to the Rothschilds in the late 1800's and was passed down from generation to generation with their collection. It was stolen during the war, thought to be lost alongside too many others, but luckily it was found and returned to the family. From there it was acquired by the French government and now it is here, on loan from the Louvre."

Charles watched her as she spoke, her eyes never leaving the painting as if she were reading the words directly from the canvas. But the history was just another piece of knowledge she stored in her brain. The more Nora talked, the more the tension in her shoulders receded, the more her lips curled.

"That is quite the story for just one painting."

Nora looked at him and frowned. "It certainly is, but people are rather obsessed with owning pretty things, Chuck."

"I suppose you're right."

And she was.

Nora had a blunt way of boiling the world down to its exact reality. There was no hiding with her nor did she run from its harshness.

She turned away from the painting, leaving Charles to trail her through more galleries. Charles listened to Nora tell him about the art like it was a good friend. She pointed out painting styles and brush strokes and imagery. She showed him all of her favorite pieces and the ones she thought pretentious. She noticed elements that Charles would have never thought to pay attention to. How if you stood at a certain angle from the center of the painting you could see the real image instead of the distorted one. She talked of the divine power of three, the influence of the Catholic church.

He was in awe of what she saw, in what she had to teach him.

The art was beautiful, but Nora was spectacular. Charles could listen to her talk for the rest of his life. She could teach him about the universe, tell him the meaning of life, and he would believe her without question.

Nora was a work of art herself.

She was dressed in her usual attire, but much like the museum they walked through, it was expertly curated–from the sneakers she wore to the black jeans that stopped just above her ankles to the cotton candy blue cardigan hanging from her shoulders. Nora's pink dipped hair that was pinned meticulously out of her face was a stark contrast against the blue of her sweater, staying perfectly down her back as they walked.

But then there was her face, the biology that made her uniquely Nora. Her gray eyes shone like a billion stars. As for the freckles that kissed her cheeks, Charles could have sworn someone placed each one specifically with the intent to distract him.

Just when Charles thought there couldn't be any more of the museum left to see, Nora led them into a massive room.

"Welcome to the Kramer Wing," Nora said as Charles realized the room they entered wasn't just a singular gallery. There was a door at the back that opened to a hallway and doors to his left and right leading to additional rooms—all of which were full of paintings. "It's all work he has either done himself or collected and donated to the museum."

Charles walked up to a bust in the center of the room on a lone pedestal. It was the marble likeness of an older man, one he didn't recognize.

The plaque read:

*This room has been dedicated to Norman T. Kramer whose generosity brought us our most frequented wing of the museum. As an accomplished artist and expert collector, the late Norman Kramer donated much of these works to the museum in the years before his death. He and his family are remembered within these walls as great contributors to the art world.*

*About the Kramer Wing: The wing consists of fourteen rooms in total, each dedicated to one of Norman's sons and his grandchildren. The hallway connecting them all has been dedicated to Norman's late wife, Roxanne. Norman handpicked the works in each room based on the person the room is dedicated to, along with a portrait of the person, painted by Norman himself.*

When he finished reading, he turned around to see Nora smiling at him. Her lips at war with her eyes as she stared past him to the bust of her grandfather.

"You have a room here?"

Her eyes shifted to meet his. "I do."

"Can I see it?" he asked softly as to not sound too eager.

"Of course. That one is Noah's." Nora pointed at the room to the left radiating a soft yellow-orange glow. "The rest of the boys are on that side. Mine is this way, with the other girls."

Charles followed her to the room on the right and the deep blue that lingered there. "Trying to keep the boys and girls separate?"

Nora laughed, "No, he was quite equal in that department. If anything, he liked us girls more—my boy cousins were mostly pricks. Aside from Carter, who followed Noah too closely to be anything but kind."

The breath from Charles's lungs escaped his body the moment they crossed the threshold of her room. The ceiling was the darkest blue, a shade just before black, and littered in constellations. The color seeped from the ceiling down the walls, the blue fading to white as it made its way to the floor and the stars fell from the ceilings, fading along with the color. Each one glittering as though they contained real light.

On the walls were some of the most dramatic works Charles had ever seen. A Monet extended the entirety of one of the walls, an amalgamation of blues and purples and greens. Several Van Goghs, a Titian, four of Norman's original paintings, a Degas, and a few others that Charles didn't know.

As he looked around the room, he understood it—it was her. The room was colorful and dark contrast and harsh composition, but it was also soft and beautiful and introspective. These weren't simple paintings, they were complex, and they were Nora.

Charles felt it all like a weight on his chest.

The portrait of her hung on the far wall, underneath was a description card that read, *'My Little Star.'* The painting of Nora was six year old her with a wide, toothy smile. Her hair had been blonder then, almost white, as it fell around her shoulders, without its current pink ends. She was in her preferred blue and still had the same round apple cheeks. A dimple he had yet to see, graced her cheesy young face.

Norman had truly been a phenomenal artist.

"Have you always had that?" Charles turned to Nora pointing to his cheek.

"I have," she said matter-of-factly. "And you will never see it."

Charles laughed, watching her suppress a smile.

But then Nora looked around the room and bit her lip. Her shoulders fell and the grip on her empty coffee cup tightened.

"Nora?" Charles tilted his head watching her.

"You want to know where my anger comes from, Charles? From this," Nora yelled, throwing her arms out to the sides, to the walls lined with her favorite works of art, works that were her. Her voice shook as she pressed trembling fingers to her lips. "Because he had to *ruin* this. Because these walls are built and adorned with his lies. None of this is real. It was all a front for the real him–the criminal he was."

"But you love him." A statement, not a question.

"Yeah. I do," Nora replied, her voice was strained and far too quiet, because it was complicated, and yet, not at all.

Charles walked over to her, standing close enough for her to feel his warmth, but not close enough to touch her. He made it a practice to let her come to him, as much as he could, because in reality, there was nothing he wanted more than to hold her in his hands and never let go. Nora's eyes burned into his chest, her knuckles turning white around the paper cup.

"You know, someone very brilliant told me something once." She didn't lift her eyes, but her mouth quirked all the same. "She said *'just because someone made bad decisions, doesn't mean they didn't love you.'*" They weren't her exact words, but they were her words all the same. "*'That everyone knows life isn't just black and white, that it is full of color and gray areas too.'*"

Nora finally looked up at him, bottom lip caught in her teeth to keep it from trembling, but her eyes were a storm of the pain she held too tightly. They were standing close enough for her knuckles to brush his stomach through his sweater, sending sparks across his skin, running around to his back and through his chest to cling to his heart. Charles could feel the beat of it in his throat, in his stomach, in his fingertips.

Nora's cheeks flushed pink and he had the overwhelming need to feel just how warm they were with his lips. If he leaned down slightly he wouldn't have to wonder any longer. Charles would happily inhale the sweet pear scent of her and blissfully melt away into the softness of her skin.

Nora's hands pressed harder into his stomach as though she was at war between pushing him away and pulling him closer. Charles brought his hand up to her cheek–it was in fact warm, but it wasn't his fingers that longed to know. Her eyes drifted closed as he brushed his knuckles over her perfectly soft skin. His fingers drifted to her hairline at the base of her neck as he lowered his face down, desperate to meet her lips.

Footsteps rushed into the room.

Nora was gone from his touch faster than he could protest

and with her went the heat in his body.

Charles felt unnaturally cold, like his blood had frozen over and the only thing with the ability to thaw it again was her. But Mr. Blake peered through his glasses at her rigid body and Charles knew Nora wouldn't come back to save him.

"Miss Kramer, I forgot to mention," said the odious Mr. Blake.

The heat returned to Charles in the form of molten ire, not thawing him in the way he needed.

"We were hoping to talk to you about a rotating exhibition in one of the other wings," he continued. A different request than what came in the mail several weeks ago.

"Another day, Mr. Blake. Charles and I were just leaving." Nora looked at him sternly, the tightness having returned to her shoulders as she picked at her thumbnail. Charles decidedly did not like the man standing in front of them.

Mr. Blake nodded. "Oh, of course, I will call you at the house next week to discuss the details."

"Perfect," Nora responded, tight lipped and clipped.

Charles and Nora stood shoulder to shoulder watching the man retreat from the room, exiting the wing. A horrifically ingenious idea floated into Charles's brain. One that if they managed to pull off, would maybe save her life and help her to forgive her grandfather at the same time.

"I have an idea, my dear Nora." Charles clasped his hands behind his back.

"And what, Chuck, would that be?" Her gaze lingered on the forgotten space of Mr. Blake.

He smirked down at her. "I think we should steal it all back."

Nora whipped her head to him and her mouth fell open, eyes forming saucers on her face, but there was a devious glint to her expression.

"Are you with me?" Charles asked, holding out his hand.

Her face broke into a wide smile, threatening to reveal the dimple he was now desperate to see. Nora took his hand, a devious smirk painted on her gorgeous face.

"Until Death comes for me."

They fled the museum.

# CHAPTER 22

## NORA

"I F WE ARE GOING to do this we have to actually crack this cipher and to do so we have to locate the right key." Nora pointed to the stack of books sitting on her grandfather's desk they had tried already.

"I have a thought."

Nora and Charlotte whipped their heads around to look at Charles.

"Well enlighten us, Charlie boy," Charlotte said, planting her hands on her hips.

He returned Nora's gaze and she felt that familiar heat wash over her chest. She willed it to not reach her cheeks, but the lifting of the corner of Charles's mouth told her that her will was not as strong as she thought it was.

"Do you remember what your plaque in the museum said?" She raised her eyebrow at him. "The one next to your portrait."

"I'm hoping you are about to tell me?"

Charles smirked and recited, "*May you still believe there to be a world inside your wardrobe.*"

"It was a nod to my love for *The Lion, the Witch, and the Wardrobe.* That is not particularly hard to figure out." Nora failed to recognize where his brain was taking them.

He clasped his hands in front of him, grinning wildly. "What if it isn't *his* favorite book that was the key? What if it's yours?"

If she wasn't actively forcing herself not to, Nora would kiss him. "Chuck, you brilliant boy."

She raced to the bookshelves to find her copy of the book. The one her grandfather had always read to her from. After he died she hadn't been able to find it, crying for days when she realized it was gone. Vincent ended up buying her a new one, but it wasn't the same, it wasn't *his*. Holding the book in her hands brought every memory rushing back to her mind.

Nora took several deep breaths to clear the unwelcome thoughts. There was work to be done. There was her life to save—a task she had not been putting much effort into these past few months. Charles and Charlotte were at the house several times a week, but they spent it mostly chatting about other topics, half-heartedly sifting through books and documents. If Nora was being honest with herself, she was avoiding it altogether.

The work felt futile.

Helping souls find their way to Heaven was much more rewarding and easier to accomplish. Yes it was draining and the desire to walk down the steps of Hell and end it all was still too great, but it gave her something to focus on rather than her own impending doom.

Saving her life felt selfish and wholly unattainable. How could she possibly think about saving herself when she hadn't been able to save anyone else, anyone who deserved it more?

As for the two people standing behind her, she was positive their lives would be infinitely easier if they abandoned this little side quest now. Charles could go back to his normal life, save himself a great deal of stress and Charlotte would be free of Nora's foul attitude. Nora didn't deserve such a light like Charlotte. She'd always thought it, always wondered why Charlotte stuck around for so long.

But the two people behind her were Hellbent on saving her, so she would indulge them. Nora begged the book in her hands to have the answers they needed, not for herself, but for Charles and Charlotte's sakes.

"Why does it look like that?" Charlotte asked, eyeing the warped cover and wavy pages.

Nora pressed the book to her chest. "I may have tried to read it in the shower when I was six."

Charles bit back a laugh and Charlotte pressed a kiss to the side of her head. "Oh Nora, you sweet, sweet, child. Never change."

"This was fourteen years ago!" Nora protested, but Charlotte nodded skeptically, patting Nora's shoulder.

Nora rolled her eyes and ignored them both. Charles was biting his knuckles to keep from laughing.

"Just tell me what the first set of numbers is," Nora quipped, slowly prying the book open. The spine groaned and the pages crinkled, the sound of it rocketing through the quiet room.

Charles read the first set from the notebook.

Nora flipped to the correct page, found the intended paragraph, and counted out the words.

"Lion," she read out loud.

The three of them exchanged a look, but kept going. The next two were the word 'witch.' Followed by another 'lion,' four 'wardrobes,' two 'lions,' another 'witch,' three 'wardrobes,' and finally one more 'lion.' There were fifteen paintings in total, five 'lions,' three, 'witches,' and seven 'wardrobes.'

*Curious.*

"So we have a clear pattern, but we still don't know what any of this means," Charlotte mused.

Nora wasn't really listening as her brain flooded with information she didn't even realize she had. She knew at least one of the paintings labeled 'lion' was in this room–the Rembrandt.

Charles protested as she snatched the journal from his hands, but she didn't hear what he said. Moving the Rembrandt to the side, Nora sifted through the rest of the paintings there, looking for the other four marked with 'lion.' Sure enough they were there.

She wanted to laugh.

Charles and Charlotte were talking around her, but her mind was on the third painting labeled 'wardrobe.' It was one she had passed idly on more occasions than she could count.

The painting in question was a Titian that hung on the far wall of the first gallery in the museum. Nora believed she knew the museum better than anyone, but this list in her hands was screaming, *Ha! You thought!*

She sprinted from the room, book and journal in hand.

"What the fuck," Charlotte exclaimed behind her.

"Nora!" Charles yelled, following her out of the room.

Nora fled down the hallway and through the foyer where Vincent gaped at her.

"Miss Nora!"

She didn't stop to tell him what was going on as she burst through the front door and down the steps. Once she was off the property, Nora took a hard left and headed through the center of town. The museum was less than a mile away, but the town was busy.

Nora dogged people left and right, skirting around a group of little kids, receiving a number of incredulous looks. Behind her, Charles was shouting as he gained on her. Charlotte on the other hand was further back, but chased her all the same.

She couldn't remember the last time she had been for a run and her body was screaming at her in protest of the forced movement. By the time Nora reached the museum, she was sweating and barely able to catch her breath, but she didn't stop until she was through the front doors and in the first gallery. She needed to set her eyes on the Titian she knew was there–confirm she hadn't lost her mind completely. On the opposite wall were two of the other paintings on the list.

"Nora," Charles said through his labored breathing, "what is going on?"

She didn't say anything, but rather shoved the journal into his hands, begging him to see it because she didn't have the words to explain it to him. Didn't have the breath for it all. Nora turned around the room in awe.

Her grandfather was one shifty mother—

"Fuck, Nora." Charlotte entered the room a few minutes later, stumbling up to her and Charles. They were all breathing heavily.

"They have been here the whole time," Nora laughed. Her laughter came lightly at first, but quickly turned hysterical. Charlotte, who was doubled over, bracing herself on her knees, pulled the journal from Charles's idle hands. He stared at the Titian on the wall, mouth hanging open from shock and lack of breath. Nora fell to her knees, unable to stand any longer.

Relief, frustration, and hope poured out of her. She couldn't believe what she was seeing and yet it had been in front of her most of her life. Her grandfather had hid the paintings in plain sight, by doing the very thing that could get him caught–giving them to the museum to display.

At some point tears fell down her cheeks, landing on the

thighs of her jeans. All it took was an afternoon. Months of flipping through books, theorizing where the paintings could be and all it had taken was for her to pay attention.

To put in genuine effort.

"They are all here then?" Charles asked, looking down at where she kneeled on the floor. His brilliant blue eyes were swimming with promise and excitement and God how she wanted to drown in them.

Nora wiped the tears from her face and smiled up at him. "They are all here Chuck. Except for the ones labeled 'witch.' The 'lion' ones are in the secret room, but the 'wardrobe' ones are all here."

"What do we do now?" Charlotte asked.

"We go with Chuck's plan and steal them all back." Nora reached up with both hands for one of them to help her up. Charles and Charlotte each took one, hauling her to her feet. The muscles in her legs had tightened from sitting on the floor immediately after her run over here.

"Are you okay?" Charles asked as Nora let out a deep breath.

Her lips pull across her face. "Yeah. I'm good." It was the first bit of tangible hope she'd had in years.

Charlotte was watching her intently and all Nora wanted was to hold onto them both. Tired of keeping herself from what she wanted, Nora threw her arms around their necks, raising up on her toes to reach them. Her friend's arms slid around her and each other as they squeezed her between them.

Charles buried his face in Nora's hair and she was instantly soothed by their smells–vanilla and cherry. Two smells she would never get used to for the sheer fact she loved them so much, finding so much comfort in them.

When Nora finally pulled away she said, "I have an idea."

"Well enlighten us, little star." Charles grinned at her, nothing but teasing in his tone. He had never used her nickname before. Charlotte's eyebrows jumped on her forehead and Nora could see her fighting to keep a comment to herself.

"I will have to make calls to the buyers to track down the paintings that my grandfather sold, but I propose we have a gala. Here at the museum. I can tell Mr. Blake I want to have an event to celebrate my grandfather's contribution to the art world." Charles bristled at her mention of Mr. Blake, but she ignored it. "We get him to move all the paintings we need into one room, get the buyers to 'loan us' the others, and at the end of the night, we take them home. Obviously we will have to finalize the rest of the details to make sure we don't get caught and all of that, but I think it might actually work."

"Fuck yes," Charlotte groaned, "finally something I can get behind." Nora rolled her eyes at her friend and Charlotte continued, "Okay, I'm behind all of it, but you know I love a good party."

Nora knew, all right. Charlotte *loved* a good party, better yet, loved one she could host. "You can plan the whole thing if you want."

"I want and I will," Charlotte demanded, "but Nora."

"Yes, Char?"

Charlotte looped her arm through Nora's and steered her towards the exit. "If you ever make me run again, I'll kill you." She leaned over and pressed a kiss to Nora's sticky forehead.

Behind them, Charles laughed, following them out of the museum and back to the estate.

# CHAPTER 23

## CHARLES

THE NIGHT HAD BEEN suffocatingly hot. Summer was in full swing and the long gone sun did nothing to cool the air around him. The four trips to Hell hadn't helped and Charles was considering spending the night in the park, rather than summon the effort to walk the rest of the way home.

His choice of souls that night were taking a toll on him. They had all been rather vicious and Charles was eternally grateful the souls lacked the ability to touch him. He was positive one of them would have wrapped their hands around his neck and squeezed until he stopped breathing.

About halfway home, Charles passed the rocky overlook his mother used to take him to have the occasional picnic by the river when it was warm out. How he wished for that now, how he'd give anything for one more day in the grass with her. It didn't matter anymore how silly it had made him feel. Charles had always been so embarrassed, always thought it *girly* and loathed the time Tessa made him sit out there on a blanket with her.

That was another thing he felt guilty for–hating their picnics–because in the end his feelings about it never mattered. In the end it mattered that he spent time with her. Charles loathed himself for ever making her think he didn't enjoy it.

Charles eased himself onto the bench that overlooked the river. It was dark and the water blended in with the night sky, but the rushing of it soothed his mind and his body was grateful to rest for a moment.

His leg muscles were like jello and there was no possible way he would be standing back up anytime soon. Charles melted into the bench and relished in the lack of aggrieved souls around.

It was surprisingly one of the only places in town that had very little activity from people and souls alike. He crossed his arms over his chest and let his eyes close for a moment.

Maybe he could sleep here for the night.

"Excuse me," called a soft deep voice. Charles wasn't going to answer. Was going to pretend he hadn't heard anything until the voice said, "You're Charles, right?"

*What the fuck?*

Charles slowly turned his head, nervous what he would see. It was almost three in the morning and he was alone near a cliff. If his mother were alive, she'd kill him for his stupidity.

It was a soul, Charles realized when he finally let himself look–his muscles relaxed again as the threat to his life dissipated. The soul was charcoal gray, the only type he could see, but when he found the face, Charles's heart skipped several beats in his chest and his hands went numb.

He squeezed his eyes shut in the hope that when he opened them again the soul in front of him would have just been his exhausted brain playing tricks on him.

That it would be any soul but this one.

*Not this one.*

*No.*

*No.*

*Please no.*

He cursed Death as his eyes opened, landing on the face he had only ever seen in photos scattered all over the Kramer estate.

"Noah." Charles's voice was distant in his ears.

The ghost of Noah held his hands up in surrender. "Please hear me out." Noah was begging him to not run from him, but Charles couldn't move if he tried. Couldn't speak either. "I just wanted to ask you about Nora."

"How do you know who I am?" Charles managed to get out through his rapidly closing throat.

"I've been following you." Noah shrugged. "I see you with my sister sometimes and I have also seen you talking to others like me, so I took a chance that maybe you'd be able to hear me."

"I really wish I couldn't right about now."

Noah laughed and God how it sounded exactly like Nora. "You and me both."

Charles shook the sound from his mind and steeled himself for the conversation he was about to have. "You wanted to talk to me about Nora?"

"I just want to know how she's doing."

The corner of Charles's mouth lifted. "She's doing well actually. I am helping her plan a gala at the museum for the beginning of October."

Noah's eyes narrowed. "Why? Did Death tell her about our grandfather?"

"She knows. She's trying to fix it–it's what the gala is for."

Relief flooded Noah's barely visible face. "Good. If anyone can do it, she can."

"It's been really hard on her," Charles said as he silently agreed with Noah–Nora would be the one to do it.

"But you are looking out for her?" Noah looked at him expectantly.

Charles nodded, offering Noah what he hope was a reassuring smile. "I am doing my best, but she does pretty well herself."

"She certainly does. You don't let her bully you, do you?" Noah teased.

It was Charles's turn to laugh. Noah of course knew exactly how Nora was and his tone suggested he was proud of it too. "Only slightly."

"Good." Noah smirked.

"She thinks you're in Hell, you know."

Noah nodded and looked at the ground. "It's best she believe that."

"If she knew you were here, she'd want to see you."

Noah turned his wide eyes on Charles. "No, she cannot know. I couldn't bear causing her any more pain. Please, you can't tell her, Charles."

Charles took a deep breath as the weight of yet another secret settled on his chest, but he'd keep Noah's. He'd keep it because even though he knew wholeheartedly that Nora would want to see her brother, it would break Nora to find out he had been out here this entire time.

Charles couldn't be the bearer of that news, but he knew someone that could. Someone whose fuck up was the reason Charles was staring at Nora's worst nightmare.

"I won't tell her, Noah."

"Thank you." He let out a heavy sigh. "Is she happy?" Desperation coated his voice squeezing Charles's heart.

"I think so. Some days are harder than others. She really

misses you though."

"I miss her too," Noah murmured, his tone indicating he was done talking, having gotten from Charles the information he needed.

Charles nodded, leaving Noah to himself. He needed to speak to Death.

*Now.*

"Nora was always the best of us," Noah told him sternly, stopping Charles in his tracks. Charles didn't have the heart to tell Noah how Nora thought exactly that of him. "She can't die, Charles."

"I won't let that happen, Noah," he promised before turning away again. Charles prayed he could keep it as he fled to find Death.

He was officially *pissed* at Death to the point he was considering killing the old man.

*How does one kill an immortal?*

*Stake through the heart?*

*Decapitation?*

Charles would have to get creative, he decided, as he pounded on Death's front door. Charles had been to Death's house once, years ago, and barely remembered where it was, but the rage coursing through every part of his body brought the memory flooding back.

Charles didn't care that Death might have been sleeping or that his neighbors might not appreciate the noise at the current hour.

He pounded even harder.

"Open the fuck up!" Charles yelled. "Get down here and let me in."

He didn't stop until a light flicked on and he heard Death yell from the other side of the door, "Relax, I'm coming!"

The moment Death opened the door, Charles barrelled in, shoving his hands into Death's chest and forcing the immortal a few steps backwards.

"What is wrong with you?" He seethed.

"What is wrong with *me?* You're the one banging on my door at nearly four in the morning!" Death stood his ground against Charles.

"How could you do that to her?"

"Do what? Charles, what the fuck are you talking about?" Death was eyeing him as if he had several heads.

"I just had a chat with Noah," Charles spat.

Death paled, if that was possible.

Didn't talk. Didn't move. Didn't even blink.

"Noah, as in Nora's brother, Noah."

"How?"

Charles laughed, "*How?* I'm fixing your fucking mess, that's how. You know the mess where you apparently didn't take people's souls to the realm they are supposed to be in."

"How?" Death asked again, a little quieter this time.

"Sam told Nora months ago, after the council informed her what you have been up to and she decided to fix it herself instead of making you do it like she should have. Nora has been killing herself for *months*, taking souls up to Heaven, and I have been taking them down to Hell."

"Charles I—"

"Don't," Charles held up a hand, "I don't need you to explain why you didn't do what you were supposed to. All I need to know is how you could do that to Nora."

Death's dark eyebrows knit together, his mouth pressing into a thin line. "I couldn't do it, Charles. I couldn't take Noah and he didn't want to go either. What was I supposed to do? It wasn't like she could have ever run into him."

"But now she could. Now she could easily spot him and what do you think that would do to her?"

"I know," Death whispered.

Another revelation hit Charles square in the chest and this one hurt most of all.

"And what would have happened had she made it into Hell that day to get to Noah? What happens if she just decides she's over all of it and goes whenever she wants? She would be giving herself up for fucking *NOTHING!* Nothing, Death. She has no idea that her brother isn't down there."

Death shut his eyes and Charles wasn't sure if the man was still breathing. "I'll fix it."

"See that you do, or I will." Charles bared his teeth. "She deserves to know the truth."

Charles was done, completely spent both physically and mentally. He left Death to stand in his modest front room drowning in the news Charles had just dumped on him, and headed home to his shower and his bed.

# CHAPTER 24

## DEATH

DEATH WAS A COWARD.

Even worse, he was an idiot.

He never thought his antics would catch up to him, let alone get back to Nora and Charles. Death wanted to lay down and die, or better yet, find Time and beg him to let him go back and fix his own mistakes. He had a hard time wrapping his head around what Nora and Charles were doing for him.

Part of him was touched that they would selflessly help him.

Part of him wanted to throw up.

In fact he had been throwing up regularly since Charles almost broke down his door the other night. The boy had been veritably irate. If Death hadn't been sick at the revelation, he would have taken a moment to admire Charles's ire.

It was all Death had wanted–for Charles to be angry again. There was no proper living in a world where a person turned off half of their emotions. It wasn't good for the mind.

Death would know.

He'd watched too many people over his years completely unravel trying to not feel.

Death walked over to the estate the next day and asked Nora to join him for coffee. She looked as though she were going to decline his invitation so he said, *"please,"* for what was likely the first time in his life.

The softness that lingered deep under all that contempt she harbored for him agreed. Nora promised to meet him Thursday afternoon at the coffee shop she and Charles both liked.

He stood out front to wait for her, dressed in his overcoat and watching people shuffle past. Had it not been for the clouds that never seemed to leave this town, Death would have been overwarm, but then again temperature really didn't have any effect on him.

So did he really mind?

Nora rounded a corner, walking slowly toward him, and Death held his breath.

He could do this.

He *had* to do this.

The alternative was letting Charles tell her, and that was not going to happen. It was not the boy's job to do so. It was not his job to break her. Death needed to talk to Nora anyway, clear the air about the main issue they had.

"Death," Nora stated, stopping directly in front of him.

"Little star," he responded, forcing a softness into his voice so as to not sound as terrified as he felt.

Her eyes fluttered. "Shall we?"

Death merely nodded, following her inside. They ordered their coffees, he paid, and the two of them settled into an awkward silence before heading to a table outside.

He cleared his throat and begged his voice to not shake. "How are you?"

"I'm fine," Nora eyed him over her paper cup, "and you?"

"Good, I'm good."

"Great."

"Little star, I can't begin to explain how sorry I am," Death blurted. Nora's face remained impassive. "I thought I was protecting you by not telling you. He didn't want you to know and I didn't want you to hate him."

Death told Nora about James then. About his previous mistakes. How he hadn't intended to fuck up this severely, but age didn't constitute wisdom, it only made people expect it. People don't just stop being idiots, and Death was certainly that.

Of course he tried to learn and grow like everyone else does over the course of their lives, but immortality was a curse and not having an end date made one boldly stupid.

"I don't hate him," Nora said after a long time. "Not anymore. And I don't hate you either."

"You don't?" Death narrowed his eyes on her, desperate to not sound too eager.

She shook her head. "No I don't. I get why you did it, and I understand his part in your decision. I just hate that you lied."

Nora spoke the word *lied* with extra emphasis which Death figured was a nod to his other lie, but he wouldn't admit he knew what she was doing.

At least not yet.

He was losing more and more of his confidence the longer they spoke and it was likely they'd get to the end of the conversation and he wouldn't even tell her about Noah.

Death was a coward.

"I hate that I lied to you too. It never got easier either. Not once did I think you would find that room of his."

"Were you just going to let me die and take me to Hell without letting me fight it all?" Nora tilted her head, observing him closely.

"In all my years, I have never heard of Lucifer letting a person out of a contract. It's not like him in the slightest." Death shook his head. "He is the devil, Nora. He didn't get that name because he routinely shows kindness."

Nora laughed and it made his heart soar. It had been too long since he'd heard that sound from her. "You do have a point there."

Death grinned against the lid of his cup. "So what are you doing to break the contract?"

"We are hosting a gala at the museum and are going to steal the art to send it back to the original owners."

"Ah, so it's simple then. I was worried it'd be complicated."

Nora rolled her eyes. "Obviously, because I'm brilliant."

"Obviously," he chided, grinning to himself.

Death would not be telling her about Noah.

He was okay with being a coward for the time being, if it meant they could talk to one another again. If he could hear her laugh.

"I have to go. Charles is waiting for me at the house." Nora smiled lightly, standing from her chair. "We are finalizing the details of the gala."

"Of course," Death urged her on, "tell the boy hello for me, will you?"

"I will, if you promise to come to the gala."

Death made her wait a moment before he answered. "I wouldn't miss it for anything."

Nora nodded and left him at the table to head home. Death watched her hurry down the street and only when she disappeared around the corner was he able to suck down a deep breath. Self loathing lingered because he had refused to tell her about Noah, but he was just a man who indeed feared the wrath of a mortal girl.

Death would tell her.

Soon.

# CHAPTER 25

## NORA

C HARLES WAS LONG ASLEEP like the rest of the house, like she should be, but Nora was entirely too restless to lie down. Two hours she had laid in bed, staring at the ceiling, attempting to read the most boring book she owned, testing out every possible sleeping position.

Despite her best efforts, thoughts swirled around in her brain like a hurricane yet to hit land, full of momentum and vengeance with nothing to slow it down.

Nora was drowning in anticipation, suffocating with fear.

There wasn't anything tangible to be afraid of, but tomorrow was the gala and Nora couldn't shake the feeling she was missing something.

Her legs needed to move.

Her mind begged her to run, unfortunately a walk around the house would have to do at this hour. She could leave the house and find a few people to take to Heaven, but she didn't want to run the risk of Charles catching her.

Nora always had trouble sleeping when she was anxious. During the day her mind had company with tasks for to complete. But when it was time for bed and she physically settled, her thoughts took over.

Running through each action and word she spoke like a

highlight reel. It showed her all of the words she fumbled over, all of the thoughts she was avoiding, all of her awkward interactions.

Worst of all it created demons from nothing.

Dark looming thoughts about situations that had never happened, that in the light of day never would. Nora only found sleep when her brain exhausted itself, only to wake up feeling worse.

There were sixteen bedrooms in the house, all of which had been occupied by a family member at one point. Vincent lived in the guest house on the west end of the estate grounds. Noah's room was across the hall from hers. Izzy's room was next to hers and Carter's–the one Charles currently occupied–was next to Noah's.

She hadn't had the heart to let Charles use Noah's room all this time, even though it was probably the most equipped to house someone of his age. The bed was bigger, the items inside more appropriate for someone older.

Carter died when he was eleven and his room remained stuck in time–filled with toys and figurines and buildable sets. Then again, Nora thought, Charles might enjoy that. Just like Charlotte who always stayed in Izzy's room because it was the room right next to Nora's, but Charlotte secretly loved the flowery pink walls.

But the room Nora was looking for wasn't on this side of the house so she quietly made her way to the west end of the second floor, located the room she needed, and pushed open the thick wooden door.

The light was already on.

The house knew she was coming.

Her parent's old room was just as it always had been. The

crimson covered room was plain save for the desk by the window and the four poster mahogany bed that was pushed up against the far wall. Nora thought she might enter, but her feet were rooted to the floor.

Nora was five years old again.

The door had been open just like this as her parents never worried about hiding their volatility from her or Noah. Or from anyone for that matter.

It had been a sticky summer day, but the heat hadn't stopped her and her brother and their cousins from spending the day outside.

Her grandfather indulged them in those days. Giving them everything they asked for and Izzy had just been gifted the bunnies she had been wanting. The boys were at the edge of the property climbing trees and the older girls thought Nora and Izzy childish for wanting to play with the bunnies. But Nora and Izzy didn't care what they thought. The bunnies had been so soft, making the girls squeal when they hopped around in the grass. Izzy's toothless grin never left, and more than anything, Nora wanted to show her mother.

"Mummy, mummy!" her little voice called as she ran up the stairs. "Come quick, you have to see the—" Nora started but the words and her excitement died on her tongue when she reached her parents' open bedroom door in time to see her father strike her mother across the face.

Her mother collapsed to the ground, but got up a moment later with a vengeance. She leapt at Nathaniel, swiping at him with her nails, tearing at his clothes. Nora watched it all from the other side of the doorway, frozen to her spot on the floor.

She might as well have been part of the house itself.

Nathaniel pushed her mother down onto the bed, jerking her

head back by a fistful of her hair. Blood poured from Nora's mother's nose, smearing over her cheek and dripping down her chin, but she bared her teeth all the same. Nathaniel leaned over her to whisper something Nora couldn't hear and the next thing she knew, Vincent scooped her up and carried her away in his arms.

"Off we go, Miss Nora."

She wrapped her tiny arms around his neck and held on until the caretaker deposited Nora in her grandfather's study, right onto his lap.

He was painting again.

It was one of his abstract pieces that he loosely called *impressionism*, but she could have sworn it was just a giant orange mess of nothing.

"Were they fighting again?" he asked after some time, not taking his eyes off his painting.

"Yeah. Mummy was bleeding." Nora picked at her thumb nail as she stared at her shoes. They were muddy and covered in freshly cut grass.

How she wished she'd stayed outside.

"I am sorry you had to see that, little star." Her grandfather continued to paint and Nora watched the brush streak across the canvas, letting its movements calm her.

"Why does daddy hurt mummy, papa?"

The brush stopped.

He set it down on the easel and turned her little body to face him. "Your father is angry, he doesn't see the light that he has."

Nora frowned at him. "But the lights were on, papa."

Her grandfather chuckled. "The good, little one. He doesn't see the good things in his life. *Light* is all of the love and good in your life and your father believes he does not have much of that so he takes it out on your mother."

"I thought he loved mummy." Nora looked up to see his thin lips pressed together, pulled down at the edges. His gray eyes mirrored hers, dull despite the sunny day.

"That I cannot say. I don't know."

"Do you love daddy, papa?"

He didn't answer and instead asked, "Do you?"

Nora considered his question for a moment. A part of her thought she should, that it was the right thing to feel for one's father, but when she thought of him, she didn't see any light at all.

Nora shook her head and said, "He is darkness."

"Some people are, but there will be people who will shine so brightly for you, my love."

Her grandfather picked up his brush and touched it to her nose, painting it orange.

"Papa!" she shrieked.

He simply touched his nose to hers, brushing it back and forth. When he pulled away, revealing his own orange nose, Nora descended into a fit of giggles that loosened all of the tension in her rigid little body. She would have slipped right off his lap onto the floor had he not been holding onto her. Her grandfather laughed with her for a long time until he wrapped his arms tight around her, pressing her to his chest.

"You are my light, little star." He kissed the top of Nora's head and she sat on his lap while he continued to paint.

Her cousins played beyond the windows until the sun went down, but Nora had long forgotten the bunnies and her desire to play outside, discarded for the soothing motion of the paint brush and the warmth of her grandfather's arms.

Nora's mother was gone the next morning.

A month later, her grandfather hung the finished painting in her room at the museum, right next to her portrait. It was a sun, the embodiment of her brother.

The plaque below it read, "*Distant stars are someone else's sun.*"

"Fears are meant to be faced, Nora," she whispered, rolling her shoulders back and taking a step across the threshold to her parents' room.

Her feet sunk into the carpet that hadn't been walked on in over a decade. It was plush through her socks, feeling like new. Their door had been shut since her father died as neither Nora nor her brother had any desire to spend time there.

She walked over to the desk and ran her fingers over the few books stacked there until they reached a singular picture frame. Nora picked it up and wiped the dust off the glass.

It was the four of them. Nora was a baby, held by her mother while Nathaniel balanced Noah on his hip with one arm, his other was draped around her mother's shoulders.

The smiles were genuine, or at least they looked it. Nathaniel's dark hair was perfectly in place and a dimple had formed in his cheek–the only piece of him Nora and Noah both carried. Nora had her mother's blonde hair, Noah had her blue eyes. Her mother had such delicate features in the photo, looking nothing like the hard, angular woman from her memories.

Nora wasn't sure why she had sought out her parents' room in the first place. Partly because she was curious, partly because she wanted to erase the old memory, partly because she missed them.

She wanted to believe they loved her, loved Noah, but she couldn't be certain. If Nora had known the people in the photo, she would have said yes, without a doubt, but those were not the parents she had known.

She returned the picture to the desk and left as quietly as she had entered.

There had only been one person whom she was certain loved her and Noah unconditionally, but he was thirteen years gone from this world and she was cross with his ghost.

The house silently pulled her towards him, to his secret room, lighting the halls that would take her there. As always, the house knew what she needed, knew her intentions. It read her thoughts and emotions better than anyone ever had, save for her grandfather.

Nora had been through everything in the room. She knew where everything was like the back of her hand and yet a stack of papers she hadn't placed there, sat on the desk.

Nora expected more terrible secrets to be concealed, but a letter laid on top of the stack of papers, like it had been placed there on purpose, intentionally set aside for her to see.

The paper stared at her, branding itself onto her soul, marking its words there for eternity.

*My Darling Nora.*

Her grandfather's worn script stung her eyes. Each stroke of his pen etched another mark of her pain. Nora wasn't sure this was what she needed, but she forced herself to read it anyway.

*October 21*
*My Darling Nora,*

*If you are reading this it is because you are all that is left of us and how I hate myself for leaving this burden to you. You are also likely aware of the deals I have made and the crimes I have committed, and for that I am sorry. But if anyone would find me out, I knew it would be you. From the tiny version of you that I am watching chase your brother through these halls, to the young woman I am imagining reading this letter, you were always the best of us. The most brilliant. The most clever. My little star.*

*You, Nora, from the day you were born, have been the best thing I have ever done. In all of the wrong. The miniscule amount of credit I can claim in the making of you, I hold on tight to. I sit here in more sorrow than I can handle, not because I am going to die tomorrow, but because of the pain I will have caused you.*

*I had a life, when I was young, that I am not proud of. I stole and lied and cheated my way through it because I was desperate to survive. But then when I could survive, I craved more. I made my deal before I met and married your grandmother.*

*She was a nasty pill of a woman, angry and vindictive, but I accepted her love because I thought it to be what I deserved for my transgressions. Your grandmother wanted a million children, whereas I would have preferred to have had none. The less deaths to mark my soul the better.*

*My sons were every bit of the worst parts of their mother. Terribly bitter and spiteful people. As you know very well. I hate everyday that I didn't spare you and Noah from your father's wrath. My sons went on to have nasty children themselves, the only exceptions being you and Noah and Izzy and Carter. You four were all the good bits of me, the few that existed.*

*When I made this deal, I thought there would be no*

*harm in it. I thought that seventy would be a long and prosperous life. What I did not think about were the people I would hurt. The people I would come to love with my whole heart.*

*One last time I must ask too much of you.*

*I must ask that you forgive me.*

*You don't have to do so now, or anytime soon. Sit with the anger that I know you feel. Be cross with me. You always had big, wonderful emotions. I hope one day you won't hold such anger towards me, but I cannot dictate how you feel anymore than I can change what I have done.*

*Know one thing without a doubt.*

*I love you, Nora Grace, with every bit that is left of my tattered soul.*

*You taught me love and light and I cannot thank you enough.*

At some point while reading the letter, Nora had backed up to the wall and slid down to the floor. The ground had become unstable and she needed to sit before she fell over. It was just like her grandfather to leave her something like this. Something he knew only she would find.

He had done it often when Nora was little, leaving her notes and clues around the house for her to crack or to simply tell her there was a treat waiting for her.

But this letter wasn't like the others. There wasn't a present to be found.

This was an apology.

An explanation.

One she didn't know she needed. One that stomped on her

heart.

Nora had been consumed with anger for so long that once she righted his wrongs she was afraid of what would be left, if there would be anything at all.

Of course she forgave him. It was easy to do now that he had asked–from beyond the grave. Part of her felt wrong to do so, felt her morals shutter slightly as she sat amidst the evidence of his felony. Several felonies for that matter.

But for everything her grandfather was, he was still the fun, kind hearted man who had raised her. He had been one of the few people who had truly loved her.

Nora couldn't hate him.

Not really.

Even knowing everything he did, the doom he had caused them all, she still loved him.

Nora cried for what felt like hours, but time in the secret room didn't exist when she couldn't see the sun–when she was surrounded by the past.

It could have been hours.

It could have been five minutes.

She let herself sob until her breathing eased, until all that was left were the tears that flowed silently down her cheeks.

The next thing Nora was aware of were soft, warm hands on her face, they wiped away the tears, but she kept her eyes squeezed shut. When she finally found the strength to open them and her vision cleared, she was greeted with ocean blue eyes and mangled hair. Sleep had made his hair even messier, if that was at all possible.

*He should be asleep,* Nora thought as she reached up to run her fingers through his hair, letting her knuckles brush over his pink-kissed cheek.

"Charles," she whispered. She wasn't even sure he heard her until she saw the flash of his brilliant smile.

"Nora," Charles whispered back, pressing his forehead to hers. "I've got you."

She didn't have any words left. Her nerves were fried and her thoughts had liquified the gray matter inside her head. Warmth like she had never felt before wrapped around her as the ground fell away.

Nora leaned into the heat and let it pull her under.

Let it absolve every terrible thought she'd ever had, every lapse in her morality.

Let it thaw her frozen soul.

# CHAPTER 26

## CHARLES

C HARLES HAD BEEN DEEP into sleep when he woke up to the door of Carter's room bursting open. The sound had him shooting up in bed before he was even fully awake. Lights were on in the hall, but when he stepped into it, he realized only certain ones were lit.

It was odd for the house to be lit up at that time of night, but Nora had always told him to trust that the house knew what he needed.

So he did.

Charles trusted a sentient house over his own logical mind and he was glad he did.

The lights led him out of the east wing and into the main part of the house, the walls pulsed with an urgent energy that filled him with nothing but dread. His feet traveling swiftly over soft green rugs to the stairs.

Lights bloomed in front of Charles as he walked, winking out as he passed each one down the stairs and into the foyer leading him quickly to the source–the secret room.

He entered the library slowly, almost afraid of what he would find and then he heard it. Soft sobs and labored breathing.

Charles ran, leaving his fear behind in the hall. He was frantic when he burst into the secret room, half expecting to find Nora hurt and bleeding out, but she wasn't. Instead Nora was slumped against the wall with knees curled to her chest, clutching a sheet of paper.

Looking up to the ceiling, he said a quiet thank you, feeling slightly ridiculous that he was thanking a house until he felt it hum in response.

He knelt in front of her to search her face, but Nora's eyes were squeezed shut, tears flowing swiftly down her pale cheeks. He had no idea what to expect when the house woke him, but he never expected this. If he found her in trouble at all, he imagined it would have been facing certain death rather than her crying on the floor.

This reality hurt his heart infinitely more.

Over the past several months Charles had more or less come to terms with the fact that he would lose Nora.

He wanted to hate her for it. The way she joked about it. The way she talked about her finality like it wasn't something to be bothered with.

It made him angry.

Angry because Charles couldn't understand being so okay with dying. Angry because she made him love her and expected him to not.

Nora had warned him. God how she had warned him, but Charles couldn't stop his need for her.

He hadn't even tried.

When he pried the paper from her grip, the words written there told him everything he needed to know about the state she was in. Those words would haunt her the rest of her days–however long she had. So Charles did what he could and wiped the tears from her cheeks.

When she opened her eyes and whispered his name, he was

thankful he was already on his knees. Storm clouds pooled in her irises and Charles was no longer cross with her because while she elicited from him some of his more regrettable emotions, she made him feel everything.

Everything he was too afraid of.

Nora was a star in all of the darkness around her and she may call him the sun but he would dim himself to bask in her light forever.

Charles wrapped her in his arms letting his warmth settle into her until she melted against him and her shaking subsided. He carried Nora out of the library and across the hall to the drawing room she loved and laid her down on a sofa next to the already burning fire.

After locating a blanket, Charles squeezed himself onto the small space next to her and pulled Nora into him. She rested her cheek on his chest, the tension in her body dissipating beneath his hands, her breathing returning to normal.

"I've got you, Nora," Charles whispered one last time into her hair, letting the heat of the fire and rhythm of her breathing lull him back to sleep.

Charles woke unexpectedly a second time to the sound of someone clearing their throat. He inhaled deeply only to be pleasantly greeted with the pear scent of Nora's hair.

When Charles finally cracked an eye open, the room was full of morning light, the fire burned low, and a very stern looking Vincent stared down at him. Heat bloomed over Charles's face and Nora stirred as he shifted. He gave her a light shake, watching as a smile tugged at the corner of her mouth.

As much as he wanted to savor this moment, Vincent cleared his throat again. Nora's eyes shot open and she pushed off Charles's chest in an abrupt motion that forcibly evacuated all the air from his lungs. Her eyes were wild, taking in Charles and Vincent and the room she had woken up in.

Nora retreated to the other side of the sofa and Charles watched the memory of the night warm her cheeks, the embarrassment she was desperately trying to hide. He sat up to reach for her but she retreated further, clutching the blanket to her. Nora's wide eyes swung back to Vincent who looked more worried than anything. Several rapid blinks later, she jumped from the sofa and took off.

"Nora!" Charles yelled after her, but it was no use. She was gone from the room in a flurry of pink hair, the blanket trailing in her wake.

Charles let out a heavy sigh and scrubbed a hand over his face only to see the disappointment had returned to Vincent's. The old man raised a dark bushy eyebrow at him before turning to leave the room as well.

*Fantastic.*

An hour later, Charles was showered and ready for the day which included much of him sitting around waiting for the gala to start. He was restless and Nora was nowhere to be found. Her bedroom door was slightly ajar, but when he knocked only to receive no response, he pushed it the rest of the way open to find it empty.

Nora was hiding and Charles suspected she would emerge only when she inevitably had to, which would likely be later that night to leave for the gala.

An absent Nora meant an afternoon to himself, which unsettled him. Charles was in desperate need to be busy.

A quick message to Andrew and Dylan confirmed they were at home and subsequently his plans for the afternoon. Charles couldn't remember the last time he had seen his friends and it was no one's fault but his.

It was a bad habit of Charles's–hyperfixation.

He would become singularly focused on one task and neglect everything else. Luckily he had friends who didn't seem to mind and were entirely too understanding. It wasn't as if they hadn't talked at all, there was the occasional text, but physically seeing each other was something else entirely.

Charles made his way out the front door of the estate to a delightfully warm fall day. The leaves had all turned to various shades of red, yellow, and orange–most of them already littering the ground. He liked the bareness of the trees, the stillness of the fall. It was all so exact, so exposing.

Charles made it halfway down the driveway before Death rounded the entrance of the estate.

"She's not here," Charles informed Death idly as he passed the immortal on the concrete path.

"Charles, please," Death pleaded.

"Have you told her yet?" Disdain laced his words, but he stopped walking.

"No, I haven't," Death murmured, refusing to meet Charles's stare.

"Then I have nothing to say to you." Charles continued down the drive.

"I am going to tell her!" Death called from behind him.

"Sure," he spat back. Charles didn't believe him in the slightest.

Not anymore.

He headed towards the university where Andrew lived just off campus. Charles had invited them to the gala weeks ago and they caught up a little then over the phone, but it was time to do so properly. It wasn't like him to go so long without seeing them, but he had been distracted. A beautiful, worthy distraction at that, despite how stressful it all was.

Lately, Charles was being crushed by his hope.

Nora had been adamant at the start that he not get attached to her and while he didn't really try to heed her wish, Nora hadn't either. She might not have explicitly said anything, but Charles could feel it on her–the desire to touch him, to be near him.

Everytime Charles stepped closer to her, he felt her heart rate quicken, saw the heat flush in her cheeks. Charles begrudgingly kept his hands to himself, but his will was fraying at the edges.

Charles had mentally prepared to never find a way to save her life, to get Nora past her death date, but hope had wormed its way into his very bones. It wrapped its grimy little fingers around his heart and waited.

Ready to pull, tear, destroy, at a moment's notice.

It was wholly his fault for letting hope in, but it's who he was!

Charles had always been hopeful. Had always been optimistic. Then this beautiful, pink haired, storm of a girl entered his life and asked him to be realistic, so he had pretended. He had pretended to expect what was right in front of him and nothing more.

But Charles was still Charles and he still believed in good outcomes.

Optimism and remorse carried him to his friend's doorstep where he waited for them to let him in. The second the door opened, Dylan and Andrew threw their arms around him and dragged him inside.

"God, we've missed you Charles," Dylan admitted steering him into Andrew's living room.

The strain on Charles's heart eased, his worry was nowhere to be found.

"I've missed you both too."

"Want to share where you've been for the last ten months?" Andrew asked, falling into the oversized chair by the window. His typically overgrown, tightly coiled hair was cut close to his head on the sides. But Andrew's eyes and skin were still the same shade of warm brown they had always been and the shadow of a smile on his lips welcomed Charles home.

"You barely even bothered to check in either." Dylan's eyes raked over him, looking for any sign of harm. He had always worried more than the others about Charles's health–always ready to jump into action at the first sign of a problem. "Then you show up here looking more stressed than I've ever seen you and we are supposed to go to a gala tonight? What is going on Charles?"

Charles wasn't sure where to start or how to explain the mess he'd gotten himself into, if he could even call it a mess. It wasn't really, it was something to be solved and Nora was the furthest from a mess. She was confident and direct and the most strictly logical person he'd ever known.

*Mess* wasn't the correct word, but he could figure that out later. Charles decided an apology was the best place for him to start.

"I'm sorry, Dylan. I'm sorry to you both. It was never my intention to worry either of you, but I've just been so busy and there's this horribly big secret I'm keeping from someone I really care about and it's eating me alive."

Andrew and Dylan exchanged a look, the former raised his eyebrows, the latter pursed his lips.

"Charles Riley, keeping a secret? I never thought I'd see the day," Andrew jested at the same time Dylan said, "Someone you really care about?"

Charles laughed, "Her name is Nora Kramer."

Andrew gaped at him. "I'm sorry, but you mean to tell us you have been spending all your time with that mysterious, billionaire heiress."

"There's no way." Dylan shook his head, disbelief swimming in his eyes.

"It's her gala you're going to tonight," Charles stated.

"How?" Dylan exhaled.

Charles shrugged. "Her and I have a mutual friend in Death and when she lost her brother last year, he asked me to check in on her. Turns out she needed a lot more help than either of us thought."

The guys knew about Death from the start. Charles had wanted them to know he wasn't completely without supervision.

"What are you keeping from her?" Andrew asked carefully.

"Something about her brother. Something Death has been keeping from her that I only recently found out about." Charles wouldn't tell his friends how he had found Noah's soul floating around by the river outlook. He was waiting for Death to tell her, but Charles wouldn't tell anyone until Nora knew herself.

It wasn't fair.

None of it was fair, but he could at least do his best to make this right. However, Charles could tell them about her situation, so he did.

He shared it all, from going to Hell, about Death leaving souls behind, the day Nora is supposed to die, how her grandfather was actually a criminal. Charles made sure to put extra emphasis on his disdain for Councilman Sam.

"Is she as dark and scary as everyone in town says she is?" Dylan asked when Charles finally finished recapping the last ten months.

Charles laughed at his friend. He had never paid attention to gossip, but this was downright hilarious. Of course the town thought Nora 'dark and scary.' People tended to believe exactly that of those who were quiet and didn't pay attention to what others thought of them. Nora kept to herself and didn't get out of the estate very often, there was no doubt the town thought ill of her.

"She is definitely *not* dark and scary. Nora *is* quiet, but she brilliant and kind. She has been dealt a really shitty hand in this life and the fact that she is still moving forward should be studied." Charles looked over both of his friends. "I mean that seriously. It is the most amazing thing I have ever seen."

Dylan's hazel eyes watched him carefully. "You haven't gotten yourself into trouble have you, Charles."

"No, Dyl. I promise." Charles tried to reassure his friend.

"Is she funny at least?" Andrew cut in.

Charles scoffed, "She is."

"Not to mention she's pretty," Andrew mused.

"Goddamn gorgeous," Charles exhaled.

"Is our boy in love?" Andrew asked Dylan.

Charles rolled his eyes.

"I think he might actually be." Dylan grinned.

"Well you'll get to meet her tonight. You'll both love her," Charles assured them.

"And she's good to you?" Andrew watched him.

Charles nodded. Nora was never not good to him. She was difficult and exacting, but she was always caring, always concerned about everyone but herself.

He was actively not thinking about how she ran away from him that morning, but he'd worry about that later.

"What are you doing tomorrow for your birthday, by the way?" Dylan asked.

Charles shook his head. He hadn't even thought about his birthday. "Trying to keep Nora out of Hell."

"Oh," Andrew murmured, "just your casual Thursday, then."

"Exactly." Charles smiled and rose to his feet. His friends followed him to the front door.

"It really was good to see you, buddy." Dylan said, raking a hand through his thick, curly blond hair. Andrew watched him, his lips pressed together.

"I'm so sorry I've been absent for so long. It won't happen again," Charles promised his friends.

"It will," Andrew mused, "but it's okay, Charlie. We will always be around."

Charles placed a hand on Andrew's shoulder in quiet thanks. He didn't deserve his friends, not after he'd been such an ass.

"And I will see you both tonight?" Charles asked for confirmation as he headed out the door.

"Of course you will," Dylan said. "No way we are missing meeting this Nora of yours or a chance to embarrass you in front of her."

*Brilliant.*

Charles deserved their derision so he simply nodded and stifled a laugh. There was much to do to get ready for tonight and no way he would be late for it.

# CHAPTER 27

## NORA

N ORA STOOD IN FRONT of the plain mausoleum and mentally screamed at herself. The door to Hell was right in front of her, but she couldn't bring herself to close the distance.

It would be so easy to get the door open. All it would take is the touch of her palm.

So why couldn't she do it?

"Fuck you," Nora spat.

She was unclear if she was directing that curse at Lucifer, Death, her grandfather, herself, or life itself. The list of people she was cross with was growing longer by the minute.

She hated that she couldn't face this particular fear. Nora wasn't even positive it was a fear rather than a lack of trust in herself.

It had been almost a full year since she had descended the steps to Hell the first time, completely lacking the desire to live. Now there were too many reasons to live, but still too many reasons to stay down there.

This past year had taught Nora a lot about herself. She enjoyed playing the piano again, the time she spent with Charlotte was too precious, and Charles made her feel more than she'd like to admit. Nora could go to the museum again without having a panic attack and walls of the estate no longer felt like they were closing in on her. Even her nightmares had been scarce.

Why couldn't she do this?

Why was this the *one thing* she couldn't face?

Noah was down there. Her grandfather was down there. Izzy. Carter. They were all down there and yet the thought of joining them made Nora want to throw up.

*Before* she had wanted nothing more than to join them. *Before* she would have given anything to see them again, to hug them again, to hear them laugh again.

But this morning she had woken up warm, with her head on Charles's chest, wrapped in his sweet vanilla scent. She had played the piano for him. She had taken him to the museum. She finally felt safe.

A year ago when Nora closed her eyes all she saw were the faces of her dead relatives, but now when she closed them, she saw Charles's messy hair. His ocean blue eyes. She heard Charlotte's carefree laughter. She could feel the warmth of her friend's arms tight around her. Vincent's eyes finally reflecting his smile again.

Nora's allconsuming doom had been replaced by guilt.

The reasons to live had tripled and yet the logic of it all dictated a different fate. Nora's wants weren't her reality and the hardest thing she'd ever have to do was accept it. She could accept the idea of wanting to live, the joy of it all, the feelings she had for Charles–if she had to.

What she couldn't accept was the reality that it would all be ripped from her hands as though it was never hers in the first place.

"Fuck!" Nora yelled only to turn away from the stone mausoleum to see Charlotte leaning against the wall of a stone statue, suppressing her laughter.

"Fighting with a tomb are we?" Charlotte's eyebrows were high on her forehead.

Nora thought about protesting, but there was no use. She *had* been yelling at a tomb. "How did you know where to find me?"

"I know who your friends are." Charlotte shrugged.

"You're my only friend, Char," Nora crossed her arms.

Charlotte pushed off the wall and crossed the gravel to stand next to Nora, examining the door. "You going to go down there?"

Nora turned back around, eyeing her friend skeptically. She hadn't told Charlotte about her ability to enter Hell. Her friend didn't need to worry about Death's problem or worry about Nora's involvement in said problem.

There was one person Charlotte talked to regularly who Nora also hadn't told, but was smart enough and close enough to it all to figure it out.

"I am going to kill that boy," Nora seethed.

Her friend smirked, rolling her eyes. "No you're not."

Maybe Nora wouldn't kill him, but they would definitely be having a conversation. About a few things for that matter–starting with the fact that Charles knew what she had been doing and not only kept it from her, he told her best friend.

How he knew, she had no idea, but Nora always had the feeling Charles knew more about her than she was comfortable with. He saw too much, read her too easily.

"Okay, no I'm not going to kill him, but I haven't decided whether or not I'm going down there." Nora sighed, "I don't think I can Char."

"Do you need to?"

"Not particularly, but I feel like I have to." Nora chewed on her bottom lip.

"I could go with you." Charlotte shrugged.

Nora shook her head. "I can't let you go down there Char, it's terrible."

"All the more reason to go together. We go down. Prove to yourself that you are still the fearless person I know you to be and then we will walk back up here." Charlotte held out her hand to Nora. "Together?"

Nora looked down at the hand outstretched before her, fighting the burning in her eyes. "I don't deserve you, Charlotte."

"You deserve good things Nora, and I happen to be the best." Her friend smirked.

Laughing, Nora took Charlotte's hand. "You certainly are."

"Let's get this over with because we have a gala to get to tonight and there is quite a bit of work to be done to my hair if I am going to be the best looking person there." Charlotte squared her shoulders to the mausoleum.

Nora bit back her retort and admired her friend. Her brilliant, fearless, gorgeous friend who never failed to be right next to her when Nora needed her. She wished to one day be half the person Charlotte Hayes was—that was if she made it past her grandfather's birthday in two weeks.

Charlotte and Nora took the steps up to the marble slab that blocked the entrance to Hell. Nora lifted her free hand to the warm stone as Charlotte's fingers tightened around hers. The slab shifted backwards and slid to the side as an unwelcome, suffocating heat poured out of the open door.

"Ugh, that's gross," Charlotte groaned.

"There's a hook for your coat inside the door," Nora said, pulling Charlotte in behind her.

"I hate that you know that."

"If it makes you feel any better, I hate it too."

"It doesn't," Charlotte said flatly.

They shed their coats, hung them on the hooks, and crossed the small room to the top of the stairs. Nora rolled her shoulders back and Charlotte's hand slid back into hers. They exchanged a nervous look, Nora dipped her chin slightly.

They could do this.

The descent was the easiest part of their excursion, but the further they got, the more Nora dreaded the eventual climb back up. The girls were silent the entire way, but when the heat became too much they were forced to let go of one another–sweat making it impossible to keep their hands clasped.

Charlotte turned in a slow circle, once they reached the platform, taking in the emptiness of the realm below. The fiery gates jolted open, rustling the smoke, causing Charlotte to jump when the ground shook.

"Heaven looks similar, just a lot brighter and it stinks of roses," Nora whispered to her friend who wasn't listening to her in the slightest.

Lucifer drifted out of the gates on a plume of smoke. His suit jacket billowed around him to expose his bare torso. Nora rolled her eyes and the Devil himself smirked.

"I was hoping you'd visit again. I am getting tired of only seeing your friend." Lucifer frowned. "He is pretty, but not as pretty as you, little star."

Bile burned in her throat.

Nora turned slightly to look at Charlotte who shook her head lightly, confirming she didn't know Charles had been coming down there either.

The conversation Nora and Charles needed to have would be

a heated one. Nora's blood boiled and she would have turned a shade of red had she not already been so ungodly hot.

"I do however appreciate him bringing all those souls to me, the ones Death was too selfish to leave behind."

She wished Lucifer would stop talking.

This was not the information she came down here to get, but now her mind was full of thoughts of Charles dragging souls down here. Nora needed to get her breathing under control and change the subject.

The heat was not helping.

"I need to know that when I fix my grandfather's mess, I'm not going to die in a week." Nora sucked down hot air in an attempt to calm herself.

*On second thought, maybe it'd be best if I didn't breathe at all.*

"I can't tell you that yet," Lucifer admitted flatly, shoving his hands in his pants pockets.

"Why?" Charlotte spat.

Lucifer turned his attention to Charlotte. "You are a pretty one too. However, I won't be able to decide if it's enough until you complete said task. But I will let you know as soon as I can, I promise." He placed a hand over his heart, but the look on his face was far from sincere.

"How is that even fair? What's the point?" Nora yelled across the open space.

"It's certainly not fair, but I said I was kind, not trustworthy." Lucifer frowned. "The point is you tried, I guess. Though if you are looking for the point, this is not the realm to find it."

"So in the end, it never mattered what I did, it was always your decision to let me go or not," Nora mused. She could feel laughter bubbling in her stomach.

"Now you are getting it. It was always my decision, but it is cute to watch you try so hard. Sam tells me that the gala tonight is going to be one worth attending."

The laughter fizzled out, doused by the fear of Lucifer joining them above. He sensed her discomfort and flashed his perfect teeth again.

"Oh don't worry, darling Nora. I have no desire to go up there. As fun as your little party is rumored to be, I have far enough down here to keep me occupied."

"Great," Nora muttered. Charlotte stiffened next to her and she could feel her friend's need to pick a fight with the being standing in front of them. Nora reached out and put a hand on Charlotte's arm, Lucifer's black eyes tracked the movement.

"Do look for my letter. I'll send it along with the post in a day or two to let you know if I approve of your *solution*." Lucifer wagged his fingers to wave goodbye before striding back through the iron gates.

The realization that it was still in his hands should have been shocking, but it wasn't. Not to Nora. Maybe to Charlotte. In the end it was always his decision. In the end Nora had already come to terms with her death.

To know that it may still happen in two weeks, despite her effort, didn't hurt. What hurt was the fact she had never been in control, that the hope she had let build was a moot point.

"So he just gets final say like that?" Charlotte leaned over to whisper in Nora's ear.

"They were his rules to begin with." Nora shrugged.

"Oh fuck that guy," Charlotte spat at the closed gates.

Nora wanted to throw up and lay on the ground, but raised an eyebrow at her friend instead. "He is the literal Devil, Char."

Charlotte crossed her arms, doubling down. "Well I hope he rots in there."

"He probably won't," Nora muttered. Charlotte scowled at her. "Let's get out of here."

"Yes please."

By the time they were halfway up the stairs, they were gasping for air and Charlotte was doubled over, using her hands to help her climb, brown hair plastered to the sides of her face. Nora loved Charlotte for going with her, but this was likely the most physical activity Charlotte had done in years, second to when she chased Nora across town a few months ago.

"This is Hell," Charlotte panted.

Nora started laughing despite herself and her horrific reality. It quickly turned hysterical and she was forced to sit on the stairs before her legs gave out. Charlotte joined Nora in her hysteria.

Nora wrapped her arms around Charlotte and they held each other as their laughter turned to tears. They remained in each other's arms until the two of them calmed down enough to move again. Nora reached up and wiped the tears from Charlotte's face.

"I hate that I might have to leave you," Nora admitted.

Charlotte sniffed. "I hate it too, but some of the best years of my life have been spent with you."

Nora's tears started anew. "Some of the best of mine were spent with you too. I'm just so sorry I was so angry the whole time."

"You sort of had a valid excuse." Charlotte inclined her head toward the way they had come. Nora silently agreed. "Plus you aren't nearly as angry as you think you are. You are enjoyable to be around, you know. Most of it is in that brilliant head of yours."

"So you don't hate me for it?" she asked timidly.

"Nora, if I wanted a friend who was more like me, I would

never have been friends with you. I would have hung out with that bitch, Sarah, down the street." They laughed. "We all have our shit. If you are looking for someone to blame you for how you handled it all, you'll have to find someone other than me."

"I love you," was all Nora could say through the emotion knotted in her throat.

"Will you at least do one thing for me?" Charlotte watched Nora from her spot next to her on the stairs.

"Anything," Nora said without a thought.

"Tell Charles how you feel about him."

Nora's mouth fell open to protest—

"Nora Kramer, if you lie to me right now, I'm making you carry me the rest of the way up these stairs."

She shut her mouth. "How do you even know that I might, *potentially*, feel something for Charles?"

"Well, for one, I have eyes," which she rolled, "second, I know you much better than you know yourself."

"You don't know how he feels about me though," Nora countered.

Charlotte smacked her on the arm. "The only person who doesn't know Charles has feelings for you is *you*. Which is likely due to the fact that you refuse to believe it rather than just accept it."

"And your proof of this is?" Nora narrowed her eyes on her friend.

"Because he is the one who planned your little birthday party and again, I have eyes," Charlotte said bluntly.

The thoughts in Nora's brain found somewhere else to be. She had assumed the idea was Charlotte's. Had believed for months that her friend had forced Charles into it and he hadn't said a word, letting her believe it was all Charlotte.

"Oh," Nora managed to say.

Charlotte nodded. "Speaking of which, his birthday is to-morrow, you know."

"I know." Her throat was closing in on itself.

"So tell him Nora. I want you to live so fucking bad it hurts, but if you have to die," she climbed to her feet, "do not leave this earth with any regrets."

Charlotte leaned down and pressed a kiss to Nora's sweaty forehead before starting up the stairs again. Nora watched her friend for a minute, opened mouthed, before she got to her feet and followed.

There was a gala to get ready for, Charlotte's hair to do, a life to fight for.

It was time they left Hell.

# CHAPTER 28

## DEATH

DEATH FOUND THE HELL Hound in his office, *pretending* to work as usual.

"Care to explain to me why Nora and Charles both have access to the gates of Hell?" Death was seething. If he could kill this demon, he would. How he wished for the ability to wield Hellfire.

*God*, it would make his life so much easier.

Sam leaned back in his plush leather office chair, folding his dark hands in his lap.

*Smug mother fucker.*

"Nora begged me and you know my inability to resist her." The Hell Hound pouted. "As for Charles, he asked, and as much as it pains me to admit this, as I am a prideful man, he made a good argument."

"You have a problem, you talk to me. You don't involve them."

Sam rose to his feet. "We tried to talk to you—you didn't respond."

Death stilled, eyes drifting to the wall behind Sam. The Hell Hound had a point, unfortunately. The council had been sending him letters. All of which he'd tossed in the bin before reading, but that was besides the point.

*Wasn't it?*

"Yeah, so I fucked up, Sam. What do you want me to do about it?" Death yelled.

"Fix your fucking mess, Death. Not that hard to figure out," Sam yelled right back.

"Oh fuck you."

"Fuck you."

Death and Sam stared at each other in a quiet standoff, murder in their eyes. It was already the most they had ever spoken to each other over their years of mutual existence. Their shared disdain for one another was perfectly okay with the both of them. Neither of them needed anything more. Death didn't respect Sam and vice versa.

It wasn't complicated at all.

"I don't like you," Death stated flatly.

"Likewise," Sam admitted. "Make you feel better to say it out loud?"

"A little." Death pouted.

"What is it you really want, Death?"

He wasn't exactly sure what the answer to that question should be. Death had no idea what he wanted, or why he had shown up to the Hell Hound's office in the first place other than to yell at him for giving Nora and Charles access to Hell.

Now that he had done so—now that he had his ass rightfully handed to him—he wasn't sure where to go or what to say.

Part of him wanted his mess to go away. Part of him wanted to punch Sam in the face.

Punching the Hell Hound would only lead to Sam doing whatever it was that Hell Hounds did and Death really wasn't in the mood to find out.

He'd never asked in his many thousands of years.

Never wanted to know.

But part of him wanted it all to be over with.

Immortality was something Death just *had*. It never made any sense. Never had any meaning to him. So many beings over his years told him how blessed he was, how lucky. But Death never felt lucky. He felt cursed.

Because that is what immortality was at the end of the day.

A curse.

Everyone wanted to live forever until they realized what it truly meant. Until they realized what a loss it all was. He knew Sam could see it on his face, the weight of all those years, the exhaustion that lived in the suitcases under his eyes.

Part of him wanted to ask Sam to finish him off right there.

To find out what it is Hell Hounds really do.

But Death was a coward.

It was selfish to leave without saying goodbye to the only two people he cared about. Selfish to leave them with the weight of the mess he'd made.

Death would go on–for now. Until he fixed it all. Until he could say goodbye properly.

"I don't want anything." Death adjusted his suit jacket. "I'll see you tonight then?"

"You will." Sam slid his hands into his pockets.

"Okay."

"Okay."

Death was out the door, determined to fix his mess once and for all. Once he was back on the street, he noticed significantly less souls lingering about–his wards had been busy.

This was something Death might have noticed had he been paying attention, but he had stopped paying attention a long time ago, stopped truly caring about what passed him by.

Death decided that in the next few days he'd drag every last one of the lingering souls to their respective realms. Even if it killed him. There was no rule stating he could only take one at a time. No law of physics that prohibited such effort.

*"Has anyone seen my dog?"*

Death walked up to a group of charcoal gray souls who were loitering around the entrance of the bank. He could immediately feel their desire—one was murderous with rage (he wanted to kill his sister for sleeping with his wife, which Death thought, *good for her*), one wanted to confront the bank manager inside the building (it was Wednesday evening and the bank was already closed), one desperately wanted a block of cheese (*odd,* but not unlike his own desires), and the last soul wanted to kill that lady's dog if she ever found it (*yikes*).

*"FUCK THESE PLANTS!"*

He listened to them all, promised them each absolution and they followed willingly. What gullible things souls were, so desperate to fulfill their needs. It wasn't until they reached the entrance to Hell that the souls started to pull away from him, but he tightened his mental grip to drag them through enough to shut the door.

Getting them down the stairs and into the disgustingly sweaty hands of the Devil himself was the easy part. Death climbed out of the depths of Hell and went in search of another group of souls to grab.

He did this several more times before he checked his watch, realizing he needed to get home and get ready.

The cemetery was quiet, devoid of souls as usual, but eerily absent of humans. On a typical day, Death encountered at least one person visiting the grave of a loved one. It was oddly comforting to not be alone amongst all these graves, but the lack of visitors put him on edge.

As he walked down the path to exit the cemetery, he passed the Kramer plots, looking over them for a long moment. Charles's mother, Tessa was on the other side and Death let out a heavy breath at the thought of them all.

The weight of their lives.

Noah was still out there–his would be the one soul Death left alone for the time being. At least until he summoned the courage to tell Nora about her brother, giving her a chance to speak to him.

God, were there a million marks on his soul.

All of the poor decisions he'd made in his long life weighed on him then, pushing him into the soft ground of the cemetery. Death frowned at this sudden moment of introspection. He had never been one to second guess himself. No matter what the decision was, he made it and moved on as his life would have been infinitely longer had he dwelled on his choices.

Maybe it was the impending death of his little star that had him melancholic. Maybe it was all the time he had spent in the warmth of his sun that forcing mild optimism onto Death.

Maybe it was the fact that Charles, the person who saw the good in everyone, even Death, was well and truly disappointed in him.

Maybe it was everything.

Maybe it was nothing at all.

*"For the love of God! Could someone just tell me what day it is!"*

Regardless, there had to be something he could do to clean the stain on his soul, something that would right all of his wrongs.

# CHAPTER 29

## CHARLES

"Y OU LOOK SMART, YOUNG man," Vincent said, emerging from the hallway to his left.

Charles was dressed in the suit Nora laid out for him, freshly shaved and hair tamed–as much as was possible. He had attempted to push it back and it stayed for the most part with the help of some gel, but it was only a matter of time before it returned to its completely unruly state.

It wasn't his fault his hair didn't adhere to normal laws of physics.

"Thank you, Vincent. You look great too." The caretaker was in a suit as well, looking very much the same as Charles save for the white shirt under his jacket, where Charles's was black. Vincent crossed the foyer and adjusted Charles's bow tie before clapping him on the shoulder.

"You have brought life back into this house." Vincent dipped his chin in quiet thanks.

Charles offered him a smile. "I think you give me too much credit."

"I don't." Pain lingered in Vincent's eyes as he pursed his lips. "She is herself again and this house sings like it used to."

"I didn't know Nora before." Charles shrugged. He hadn't known her before last year and knowing her now, Charles couldn't imagine Nora had changed too much since then—stubborn as she was.

"She was quiet," Vincent started, "very quiet, and she hated any bit of enjoyment that came her way. Nora pushed Charlotte away as much as Charlotte would let her." Vincent smiled and Charles found he was too—there was no getting past Charlotte's will. "She fought with Noah so much in his last few years that I worried she would break when he died, because through all of that fighting, he grounded her. He at least made her fight to live."

"I thought they were close," Charles mused, unable to imagine the two siblings at odds.

Vincent laughed, "Noah intentionally antagonized her. I asked him why he did it after a particularly nasty blowout one afternoon," Vincent rolled his eyes at the memory, but his smile remained, "and he told me it was to prove that she still cared. That he didn't mind her ire as long as she still had an opinion about life."

Charles didn't know what to say. He couldn't tell Vincent that having met Noah, he had discerned as much because no one knew Noah's soul was out there floating around besides him and Death. Charles felt a deep appreciation for Nora's older brother and his efforts to keep his sister alive as he was desperately trying to do the same.

Maybe Nora had changed.

But Charles had changed too.

Charles was not the same person he was a year ago. He was fuller, more complete, less afraid of his volatility. Anger, he learned from Nora, was a necessary part of grief. A necessary part of living. It was important to acknowledge it or else it burned everything it touched.

Nora may say she is consumed by hers, but Charles knew she was mainly using it as a weapon to guard her heart, in much the same way that he used his positivity to guard his mind.

Both were important to protect, but both were important to feel too. Charles's anger didn't mean he didn't *love* his mother, but rather proved he did. If he didn't care about what she did, he wouldn't care that she was gone. Charles always believed that if he'd had more people than just his mother, it would have been better, but this very house proved the opposite.

It had been full of people at one point in its history, but happiness had been scarce. The Kramer's hadn't been the best to each other. They fought, they abandoned each other, they were selfish, and they were all dead because of it.

Being angry didn't make Charles a bad person. It demanded to be heard, to expect better from those he loved, better from himself.

It proved he was alive.

"You make her fight too, Charles," Vincent said, bringing him back to their reality. "I am not telling you this to put any pressure on you, but rather to say thank you. Thank you for pushing her, for making her want to live again."

The caretaker choked out the last few words and Charles's own throat closed, but he managed to say, "of course," as he shook Vincent's outstretched hand. The two of them stood in quiet understanding until the front door creaked open.

Death entered the foyer, flashing his watch. They were going to be terribly late–that was if they left at that exact moment, which was unlikely considering Nora was still yet to join them downstairs.

Charles and Vincent exchanged a knowing look.

"Miss Nora!" Vincent yelled through the house. "We do need

to be going!"

"I know, Vincent. We're sure I can't wear sneakers?" Her voice called back from deep in the house.

Charles rolled his eyes. "Nora!"

"Fine," she groaned in defeat.

But a moment later she descended the stairs.

And his mouth fell open.

Nora wore a silver floor length dress that rippled around her like water. Each movement made the dress shimmer under the light. It was hypnotizing and was certain to distract him the entire night–for several reasons.

The main reason being the plunging neckline which descended low enough to stop his breathing. Her shoulders were bare, save for the straps holding the dress on her body. Nora's hair was pulled up in a loose bun on top of her head, pink weaving with the blonde and a few pieces hanging loose around her face.

She reached the bottom of the stairs, making her way towards the group of them in what felt like slow motion.

"Close your mouth, Charlie boy, it's unbecoming." Charles jumped at the sudden voice whispering in his ear. Death stood just behind him, leaning in close, his watchful eyes trained on Nora.

"Hi," she whispered, eyes locked on Charles.

Charles swallowed. "You ready?"

"I think so." Nora's lips pursed.

Somewhere behind him, Death and Vincent murmured their agreement to head to the car, leaving the two of them in the foyer.

Completely alone.

The room could have been on fire for all he cared, but he

didn't. Couldn't even feign interest in anything else. Not when Nora was standing in front of him looking like that.

Looking *at him* like that.

He was suddenly too aware of the angle his bowtie sat on his neck, too worried there was a wrinkle in his crisp black shirt. There had to be lint on him *somewhere* that he'd missed.

Was he even dressed appropriately?

*Of course I am, Nora picked it all out for me.*

Was he missing something?

Were his shoes on the correct feet?

Charles ran a nervous hand through his hair.

*Fuckkk. His hair.*

Nora's pink mouth ticked up on one side as if she could see right through to his brain and the argument he was having there, the panic that was ensuing.

"You look–" Charles attempted, but there weren't words for how she looked and saying *'you look fucking spectacular,'* wasn't enough and it also seemed mildly inappropriate–though he couldn't pinpoint why.

Nora rolled her shoulders back and said, "You look great, Charles."

"Ah well I had some help with the clothes," he stammered as her eyes traveled up to his hair. "I tried everything I could to fix it, but unfortunately, this is the best it's going to get."

She stepped forward and the shimmer of her dress rippled, sending a wave of silver sparkles across her body. Nora reached up to run her slim fingers through his hair and the sensation was enough to send him to his knees before her.

And he would too.

Charles would kneel before her and beg, grovel, heed her every command just as long as she kept touching him. His mind was drifting to unsavory places.

He grabbed her hand, groaning as he removed it from his head.

"You have to stop doing that," Charles tugged on her wrist, pulling her closer to him, "or we are not leaving this house."

Nora's throat bobbed and her eyes settled on his mouth. Charles trailed his fingers, painstakingly slow, up her arm to trace the line of her collarbone and settle on her neck. Her skin was soft under his finger tips, begging him to find out how it would feel against his lips.

God he wanted to kiss her–he wanted to do well more than kiss her–a desire he had been struggling with for months–but if there was ever a time to act on the thoughts swimming in his brain, it was definitely not now.

In Charles's imagination he carried her upstairs and ripped her gorgeous dress off, sank his fingers into her hair, and ruined her makeup.

In his imagination they never made it to the gala.

*Darn.*

*How tragic.*

"You're right, we should go," Nora whispered, stepping around him to head out the front door. Charles could have sworn he saw the corner of her mouth kick up. She knew exactly what she was doing to him.

*Absolutely diabolical.*

It was going to be an excruciatingly long night, Charles concluded, as her dress dipped down to expose the majority of her back. Charles groaned at the ceiling before following her to the car.

He could have sworn the house hummed in agreement.

Nora didn't settle the entire ride to the museum. She shifted in her seat, fidgeted with her rings, picked at her pink nails, checked her watch over and over. Charles was nervous too, but knowing Nora, part of her uneasiness was because of the previous night and their ill fated morning.

He physically couldn't take the silence any longer.

"Nora," Charles said softly as to not spook her.

She took a deep breath and finally looked at him, worry creasing her brow. Before he could speak again, before he could put her mind at ease, Nora said, "I am sorry about last night. I never meant for you to see me like that."

It struck him then that this was the first time Nora had ever apologized to him about anything and the fact she was apologizing for him seeing her cry made his stomach do a backflip. Nora didn't apologize for her actions or her words as she never acted without logic or reason, but there she was, apologizing for how she felt and it didn't sit right with him.

"You don't have to hide from me. I am happy to help you, if you'll let me," he pleaded with her.

"You are helping enough. Tonight is enough as it is." She looked forward again.

Charles turned in his seat to face her. "It doesn't have to be."

"Charles." Nora turned to fully face him again.

Her use of his full name startled him. She wanted his full attention as though there was ever a moment where she didn't already have it. Charles could count on one hand the number of times she had used his full name.

He didn't dare speak.

Nora's eyes fluttered closed for a moment, but when they found his again, they were full of force and determination.

"I warned you."

Charles's heart pounded low in his chest. "So you did."

She leaned slightly into the space that separated them and he joined her. He could feel her on his skin despite the distance between them. But he didn't need her near to know how she felt. Nora shifted his universe in a way he would never be free from.

Charles was certain her death would be the end of him. The force of her existence was enough to destroy the universe and he would gladly give himself up to be consumed by it all.

Was certain it would be bliss.

The car rolled to a stop and the seconds of quiet ticked away before they threw themselves into the depths of chaos.

Time stilled completely.

Her eyes weren't on him but rather on the seat beneath them so Charles let his gaze drift to her pink lips. The bottom one was caught between her teeth–she was thinking. He was just about to touch his lips to hers when she looked up at him, stars sparkling in the gray of her eyes.

"Hey Chuck?" She smirked.

Charles knew where this was going.

He reached up and caught the pink end of her hair.

"Yeah, Nora?"

But maybe he didn't know anything at all because the next thing he knew was her hand slipping into the base of his hair and her lips on his. Charles melted into her, drawing his arms tight around her, and deepening the kiss.

He needing more of her. He needed to imprint her on his soul because he surely wouldn't survive a day where he forgot how she tasted. How she smelled. How she felt in his arms.

Nora pulled away after what was the longest and yet shortest moment of his life, leaving him breathless, with a smile on her perfect face and a devious glint in her eye.

"Are you with me?" she asked against his lips.

"Until Death comes for me," he promised.

She slipped from his fingers and out the car door, leaving him with no choice but to follow her into the night.

# CHAPTER 30

## NORA

THE GALA WAS PERFECT, thanks to Charlotte.

Nora had hand picked several paintings from her family's wing, including the seven from other galleries she would be taking home with her later that evening. The paintings from the buyers had all trickled in over the last few weeks and were resting safely in the secret room.

She chose to hold the gala in the expansive courtyard of the museum–this way, no room would have to be altered for the event, the paintings could be brought into the courtyard, then removed to storage at the end of the night. They would wait in storage until the museum team put them back in their original places the next day.

There would be seven less to replace come the morning, but that information was reserved for her, Charles, Charlotte, Vincent, and Death.

Five people was entirely too many people to know the plan and it made Nora uncomfortable that such precious information was floating between them all, but it was necessary for each one of them to know.

Charlotte and Charles were her accomplices and the three of them couldn't very well bring stolen art into Vincent's home without telling him. As for Death, well, he was Death—there wasn't anyone alive for him to tell.

The real issue were the council members floating around the room.

Two weeks prior, Nora had paid them a visit. It was important they have a light understanding of what was going on because she needed them to keep their noses out of it, and she was banking on their greed and general moral corruptibility to do just that.

"As I am sure a few of you are well aware," Nora addressed the council as she stood in front of their dias, "my grandfather bargained with the Devil." She paused to look at each of their faces. Sam and Lily were the only two that looked genuinely upset, the rest were completely impassive.

"Your blatant shock aside, I wanted to inform you all that I am working to fix this mess of a life I have been given and all I need from you is to turn a blind eye when it inevitably lands on your desk."

"What is it that you will be—" Gabe started.

Nora held up a hand to stop him. "The details are not important to you. However, if you want to continue receiving funding for your campaigns and this council, you simply need to mind your own business. I am merely telling you as a courtesy to you all and a favor to myself."

The Archangels erupted with disgust and contempt while the Hell Hounds murmured amongst themselves. Sam smirked at Nora and Lily looked down at her hands, trying her hardest not to laugh.

"You do realize this is a quid pro quo. We could be indicted for something like this," Mike seethed, leaning over his desk to peer down at her.

*An interesting time for them to stray from their loose morality*, she thought.

Nora studied her nails, she would need to get them done before the gala–her thumb nail was looking rather rough. "Councilman, I don't believe you are arguing with *me* about this council's integrity now are you?"

Lily snorted, clapping a hand over her mouth to staunch the sound, Sam looked at the ceiling, taking a deep breath. Mike and the other Archangels looked at her in shock, mouths hanging stupidly open.

Nora continued, "I am choosing to trust you all to keep me out of the mess I am about to create in order to fix the mess my grandfather made. If any of you would like to discuss your faulty morals, I am happy to tell you where my money will *not* be going in the next election cycle. As always, I appreciate your time. I will see you all at my gala in two weeks."

Nora winked at Lily, nodded at Sam, and left the council chamber.

Now, two weeks later, thirteen city councilors ambled about the room–all of them in black suits, aside from Lily who wore a stunning burgundy dress. It complimented her midnight black hair and pale skin. The Hell Hound floated across the room to kiss Nora on the cheek as they exchanged equal sentiment for the other before parting ways.

Nora liked Lily for that reason, she was kind despite her Hellish nature and always had time to speak to Nora.

Charlotte was in the opposite corner with Charles and what Nora was assuming were the friends he had invited. She was relieved to find out they were real and not imaginary. Charles had been telling her about these boys for months now and they had yet to materialize, she was thrilled to see them in the flesh.

Dylan and Andrew were loud, comical boys and Charles was a different person around them. Not different in a negative way. In fact they brought out more of his personality, he laughed easier, talked a little louder, moved a little freer.

It only made Nora love him more.

It only made her loath herself.

She shut her eyes at the thought. How stupid she'd been. How selfish. How terribly dark and gloomy must she be for Charles to not feel this comfortable around her.

Even worse, Nora had allowed herself to fall for Charles, to let him in and make a home in her heart. If this all went poorly, like it was bound to, Nora would have to excise him from her chest and there was no way to do that without killing herself and damaging him in the process.

As if Charles felt her thinking about him, he looked up and met her eyes. Nora's breath caught in her throat, as his blue eyes rippled like the deepest part of the ocean. They were brilliantly deep in the low light and she imagined drowning in them to be the sweetest way to die. Charles's hair was slowly freeing itself from the light hold of the gel as a piece of it fell down his forehead.

He didn't seem to notice as his attention remained on her. His friends and Charlotte were talking around him, but he didn't seem to care. Not to mention the paintings–they were surrounded by priceless, awe-inspiring, soul shattering paintings and yet his eyes never left her.

Warmth bloomed over her chest, creeping up to kiss her cheeks. The only indication that he'd noticed was the slight pull at the corner of his mouth.

But Charles's smile faded as quickly as it arrived when an ungodly warm hand pressed into her back. Nora watched

Charles's face harden, as he registered the Hell Hound now at her side.

"You are breathtaking, sunshine," Sam purred in her ear, slipping between her and Charles.

Nora ground her teeth together.

"Dance with me?"

"Absolutely not, Sam." Nora narrowed her eyes on his flawless face.

Sam pouted. "Please? One dance before you run off into the night with pretty boy over there."

The Hell Hound inclined his head over his shoulder to where Charles stood with his group. Nora looked in his direction just to watch his gaze drop to the floor. A wave of hurt crashed through her chest, but she nodded to Sam all the same.

She did this to herself.

The pain Charles felt was Nora's to carry all because she didn't follow her own rules.

"Don't get attached to me, Chuck," she had said and he'd agreed. But Nora hadn't even tried to do the same. Hadn't even tried to make him hate her and now his pain would be her fault. Nora knew pain, she knew heartbreak, but Charles didn't deserve that.

He was too good, too bright.

And she was selfish for darkening him.

Maybe she was a little too full of herself to think that the loss of her would hurt him so, but she felt it. Anytime he was near, Nora felt Charles's need to touch her, his need to ingrain her in his soul and the only reason she knew his needs so intimately was because they were her needs too.

Nora would forever hate herself for ruining his light.

"You are in love with the mortal boy, aren't you?" Sam asked, bringing her back to the courtyard from her thoughts. Nora realized they hadn't moved. Sam was still standing in front of her and she was still staring blankly over his shoulder at Charles.

She rolled her eyes. "Sam."

He brushed a strand of hair away from her face. "Oh come on now, sunshine."

Nora didn't know what to say so she asked, "There's no point is there?"

"I don't know. I have lived a lot of years and have loved many people just to turn around and lose them all in one way or another. It never gets any easier," Sam tilted his head and finally Nora let herself meet his black eyes, "but it is always just as sweet."

"And the pain is worth it?"

Nora was begging him to say yes.

Begging him to say no.

Wholly unable to decide what it was she wanted to hear.

Sam leaned down to kiss her softly on the cheek. "It's worth it for the right people."

He left her there to ponder his words, ponder what she wanted.

Nora had spoken to the last councilmember and was finally standing alone in front of one of her grandfather's stolen paintings. It wasn't an internationally known work, but it was valuable to say the least. The painting itself had bounced around private auctions for years, sold over and over for several million–that was until Norman stole the painting from one of the collectors, fenced it for twice as much, stole it back and donated it to the museum as an anonymous benefactor.

Again, her awe of him was in a brutal war with her fury.

Out of the corner of her eye, Nora spotted Mr. Blake heading

in her direction. The thought of speaking with him straightened her spine, causing a thin sheen of sweat to form on her
back. Her friends must have spotted him too because at the same
time, Charles and Charlotte descended on her.

Charlotte looped an arm through hers as Charles briefly
slipped his fingers into Nora's before heading off to intercept
Mr. Blake.

Charlotte steered her in the opposite direction to where Dylan and Andrew stood at the edge of the courtyard, whispering
to each other. Nora hadn't officially met them yet as she had
been busy all evening, but now was as good a time as any.

"Guys, have you met Nora yet?" Charlotte asked, even
though she knew the answer.

Dylan seemed skeptical of Nora, looking over her as if to
assess a potential threat. Andrew however stepped forward and
pulled Nora into his chest, arms tightening around her. She did
her best to match his enthusiasm, but hugging people she didn't
know was not something she enjoyed, or regularly did.

"No, we haven't been introduced yet, but it is wonderful to
meet you." Andrew released her, smiling wide. "Charles has
told us all about you."

"Andrew, right?" Nora asked despite already knowing and
he beamed. "And Dylan?" He nodded, reached a hand out for
her to shake, and offered her a smile. She hoped her own smile
put him at ease, but a relaxing demeanor was not something
she was known for. Meeting new people for the first time never
went well as Nora's quietness general skepticism made people
think she was judging them harshly when she wasn't.

"Well, we hate to have kept Charles from you for so long,
but he has been immensely helpful with all of this." Charlotte
gestured around the room, her long, perfectly wavy hair shifted

down her back. The dark cherry dress she wore complimented her complexion, making her look even more beautiful than ever. Andrew couldn't take his eyes off of Charlotte and Nora couldn't blame him. Nora suppressed a grin, hoping Andrew wouldn't notice her observation.

"We could not have done this without Charles. I could not have done this without him." Nora let out a deep breath.

"He is a good person to have around," Dylan said. Was that jealousy Nora heard in his voice? Concern? Warning?

She shook it off and let Charlotte direct the conversation. They talked about the museum, the art pulled for the gala, what Andrew and Dylan studied at university, how long they have known Charles.

Nora looked over her shoulder, expecting to see Charles still speaking with Mr. Blake, but instead he was chatting with Sam in a rather hushed, animated conversation. She scanned the rest of the courtyard quickly to find Vincent sitting at a table with Lily, and Death leaning on the bar, pretending to sip his drink while his eyes watched Charles and Sam.

Death clearly wasn't a fan of the two of them talking either. Watching the two of them together reminded Nora about Charles's ability to get into Hell and who would have given him that access.

*Fucking Sam.*

Sam would have been the only one to have given Charles permission. The only one who would have told Charles what she was doing. The only Hell Hound who would have felt vindictive enough to pull Charles into this without a single thought to his wellbeing.

Nora's jaw tightened with the revelation and she wasn't sure who she was more angry with–Sam or Charles.

*Both.*

*Decidedly both.*

But now was not the time, she told herself, taking a deep breath. Nora turned her attention back to the group–Andrew and Charlotte were talking animatedly–and found Dylan's eyes on her, watching her closely. She tried as hard as she could to relax her face through the rage burning through her veins, but turned her eyes to the floor. Nora couldn't bear the look of disappointment on Dylan's face. The look that he could see right through her, that she had put their friend in danger.

*If it's any consolation,* Nora thought, *I hate me too.*

Not five minutes later, she felt Charles moving towards her, as if the air was giving her a heads up. Nora felt his warm hand slide to the small of her back and the touch was almost soothing enough to forget her anger.

"What did I miss?" Charles interjected with his typical buoyant tone. His thumb started a distracting back and forth motion on her skin. It had her discarding her urge to rip into him, replacing it with the overwhelming desire to pull him away from the courtyard and see what his hands could really do.

What his mouth could do.

Nora was desperate for air.

"I'll be right back," Nora muttered to no one in particular and retreated from the group. She could feel Charles's eyes on her, but she refused to meet them. The courtyard of the museum was an enclosed space, but there were doors at the back that led to a topiary garden and the air she needed.

Nora fled through the doors and into the garden, gulping down chilly, October air. Her watch told her it was almost midnight and thankfully in a few minutes, Mr. Blake would be asking everyone to leave.

Once everyone cleared out, including Charles, Nora would tell Mr. Blake that she wanted to see for herself that the paintings made it to storage. After the staff moved the paintings and left, she would make her way to the loading dock where Charles would be pulling a car around. Nora would let him in the back and the two of them would move all seven paintings to the car and head home to the estate.

*Easy.*

At least she hoped it'd be easy.

Thought, the act of stealing the paintings from the museum was going to be infinitely easier than waiting for Lucifer's impending decision. Nora was never very good at waiting. Never had the patience for much of anything. It was the not knowing that heightened her anxiety.

But none of it was in her control, not really anyway. She could steal the paintings and return them to their rightful owners, but that didn't mean Lucifer had to grant her freedom.

If Nora was being honest, she was fully expecting him to send her a letter in a few days time informing her he'd be collecting her himself.

There was not enough air in the world to calm her down, to slow her breathing. Nora didn't know how to tell Charles their efforts may be completely futile. Not with how much he'd helped her get to this point, how much he'd helped her in other ways too.

It's what made the look in Dylan's eyes all the more painful. He was worried for his friend and Nora was too, but there was no way for her to make it right for any of them. To make it right for herself.

"Nora?" Charles's sweet voice called from behind her. He was holding her jacket, worry and concern swimming in his eyes.

The sight of him made her want to scream.

Made her want to cry.

Made her want to be another person, in another life, where she could love the boy in front of her for the beauty and kindness that he was without the potential to harm him with her inevitable destruction.

The combustion of her would destroy everything in its path and she wanted nothing more than to keep him safe.

"It's time," Charles said, walking over to help her into her coat. She rolled her shoulders back and walked into the museum to find Mr. Blake.

Nora was no longer moving forward for herself—she did so for Charles, for Charlotte, for Vincent and Death—to minimize the mess she'd leave behind.

# CHAPTER 31

## CHARLES

NORA WAS NOT OKAY.

Charles knew something was wrong from the moment he joined her and his friends. He could feel it on her skin, like the shock you get after shuffling your feet across a carpet. Then she excused herself and Charlotte told him Nora would be fine, but he wasn't convinced, even less so when he found her standing out in the cold staring into the dark garden, in nothing but her too thin dress.

Charles didn't want to leave her alone, but their plan was in full motion and he had a job to do. He took everyone back to the estate only to turn around and drive the car back across town to park it in the loading dock at the back of the building. The museum had cameras, but Charlotte turned those off on her way out, convincing Mr. Blake she had left something in the security room.

The girl could talk her way into, or out of, anything.

The back of the museum was completely empty with all the lights off save for a single flood light above the dock door, just as Nora said it would be. Charles switched off the car and waited, watching the door in the rearview mirror for any sign of her.

After the longest three minutes of his life, the loading door creaked open. He jumped out of the car and popped the trunk.

Nora didn't say a word, but handed him her coat, which he threw in the back seat, before she disappeared through the door again. None of the paintings were overly large which made the process of getting them out of the storage room all the more easy.

She emerged from the door, painting gripped in her hands and lowered it to Charles. He slid the painting into the trunk as carefully as he could. The museum staff thankfully wrapped all of the paintings in protective cloth already so they didn't have to worry about that part of the preservation process. It would also make shipping them easier.

Painting after painting was hauled out of the museum and loaded into the car until all seven were securely in their possession. Nora closed up the museum and Charles shut the trunk as softly as possible after making sure their contraband was secure. The last piece of art to collect was Nora herself, who was sitting on the edge of the loading dock, waiting for Charles to help her down.

The slit of her dress parted to reveal the length of her left leg, which Charles had every intention of exploring later. For now, they needed to make it home. He reached up and grabbed her hips as she rested her hands on his shoulders.

Carefully, as it would be a shame to rip her dress unintentionally, Charles lifted her off the platform and set her on her feet in front of him. He wasn't used to her at this height, the heels she wore added several inches.

Nora's gray eyes swam with a storm he couldn't place. Too many emotions at war with each other to pinpoint just one.

Charles brushed a strand of her hair from her cheek, it would not do to only see part of her face. Nora's hands slid from his shoulders, down the lapels of his suit jacket to rest on his chest. Her own chest rose and fell heavily with every breath she took.

Just when he thought he might lean down to kiss her, she slipped past him, silver dress shimmering in the moonlight.

"We should go," was all Nora said before she slid into the passenger seat.

He blew out a frustrated breath, but joined her in the car. Nora kept her eyes forward, not looking at Charles as he started the car and drove them away from the museum.

She was nervous.

Fuming.

On the verge of tears.

She was a lot of things and Charles didn't know why, as she wouldn't talk to him. They were barely off the museum grounds when she turned to him with what was definitely rage—silver fire burning in her irises.

"Want to tell me what you and Sam were discussing this evening?"

Charles's mouth fell open. It took all his strength to keep his eyes on the road and not face her. Sam had come up to him earlier that night to ask him how everything was going and Charles had responded by asking Sam what it would take for him to keep his hands off Nora.

He hadn't intended to even discuss the issue with him, but something about seeing the Hell Hound's hands on the girl he loved had ignited a fire in his stomach and no matter how hard he stomped on it, it wouldn't go out.

It wasn't his finest moment.

Sam's presence at the house these last few months and his late nights with Nora had been eating through his sanity faster than he could control. Charles had never known this type of irritation, this type of jealousy. Charlotte saw it, of that Charles was certain, by the way she watched him when Sam was around, careful to distract him from the Hell Hound's existence, but she never said anything.

The jealousy felt wholly irrational. Nora wasn't *his* in any sense, but still Charles couldn't shake the feeling that she was, that he was undoubtedly *hers*.

"All of a sudden you are worried about Sam, as if you aren't the one spending time with him?" The words were out of his mouth before Charles could think better of them.

"Excuse me?" Nora seethed.

This was not the time nor the place he wanted to be having this conversation with her. Charles thought it would be in a more relaxed setting where it was just the two of them, it would be a normal day when they were both calm, but there they were—well past midnight, both exhausted, with a trunk full of priceless stolen art.

"I know what you've been up to."

"I imagine it is exactly the same as what you have been up to." Nora faced the front again, crossing her arms over her chest.

Charles didn't have a chance to answer her or even think of deflecting before she continued. "You aren't as sly as you think you are, Chuck. Did you really think I wouldn't find out about you dragging souls down to Hell? How long have you been doing this?"

"Since before your birthday." His voice was distant in his ears as his knuckles turned white around the steering wheel.

Nora scoffed. "You can't be fucking serious. Do you have no concern for yourself at all?"

"I could ask exactly that of you, Nora."

"It's not the same and you know it."

"Someone had to tackle Hell, since you weren't doing it." It was a low blow. They both knew it.

Charles immediately hated himself for it. Hated how irrational he felt.

"I couldn't go down there." The fight had all but drained out of Nora's voice and the sudden lack of ire hurt more than Charles thought it would.

"I'm sorry. I shouldn't have said that."

"Does Death know?"

"Yes."

She sighed, "How did you get Sam to give you permission?"

"I confronted him," Charles said matter-of-factly, as though there would be no question how he got permission. As though confronting people was something Charles did regularly and was good at.

Nora huffed a laugh.

"He is not a good person, Nora," Charles stated.

"You think I don't know that?" She spat back.

"Not to mention, he wants to sleep with you." The words tumbled from his lips in instant regret.

Nora's mouth pressed into a thin line and the fire returned to her eyes, tenfold. "You're an idiot."

They had finally made it back to the estate. Charles put the car in park and doubled down. "Maybe I am, but that doesn't change the fact that he does, that maybe you want to too."

Jealousy rippled off of him in disgusting waves, drowning out the rest of his concerns. He didn't like this version of himself, had never encountered it before, but there was something about Sam and Nora that dismantled his sanity.

Charles opened his mouth to continue, but she was out the door in a rush of silver starlight, disappearing up the stairs of the estate.

He slammed the car door and ran after her. She wouldn't get away from him that easily.

# CHAPTER 32

## NORA

"**F**UCKING COME off it, Charles," Nora yelled as she stormed to her room, heels digging into the soft carpet. "No, Nora, I don't think I will," he yelled back, stomping up the stairs after her.

It was a childish argument they were having, one that would produce no winner, rendering them both miserable piles of themselves. Nora burst into her room attempting to slam her door behind her, but Charles caught it to slam it behind him. The sound rattled the walls of her room, no doubt echoing through the house.

The lamp on her desk flickered on instead of the overhead light and the hearth remained cold. It was as though the house could sense her rage and deemed it hot enough already.

"So that is what this is really about then. Your jealousy of Sam?" Nora whirled on him, standing her ground.

"Oh I am not jealous of Sam," Charles snarled his blatant lie. It was cute of him to try.

"Then explain it to me." She stepped out of her heels. Her feet felt stiff being flat again after such a long night and the return of their full height difference only made this argument more comical.

"The real problem is you didn't tell me what you were doing.

You have been killing yourself for months, but I'm here Nora! I'm right fucking here, willing to help you, but you won't let me." Charles was shaking, hands clenched at his sides. "The only thing that makes this all worse, is that you let *him*."

"What was I supposed to do?" Nora yelled back. "You and Death have always had a good relationship. How was I supposed to ruin that for you? How was I supposed to tell you that he wasn't this all powerful being you thought him to be? I was trying to protect you."

"You think maybe I could have made that decision for myself?"

"Well you got your way into Hell anyway. You've accomplished helping me without me even asking. Good for you, Chuck." If he wanted a fight, she'd give him a fight.

"Would you have ever asked?"

Nora wasn't expecting the pain that sharpened his beautiful face. She wasn't expecting the worry that settled between his eyebrows. The tightness in her chest threatened to take her to her knees. She thought that if she could make him hate her, her loss would be easier on him, but this was decidedly worse.

This current and very present anger was not something she could handle, as it wasn't something she knew how to fix. Nora thought about lying to him, telling him that she would have asked eventually, but the truth couldn't make this worse than it already was.

"No, I wouldn't have ever asked," Nora muttered.

Charles nodded, raking a hand through his messy hair. He wouldn't look at her and she didn't blame him. Nora couldn't look at herself most days either.

Suddenly, before she could stop herself, she had an overwhelming need to explain herself.

"I wouldn't have asked because I couldn't risk you." The confession slipped out too harshly. Charles stilled his fidgeting, but kept his eyes on the ground. "None of this was supposed to happen, okay? I was supposed to be *alone*. I was supposed to die in two weeks, right on schedule with everyone else. I tried to minimize the damage, to keep you at a distance, but I failed horrifically."

His blue eyes were on her now, searing into her chest as if to confirm she indeed had a soul, verifying it was black. "What do you mean keep me at a distance?"

"Exactly that," she exhaled. "If I could have kept from getting close to you, from knowing you, then this all would have been easier in the end. You would go back to your normal life, free of my mess and not have to worry about me again when this all inevitably blew up in my face. But then you come in here with that hair, and those eyes that see right through me, and that positive fucking attitude and it diminishes my willpower to nothing at all and I can't help myself."

Charles stared at her incredulously, completely frozen to the spot.

"You truly think there is a world in which I go back to my normal life and forget you ever existed?" he laughed. "There is no freeing myself of you and I don't even want to try. And now you are the one who can't help yourself? Help yourself what, Nora?" Charles was begging Nora to admit it, but she wouldn't.

Had he not heard the rest of what she had just said? How it would be nothing short of disaster? How terrible she was?

Couldn't he see it?

Couldn't he see her?

"Charles," Nora barely breathed.

"You are the one who told me not to get attached to you."
He took a tentative step closer.

"I did. And you should have listened to me. You should have
left me a long time ago." Nora was shaking now. Her entire
being wanted nothing but to be loved by him, to love him back,
but it was her brain that screamed in protest. It was pounding
on the inside of her head, demanding to be heard.

Charles stared at her, at war with himself too. Nora watched
as her own frustration and need reflected in his eyes. The hurt
and want that lingered there.

"Did you ever once think about what *I* wanted?"

"Tell me what it is you want then, Charles," Nora spat at
him. She'd force it out of him. She'd make him tell her that he
wanted her and she would tell him how terrible it would be.
That maybe she wanted him too, but there was nothing but a
bad ending for the both of them.

Nora could be the villain if she needed, certainly possessing
enough ire to make him hate her. It would be her last stand, her
final act–to make Charles hate her for his own good, so that her
death hurt him less.

Speaking the words out loud would convince him of their
doom.

They would convince her too.

*Maybe.*

Charles paced around her room, the old carpet tracking his
movements. Nora had never seen him this angry before, never
seen him anything other than happy, really, as it wasn't an
emotion he particularly liked.

One he avoided. One she leaned into.

But Nora found she liked him angry. She liked the differ-
ing heat that rage brought to his face. His hair became more

frayed–if that was even physically possible–and his blue eyes blazed with the force of a vengeful ocean.

Nora knew why he was angry, he hadn't hidden that from her, even if he masked it with a different argument, but it wasn't something she could change. It wasn't up to her whether she lived or died and the reality of it all was debilitating. It didn't make sense and there was nothing to grab onto and pull her in the right direction.

Charles could save himself, even if Nora couldn't.

She could feel his pain as if her physical makeup was being dismantled and stitched back together to accommodate for his presence in her soul. Charles manipulated her universe in that way, where only her soul could recognize him.

Pain. Grief. Understanding.

Nora knew it all well

It belonged to him, but it belonged to her too.

Charles walked over to lean against her desk, letting his head fall between his shoulders. His knuckles turned white where he gripped the edge. Tension pulled his shoulders in as his back rose and fell with shallow breaths. When he finally lifted his head, his eyes caught on one of her shelves and the book resting there.

*Shit.*

His birthday present.

Charles slid the book off the shelf slowly, turning it over in his hands to examine it. "What is this?" His voice was barely audible, like he was trying desperately to hold himself together.

"Charles I—"

He slid the note out of the front cover. Nora didn't need to see it to know what it said–she had written it only several hours earlier.

*Charles,*

*I know it's not your mother's original copy, but maybe*
*this will allow you to continue your reading without*
*the worry of destroying her beloved original.*
*This one was printed in the same year as hers.*
*Write in it. Fold the pages. Read it in the shower.*
*Cherish your mother's, ruin this one.*

*Happy birthday.*

*Yours,*
*Nora*

He turned to her, note in one hand, book in the other,
with tears brimming in his eyes. His beautiful lips were parted
slightly. Nora cast her eyes on the floor, suddenly self conscious
of the gift.

Of herself.

"It's for your birthday tomorrow. Which is technically today, I guess. I had planned to give it to you in the morning
sometime, but it's technically tomorrow now, so…surprise, or
something. I was trying really hard not to ruin your birthday."
Nora continued with a string of nonsensical confessions until
not even she knew what she was saying. Until her words faded
away into a whisper.

Into nothing.

She hadn't seen Charles cross the room. Hadn't heard him.
Had no indication he had moved until his lips crashed onto
hers.

It wasn't forceful, or greedy. It was combustible desire. It ignited everything she felt for him since the moment she met him. Everything about him that intrigued her. Everything she pretended wasn't there.

But Nora couldn't pretend any longer–no matter how hard she tried. She was just one person, capable of forcibly rejecting only a certain number of thoughts and feelings before her brain gave in to want, into desperation.

This wasn't the kiss from the car, this was need. The book and note had long been left behind on her desk as Charles's hands found her waist, her face, her hair, her neck. They were everywhere all at once and yet they took their time. They lingered as heat seared into her skin and she needed him closer.

*Damn it all to Hell*, Nora thought.

Her will was nothing strong anyway. If Nora was going to die despite her best efforts, she wanted to know him–in every way.

Was this completely at odds with the words she had just spoken, the thoughts she'd had? Yes.

But she was past the point of no return. Her body had outwitted her logic this round, so she surrendered to defeat and kissed him back.

They found the bed, divested themselves of their clothes, and continued. Nora hadn't realized how badly she craved to feel something other than rage. How desperate she was for love. It was just a shame it all had to end so she savored it, committed him to her memory, tucked him away into her soul, and let him heal her.

Minutes, hours, an eternity later, they laid there with their limbs tangled in one another, quiet in order to catch their breath. Comfortable in the silence as always.

Nora felt relaxed for the first time in years as she lay there with her head on his chest with his arms wrapped tight around her. She had never felt so warm. His skin was soft under her fingertips and she relished in the goosebumps that her fingers left behind as she traced them over his chest. Charles's arms tightened further as he tilted his face into her hair and took a deep breath.

"I'm sorry," Charles exhaled.

Nora's hand stilled on his chest at his whispered confession.

"Sorry for what?" she asked, unable to find in her brain what he would be apologizing for.

"For being so angry with you earlier. I shouldn't have yelled like that. I shouldn't have said some of the things I did."

Nora tilted her head up to look at him. The crease between his eyebrows deepened and she wanted desperately to ease his worry, smooth it away with her fingers, with her lips, with her words. "Do not apologize for your anger, Charles. Not to me."

She attempted a smile, anything that might lighten the pain in his heart. Charles lifted a hand to her face, resting it on her cheek.

"You told me not to get attached to you, Nora, and I tried. I really did. I pretended for as long as I could that I don't love the way you smell or the way your brain works or that I'm not at a loss for words every time I look in your eyes. You can push me away all you want, but I am not going anywhere." Charles took a deep breath before he continued, "You can't control how I feel, Nora. It's not fair. It's my choice and I want to be right next to you until the bitter end."

"I'm sorry too," Nora whispered. "The last thing I ever want is to hurt you. I just thought if I could make you hate me, the end would be easier for you. It was wrong of me to not ask what you wanted, to not let you decide for yourself."

"There is not a world in which I hate you, Nora Kramer. I just don't want to imagine one without you in it." His eyes traced her face, catching on her lips. Nora pulled him into her, pressing her lips to his. Soft and light and familiar.

"Then don't. Don't imagine it, Charles," she pleaded against him. "I'm still here–for now. Let that be enough."

Charles pressed his forehead into hers, squeezing his eyes shut. Nora could feel his body tighten with words that died on his tongue as silence fell over them again.

There was still a lot to do. They needed to make sure their plan worked and all the paintings made it to their respective ends.

And then they needed to wait for Lucifer's letter.

But in this moment, Nora was content to simply *be*. Her doom was imminent, but this moment was simple and for once in her life she let herself enjoy it–the simplicity of it, the joy of it all.

Joy and pain, she realized, could exist in tandem, that the presence of one made the other sweeter. Nora's only wish was that she had realized it sooner.

Everything she had missed by not letting herself enjoy parts of her life would certainly linger with her for an eternity.

# CHAPTER 33

## CHARLES

THIS WAS THE SECOND time in as many days Charles had woken up with Nora wrapped in his arms and he was certain this was how he needed to start the rest of his mornings.

Everything was simple when she was breathing softly against his chest. Heaven and Hell were irrelevant to him in this moment. The souls that lingered around town didn't distract his thoughts and he could pretend the girl he loved wasn't bound for Hell. All because she laid against his chest and he could feel her skin, finally warm, under his touch.

Nora's hair fanned out over his arm, the pink ends licking the pillow she wasn't using. The sheets of her bed were as soft as her skin and almost the same shade as her hair. It was the most comfortable bed he'd ever slept in, as if it were a cloud.

Nora stirred in his arms, groaning as she did so. Her arm tightened around his middle and she nestled closer to him. Charles reached up to tuck her hair behind her ear as she shifted to look up at him through her dark eyelashes. She still had her makeup on from the gala the night before, which despite his best efforts was still in near perfect condition.

"Good morning," Charles whispered.

A smile tugged at the corner of her mouth. "Good morning."

"You aren't going to run from me now are you?" he teased,

nipping at her nose with his teeth.

Nora rolled her eyes, swatting at his chest. "That was a one time occurrence, never to happen again."

"Good. You are welcome to try, but I don't plan on letting you get very far." Charles rolled over, pinning Nora beneath him.

She laughed and if death could be a sound, he'd want it to be that. There would be nothing sweeter than to drown in her laughter, just as long as she kept doing it. Charles was content to lay there for as long as possible, putting off the world that lingered on the other side of her thick, bedroom door.

Unfortunately, their moment of blissful neglect was short lived.

A pounding on her door had Nora pushing Charles aside and bolting upright, clutching the sheet to her bare chest. Charles raked a hand over his face as a familiar bubbly voice yelled from the other side of the door.

"Nora! Get your ass up. We have work to do. And Charles, I know you are in there, I already checked Carter's room and found it empty. You are involved in this too or have you forgotten?" Charlotte's voice was entirely too accusatory for his liking.

"I haven't forgotten," Charles called back and Nora buried her face in her hands.

"I'll see you both downstairs, properly dressed, thank you," Charlotte quipped before retreating down the hall.

"Sorry about her," Nora groaned, turning to peek at him through her fingers. Charles sat up to join her, brushing the hair from her shoulder to plant a soft kiss to her skin there. His body screamed at him to pull her back down to the bed and spend the day there, but Charlotte was right, they had work to do and if he wanted more of these days, they would have to fight for them.

Nora would have to fight for them.

"You know she doesn't bother me in the slightest," Charles admitted, earning him a brilliant smile.

Nora's gray eyes raked over his bare torso before she said, "I wish we didn't have anything to do today and we could just stay here."

"You, my beautiful girl, are reading my mind." Charles placed a hand on her cheek and pressed his lips lightly to hers, forcing himself to keep it just that. "But we have a certain dark lord to impress if we want to keep you on this side of life, which I fully intend on doing."

Nora nodded, planting one more kiss on him before slipping from the bed to find a sweatshirt and a pair of jeans. He laid back on the bed to train his eyes on the ceiling while she padded around her room naked or he'd abandon all hope of making it downstairs.

Distantly he heard her bedroom door open and shut. He sat back up in her bed, frowning at her absence, light pink sheets pooling around his waist. A few seconds later, Nora was back wielding one of his sweatshirts, jeans, and a pair of his boxers.

He tilted his head in a silent question which Nora answered with a shrug. "I figured you wouldn't have wanted to cross the hallway naked."

"You would be correct there. The last thing I need is for Vincent to see my bare ass sneaking out of your room," Charles remarked.

Nora grimaced, handing him his clothes. "Speaking of, I am going to go down and get a jump on the situation, field Charlotte's questions to spare you as much as I can."

"How can I ever repay you?" Charles asked, placing a hand over his heart.

"I can think of a few ways," Nora murmured, flicking her eyes over his body.

His hand tightened around the clothes he was clutching. "That mind of yours is a wicked place."

"It might be, but you like it."

"I love it," he corrected.

Nora's eyes narrowed, smirk playing at her lips, and she left him there to get dressed, closing the door softly behind her. Charles slipped from her bed and pulled his clothes on.

He took a few moments to straighten up her room, made her bed, picked up their discarded clothes from the previous night–draped his over her desk chair and hung up her dress in the closet.

On her desk was the book she had gotten him. The book that made him abandon his will and give himself up to her.

He needed her to survive more than anything. Charles had been forcibly reminding himself for the past year that this was the likely outcome, the scheduled outcome, but his need for her to survive was now drowning out his logic and he wasn't sure he would survive it. But he would do his best for her because it was what she wanted.

Nora was more prepared for her end than anyone he'd ever known. She had told him numerous times just how *okay* she was with it all. How if Lucifer didn't accept her attempt to fix her grandfather's contract, she would be fine with going. That Noah and so many other people she loved would be with her, that she wouldn't be alone.

Nora and Charles had spoken about it ad nauseam, but the bravery he found in her, was nowhere to be seen in himself.

He was selfish.

Selfish for her.

The logical thing was to accept it all like Nora had, but he had forgotten his logic miles ago when it came to her.

Nora's note told him to ruin this copy, but Charles knew he wouldn't be able to when she was gone. He'd have to get a third. Charles swallowed the pain creeping up his throat and headed downstairs to the library where he assumed everyone would be, only to find it empty.

"Nora!" he called once he was back in the hall.

"In here, young man," Vincent said, peeking out of the drawing room.

Charles was greeted in the drawing room by the three people he was expecting–Nora, Charlotte, and Vincent–along with Death, Andrew and Dylan. Each of them had a grin plastered on their faces. Nora's bottom lip was caught in her teeth, fighting the smile that pulled across her face.

"Happy birthday!" Charlotte yelled, throwing her arms out wide. Before her was a blue frosted cake.

Vincent walked up and extended his hand, Charles shook it. "Happy birthday, young man. It's been nice having you around."

"Thank you, Vincent. I'm happy to be here."

Death was next, pulling him in for a hug, making him briefly forget their quarrel. He was still rightfully pissed at the old man, but he was grateful to have him there, nonetheless.

His friends were next, followed by Charlotte who nearly took him to the floor as she threw herself onto him. When she finally released him, she retreated to the other side of the room to stand suspiciously close to Andrew who watched her with a devious look on his face. Charlotte ignored his stare, but a shadow of a smirk played at her lips as her cheeks blushed.

Nora was next, she wrapped her arms around his middle and held on tight. Charles buried his face in her hair and inhaled, letting her sweet scent calm his very being, the worry in his chest.

"Honestly Charles, if you don't kiss her, then what is the point of anything?" Charlotte huffed and distracted herself by cutting the cake.

But she made a fantastic point so he pulled away from Nora slightly, sliding his hand up to her cheeks, guiding her lips to his.

"Thank you," he muttered against her mouth, feeling her grin.

"How do you know it was me?" Nora pulled back to look him in the eye.

Charles glanced around the room, "For starters, there are no streamers, which is a signature Charlotte touch."

"Should I have gotten streamers?" Nora's face dropped.

"No, it's perfect," Charles laughed, kissing her forehead.

They joined the others for cake and talked well into the afternoon. It was a far cry from his celebrations with his mother, but it was all Charles could ask for. He knew Tessa would be proud he had found his people.

After Vincent had forced them all to eat real food for lunch, they all took a collective nap in the drawing room. The early morning sugar high was not a proper way to start their day and that coupled with last night's activities left them all exhausted.

Nora curled up with Charles in the overly large chair next to the hearth, Dylan was long gone on the settee, and Charlotte was stretched out on the sofa with her feet in Andrew's lap.

Death was long gone, muttering under his breath about

work he needed to get done. After Dylan and Andrew headed home Charles helped Vincent to retrieve the paintings from the car while the girls took inventory, marked off the paintings now in their possession, and prepared them for their final destination.

Nora wrote a note to each of the curators of the museums the paintings belonged to, explaining how each of the paintings had been anonymously donated years ago to the museum here. How after lengthy discussions, the board of directors wanted to make sure they found their proper homes. She signed the letter as though it came from the board themselves.

Mr. Blake called late that afternoon, frantic that seven of the paintings were missing, stating he had no idea who could have done something like this. Nora suggested he give it a few days, file a case with the police, and maybe some news would come in about what happened. The man thanked Nora for her brilliant idea and happily left her alone.

As for the paintings for the collectors, Nora emailed them to let them know their shipments had been flagged by customs and would follow up with an update when she had it.

The next day, Death was back to help them box up and ship the paintings back to where Norman had stolen them from. They had done all they could do and now they had to wait patiently until Lucifer sent his decision.

It all seemed so simple in the end.

Maybe it was.

Maybe it wasn't.

Nora told Charles, one night, about her visit to Lucifer with Charlotte on the day of the gala. They talked for hours about what the Devil had told her, how it was never in her hands to begin with.

At first Charles was angry, he wanted to run to the cemetery and down those stairs just to tell Lucifer to fuck himself, but Nora was calm and it made the hand squeezing his heart lessen its grip.

She was content with the life she had been dealt. She told him about the things she wished she'd been able to do, but more importantly all of the things she was happy she'd got the chance to experience.

They talked a lot of *'ifs'* during those nights. Charles would sit in her bed and comb his fingers through her hair and they would exchange all of the things they wanted to do *if* she survived her death date. Nora laughed and smiled more than he'd ever seen and *if* those were his final moments with her, he'd be content too, knowing he spent them wisely.

Despite Nora's calm, everyone was on edge. A tense air had fallen over the estate, getting thicker and thicker with each day they waited to hear from Lucifer.

Three days before her grandfather's birthday, the letter came.

Crimson paper folded neatly into the same menacing crimson envelope, smelling lightly of smoke. The five of them, Nora, Charles, Charlotte, Vincent, and Death crowded in the foyer, anxious for its verdict.

Nora carefully opened the envelope, as if it would burn her otherwise. She slid the paper out and unfolded it to stare at the words for a long moment. Her eyes closed as she swallowed hard.

Nora thrust the note away from her body, as if she wasn't the least bit surprised at what it said. Charles grabbed the letter from her and watched her walk away from them all to disappear down the back hallway.

Only when she was out of sight did he look down at the

paper and the words scrawled there.

> *A brilliant effort, little star. I was very impressed with your creative abilities in this endeavor. I hear you looked stunning—I would have loved to see you in your dress. But I do regret to inform you that after long consideration of your case, I cannot grant your wish to stay above. I am short a few souls, so I have to take what I can get and you are too sweet to pass up. See you soon.*

XOXO,
Lucifer

The four of them were stunned into silence. Vincent left the group too, opting to head outside, rather than stay in the house. Death followed him, but Charles knew they weren't headed anywhere together.

Charles's eyes fluttered closed, a tear making its way down his cheek. When he opened them again, he found Charlotte silently crying in front of him. The pain on her face was enough to crack his chest open and rip his heart out, but Charles fought the urge to fall to the ground and instead pulled Charlotte into his arms.

They cried together, arms tight around each other. Charles didn't know how long they stood there, but at some point the sound of the piano filtered down the hall.

'*Listen well, Charles Riley, I may never play again.*' Nora had told him once.

This song was a sad one, downright depressing, but still he listened, committing every note to his memory, just like he had the first time because the music was hers. He wished it would never end, but it would.

Nora would leave this earth, taking her music and a part of his soul along with her.

Charlotte released her hold on Charles to head up the stairs, leaving Charles alone in the foyer, clutching the cursed letter. He discarded it on the table and followed the beckoning of the piano.

When he found her, she wasn't crying. All of Nora's focus was on the keys beneath her fingers. Charles crossed the library to sit next to her on the small, black bench, and waited for her to finish. Only when Nora was done playing did she look over at him, her eyes a raging storm, threatening to destroy him.

*Please,* he begged.

*I am already ruined.*

"I want to go today." Nora's voice cracked over the words.

Charles nodded his understanding despite the protest screaming in his chest. Nora would do this on her terms, like she did everything and he would accept it because it was her decision. She was claiming the last bit of control she could over the situation and Charles could not love her any more than he did in this moment.

The one regret he would have when she was gone, would be not telling her he loved her properly. Maybe it would slip out, maybe he would give in, but he would not make this harder for her.

If keeping those words to himself meant her walk down the steps to Hell would be easier, Charles would keep his mouth shut.

But there was one last thing Charles needed to do because if she got to where she was going only to realize he wasn't down there, she'd never be at peace.

"There is something I have to show you first."

# CHAPTER 34

## NORA

"WHAT IS THIS?" NORA looked between the charcoal gray ghost of her brother and Charles's pained face, desperate for an explanation. "What the Hell is going on?"

"Nora." Noah's voice cracked and the sound was that of her nightmares.

Her brother's voice.

The demons from the depths of her mind had found her in the daylight and it was all she could do to not run and hide.

Charles had brought her to the rocky outlook by the river, the late fall air whipping off the water to bite at her cheeks. Nora had been here once before with Noah–too long ago. It had been one of his favorite places in the town. She hated how he loved it, convinced he'd fall to his death.

Nora shook her head, refusing to believe what her eyes were seeing. She couldn't do this, couldn't talk to him.

He wasn't supposed to be here.

"No," she gasped, retreating a step.

"Please, Nora." Noah was crying, or would have been if the ghost of his soul was capable of such an act. "God I've missed you so much."

"You're dead," she clarified for him. For herself.

"Yes."

Charles backed away several yards to give them privacy. Nora knew he wouldn't go far in case she needed him. She wanted to turn and yell at him for bringing her here, for not telling her sooner, but she couldn't.

Charles had brought her this gift, this fear to face, and Nora was nothing but thankful despite her dread.

"You shouldn't be here," she sobbed.

Noah let out a heavy breath. "I asked Death to let me stay."

Her blood turned to ice. Nora had been cleaning up Death's mess for *months*, and not once did she believe she'd have to take her own brother down to Hell because of his fuck up.

She wouldn't.

*Couldn't.*

"I cannot believe he—"

"Don't blame him, Nora. He did what I asked him to do. This is my doing. Not his."

Nora's lip trembled. "I thought you were down there all this time."

"Death told me everything our grandfather did–the person he was. I didn't believe him at first, but when I realized he was taking me to Hell, I realized he might be right. I had done everything I could to be good, to get into Heaven where I knew you would eventually end up, but there I was–being walked to the gates of Hell. Death said everyone was down there too–Carter, Izzy, *dad.* Then he gave me the option: to walk down those steps with him or to stay in this world. To stay with you."

"You should have gone with him, Noah," Nora whispered.

Noah frowned. "I wanted to keep an eye on you. I wanted to watch you live. Watch you love. Watch you enjoy life." He was smiling then. "I have never been more proud to watch you over this last year, little sister."

Nora's heart broke in two and the pain of it was unbearable. Her knees threatened to give out, unwilling to support her body any longer.

"I miss you Noah." Her tears had stopped. "More than anything."

He nodded. "I know."

"I couldn't fix it. I really did try, but it was never my mess to fix."

"But you made the effort and that was more than I could have asked for. You did promise me, remember?" Noah smirked at her, it was the same look he used to give her when he knew he caught her in an argument. How much she wished to argue with him again, how much she wished to be wrong.

Nora choked out a laugh. "I remember."

"You are going down there aren't you?" He asked even though he knew her answer. Noah had always known what she was thinking.

"I am."

"Take me with you then," Noah said.

It was simple really, this end.

Nora had failed to save herself and while she was leaving people she loved behind, she wouldn't be doing this alone.

She'd see her grandfather again. Izzy. Carter. The rest of them.

This was the best case scenario, really. There would be no dragging Noah anywhere because they would go together. Her sun and his star would spend eternity by each other's sides, exactly as they were meant to. Shining on one another, basking in the other's light.

"I really thought I could beat this, Noah."

"I know, little star."

Tears burned in streaks down Nora's cheeks. "I'm so sorry."

Noah's face twisted in confusion. "Why are you sorry?"

"Because I promised you. I promised you that I would find a way to live and I failed." Nora's hands were numb, but she was sweating under the layers sheilding her from the cold.

Noah tilted his head. "Didn't you though?"

Nora stilled. Noah always had a way of saying exactly what she needed to hear with the least amount of words. She *had* lived—just not in the way she thought he'd intended.

Nora thought the promise to her brother meant her life, to survive this wretched curse and not join her family in Hell, but he hadn't meant that at all.

Realization flooded her bones that Noah's goal wasn't for her to survive, it was for her to *live*. Living was different from surviving in that way—where surviving simply meant that one was alive, breathing, heart beating, but living was putting in effort. It was being present. It was enjoying it all.

Nora's eyes drifted over to where Charles stood, hands shoved in his pockets, with his perpetually blushed cheeks and shadow of a smile on his face. She laughed at herself thinking about how a year ago she wanted nothing to do with the sunshiney boy who showed up at her door and now Nora felt there wasn't enough time in the world to know him as thoroughly as she needed too.

"I guess, in a way, I did."

"Then be proud of yourself, Nora. Know that I am." Noah grinned at her, showing off the dimple they shared, the one remaining trait of their father. "Are you ready?"

She let out a deep breath to steady herself. "Let's do this."

Nora looked back over to Charles and nodded. The three of

them walked silently to the cemetery. The town was quiet, as if the souls knew what they were doing, as if the people did too.

A silent march.

A mournful goodbye.

The wind picked up behind them in a gentle urge to keep going. The three of them walked through the park, rounding the entrance to the cemetery. Not a single person lingered at any of the graves and Nora thought for a moment that she needed to stop and say goodbye to Noah—but he was right next to her, walking (well floating) on her left.

Nora thought of each of her "goodbyes" and the letter she had left Charlotte in Izzy's room. Saying goodbye in person would have rendered her incapable of leaving at all. Her friend deserved more, infinitely more than Nora had to give her. The letter had been short and to the point, because in the end it was simple.

> *Char,*
>
> *I love you.*
> *There isn't much more to it than that. You are my best friend, and there are not enough words, not enough lifetimes, to properly express what you mean to me. You have altered my life, Charlotte Hayes, and I am eternally grateful.*
> *It was my greatest pleasure to know you.*
>
> *Eternally yours,*
> *Nora*

She had left Vincent a note too, but there weren't enough

words for the caretaker either. He deserved the world and more, all of which he would find when the lawyers read him the will. Nora had left everything to him to decide what to do with. He needn't keep the house if he didn't want to. Could burn it to the ground for all she cared, just as long as he found peace in it.

Nora had said all she needed to say to him that morning after the initial shock of Lucifer's letter had worn off. Neither of them cried—they were prepared for this. The old man simply hugged her and thanked her and told her he loved her.

She echoed it all.

The two of them had lost them all together and managed to get through it. Nora had no doubt Vincent would get through this too.

. As for Death, he had been nowhere to be found. After he heard her fate, the immortal disappeared and Nora hadn't seen him again. Charles promised to say a proper goodbye for her and give Death the letter she left for him.

The three of them came to a stop in front of the mausoleum, Nora pressed her palm against the warm stone. The marble slab shifted under her touch one last time as Noah floated through the open doorway.

"Take your time, little star," Noah said over his shoulder, making his way to the back of the chamber to wait.

Nora and Charles stood hand in hand on the threshold of this world and the next, neither of them able to move. Charles squeezed her hand, but it felt like he was squeezing her heart.

Her chest tightened, catching her breath in her throat and Nora realized she had to tell him. Even if telling him would damn him, break him. Even if her words cleaved his chest in two. She had to do it because if Charles had taught her anything, it was that you had to take your joy where it was. Regardless if it was hard to find.

*Especially* if it was hard to find.

Love was the reason for all her pain. There was no love without pain and subsequently no pain without love. The two sweetened each other in that way–each the byproduct of the other. To experience one was to endure the latter.

Nora thought she could avoid the bad, if she avoided the good, but that was no way to live. In the end she was grateful for the love in her life, despite the fact there was no piecing her soul back together. It would remain broken like a vase shattered on the ground.

This was the unfortunate side effect of the last year–this hurt that she had been putting off and pretending wouldn't come because Charles had made her *hope*.

Made her hope it wouldn't end this way.

Nora turned and pulled his face to hers. His arms wrapped around her pressing her tight to him. Slowly, warmth eased into her bones, softening her muscles. The frost that coated her heart melted off and as it did, she felt the joy that had always been there. It was an overwhelming bliss that bloomed in her chest whenever she saw Charles's messy hair, or caught him looking at her like she was the sun herself and not some distant, dimly lit star.

"I'm out of time," Nora breathed when she pulled herself from Charles, but she didn't get far as his arms refused to let her go. "And in a terrible turn of events, I want more of it. I want more time with you, Charles. It is not enough to know you today when I crave to know you tomorrow too."

He rested his forehead against hers and shook his head lightly, the movement brushed his nose over hers, wetting it in the process. Nora hadn't realized he was crying. Hadn't realized she was crying too.

"I should be cross with you for making me love you, but not even the smallest part of me can. Because from the first time I met you, I knew there was no going back. Your mind, your heart, your fury. You are marked forever on my soul and I love you, Nora Kramer."

She pressed her lips to his again, lightly this time. An action far too familiar. Far too foreign. "I love you too, Charles Riley," Nora whispered against him.

"Find me in your next life," he smirked, "if you remember me."

"I'd know you in any lifetime," Nora admitted in benediction. "There is no making of me without you."

Nora pried herself from Charles and the absence of him chilled her bones. He had promised to stay on this side of the door, that he wouldn't enter with her, and she knew he would stay put, even if it tore his soul in half. Because despite his unrelenting need to do the right thing, to exact optimistic permanence, he would heed her wish for him to live.

Noah floated down the stairs in front of Nora's final descent into Hell. The landing was familiar. Damp and smokey and sweltering. Nora and Noah exchanged a look as the gates shuddered open and she wished more than anything that she could hold onto him in this form, but she stood quietly next to her brother and waited for Lucifer to emerge from his realm.

The cacophony of voices tumbled through the gates with a plume of smoke. Lucifer emerged buoyantly, crossing the platform to greet them.

The Devil was wearing his usual crimson suit and no shirt. His pale, bare chest glistened in the dim orange light. Nora couldn't decide what made her more uncomfortable about his presence–his lack of shoes or the sinister smirk that never left his face.

"I am happy you were so amenable to my decision. I would have hated to come to get you myself." Lucifer's black eyes slid over her like he was imagining just how sweet her soul would taste. When he was satisfied with what he saw, his attention shifted to Noah beside her. "Even better, you brought me your brother. I have been missing him."

Nora's muscles shuddered as she watched the Devil lick his lips. She wanted to smack the look off his face, but she told herself she'd go quietly–for the most part.

"You could have mentioned my brother wasn't down here this whole time," Nora seethed.

"Where would be the fun in that?" Lucifer pouted.

Distantly, from the top of the stairs behind her, Nora heard screaming. She decided to ignore it as it was too far away to make out what was being argued about.

"I was going to give myself up to you in exchange for my brother's soul—"

"Nora," Noah breathed.

"And you would have let me, knowing full well he wasn't down here."

"Yes," Lucifer said simply.

Nora bit her bottom lip. The heat was cooking her, or rather her anger was boiling her from the inside out.

"Perfect. Let's just get this over with." She looked to Noah who was watching her, his eyebrows were pulled together and his grayed out blue eyes were glassy. Nora knew he was crying again, she could feel his pain as if it were her own. In a way it was, but as for her own tears, she'd shed them all.

She was empty. Even the ever present rage inside her had finally fizzled out.

Lucifer's smirk twisted even further, darkening his face. "Right this way, then."

Nora took one step forward when the shouting behind her rushed down the stairs.

"STOP. DON'T GO WITH HIM!"

She turned to find Death, frantic and disheveled. His perfectly combed hair looked more like Charles's, his green eyes bloodshot. Nora had never seen Death like this, never thought it possible. It was more alarming than the fact that she was about to willingly walk into Hell and surrender her soul.

"Don't go, Nora. Don't go." Death's breaths heaved out of him as he reached the bottom of the stairs and ran over to her. Before she could register, his arms were around her, pressing her into his chest. Death smelled of burnt sage and Nora realized that in all her years of knowing the immortal, she had never once hugged him, so she wrapped her arms around his boney body for the first and last time.

"I have to go, Death. It's already done," Nora muttered into his chest.

"It's not and you don't have to." He released her to hold her at arm's length.

"We've known this was coming," she reminded him, confused how she ended up the more logical of the two of them.

Death shook his head frantically. Nora looked to her brother who just shrugged. Lucifer on the other hand, tapped his foot and checked a watch he wasn't wearing.

"You aren't hearing me."

"You aren't making sense."

His breathing finally relaxed as he said, "It's me for you. *That* is what I am saying."

Nora's mouth fell open and she tried to take a step away from Death and his lapsing sanity, but he held on.

"Oh, intrigue," Lucifer said from behind Death, his voice like hot oil.

"No," she stated, she couldn't let him do this.

"I've thought about this Nora. I am a coward and an idiot and many other things, but *this* I can do. I can make all of it right by doing this one thing. For you."

Nora's mind was reeling from his words. She heard him clearly, but she wouldn't accept it. "You can't just give yourself up to him."

"He most certainly can," Lucifer unhelpfully chimed in at the same time Death said, "I can."

"What do you mean?" she asked.

"Listen to me, Nora. You are going to walk up those stairs and get the fuck out of here and never come back. I am going to go with Noah and Lucifer." She tried to shake her head, to protest, to do anything that would result in him giving up this insane idea, but her body wouldn't move. Paralyzed with fear, with oncoming grief, with morbid relief. "You don't deserve this. None of you deserved this," Death looked briefly to Noah, "but you can live. You can find out the person you are without all this pain and horror."

"I can't leave Noah." Tears Nora thought she had run out of slipped like molten lava down her cheeks.

"You can," Noah spoke finally, pulling her attention to him. "Do what he says Nora."

"I haven't always made the best decisions," Death admitted, "but I can do this and you can have your life."

"What am I supposed to do without you?" Nora sobbed.

Death laughed, "Little star, you have so much waiting for you, so much you shouldn't have to give up just because someone else made poor decisions. I have lived a long, long life. There is nothing more out of it that I need. You, on the other hand, won't live as long as me, but you still have many years ahead of you. Years that will be good to you, years that you will love."

Nora didn't know what to say to him, didn't know how to protest, didn't know how to thank him.

"Noah." She looked to her brother and Death finally dropped his hands.

"It's okay Nora," Noah assured her. "It's okay that you want to live. You promised me, remember?"

She nodded, unable to audibly confirm, wishing she had never made such ill thought promises.

"Then go, let me go."

"I love you, you know that?"

Noah smiled fully, showing off his dimple one last time. "Of course I know that, or you wouldn't be you. I love you too, little sister, you were always the best of us."

He floated over to join Lucifer as a sob ripped from her throat. Nora's mind jumped to Charles–on how Death's absence would affect him. It wasn't fair he would have to lose Death because of her. Nora always had an expiration date and Charles knew he would lose her at some point, but not Death.

Death wasn't supposed to leave him.

"Wait, what about Charles? " Nora's tears burned down her cheeks as she faced Death one last time.

The immortal placed a hand on her cheek and she realized for the first time that his hands were cold. "You, little star, have done more for that boy than I ever could and I know you will take care of him, just as he will take care of you."

"You can't leave him," Nora choked.

"I'm not leaving him," Death smiled fully, his voice hoarse, "I am giving him you."

With his final words, Death kissed Nora on the forehead and strode across the platform to follow Noah and Lucifer. She sank to her knees as the gates closed, shutting two parts of her soul behind them. Nora looked to the stairs that would take her home and wondered if she could make it up.

But Charles and Charlotte and Vincent were all up there. They were all waiting on her to come back to them and finally there it was–the strength she needed to get to her feet and climb.

To fight for her life one last time.

# CHAPTER 35

## DEATH

THE THIRD AND fINAL time Death was sweet to Nora, he saved her.

In the end it wasn't a hard decision.

In fact it was very simple.

Death's life for Nora's.

He had lived a long, exhausting, seemingly insignificant existence. In truth, Death was tired. He was tired of his job, of doing nothing, of watching people leave him. A part of him hated himself for leaving Nora and Charles, felt selfish for it.

The boy had protested and screamed and begged him not to go, but Death was certain he'd understand eventually. Death may be leaving him, but ultimately he was giving him a sweeter gift.

In the last year Death watched Nora–from a distance, of course–fall in love with life, fall in love with Charles. He watched Charles–from a closer distance–accept the sharper parts of himself and learn to fight for what he wanted.

Nora was the best version of herself. The years had not been kind to her, that was obvious, but she was fighting again, fighting to live. She was no longer just surviving, getting by on the sheer fact that her heart was beating inside her chest, but rather craving new experiences. Nora was going to the museum again, she was playing the piano, taking photos, willingly spending time with people. Death couldn't ask for more from her if he wanted to.

Charles on the other hand was fighting too–albeit in a different manner. His usual nonchalance was flooded with feeling, coated in opinion without censoring his rage. Part of life was being angry with it. To show interest instead of rolling over to say, 'I don't care," because Death knew Charles did. Charles had opinions and they were *important* and to hear them without abandon was music to Death's ears.

He would miss them both, there was no doubt about that, and he would despise himself for the pain he knew he caused them, but nothing brought him more peace than knowing they had each other. That they both had their *life*.

Death knew they would live fully.

Knew they would bask in the days they had ahead.

He could not be more proud of the people they were, the people they were still becoming. Nora and Charles deserved the world and Death was happy to provide.

Immortality had never meant anything to him anyway. Life without consequence, without purpose, was no life at all and a life without death was just that. The promise of death forced a person to live. It forced them to make decisions and face their difficulties.

Immortality didn't afford happiness. It afforded ignorance. Complacency. Arrogance.

There was no reason for Death to care about anything when there were no ramifications for his actions. Death had to force himself to care, to have morals. The rules he had in his life were all rules *he* had put in place, which made them entirely too easy to disregard. The laws of the universe governed all living things except immortals and Death was tired of it. He was happy to surrender his immortality, especially for something this good, this sweet.

Death's morality had never been an exact science. It had never had rules or boundaries to contain its fluidity. It molded itself and formed new shapes when it needed to evolve, but mostly it was lacking. His *goodness* was lacking.

But this could be good, and it could be right, and it could be simple.

Giving himself up would be his final stand against his cursed existence. Death would walk through the gates of Hell and stand face to face with every soul he had dragged down there.

He would tell Charles's mother, Tessa, how feeling her son was.

He would tell Norman how strong his little star had become.

And he'd have the lot of them to keep him company, to relish in the memories of the people they loved–in those who loved them.

Se went with Lucifer willingly, knowing his sun and his little star were up above, burning brightly for one another.

Because in the end it wasn't difficult.

It was very simple indeed.

# Epilogue

T HE CEMETERY WAS QUIET.

*It would be odd if it wasn't, Chuck,* Charles could hear Nora saying in his mind. The sun shone uncharacteristically bright for a late November morning. The birds that lingered, sang in the trees as though the winter wasn't already here. Leaves crunched under their feet as Charles and Nora walked hand in hand across the grass coming to a stop in front of his mother's headstone.

*Tessa L. Riley.*

It had been years since Charles had last been there. He went a few times at first, but then thought it too strange a practice and stopped. Charles knew she was listening whenever he wanted to talk to her–he needn't be at her grave to do so.

Nora stood next to him for a few long moments before she rested a thin hand on his cheek. The warmth was a welcome comfort against his wind chilled skin.

"I'll give you a minute." Nora smiled, gray eyes falsely blue against her navy coat. Charles leaned down and pressed his lips softly to hers.

A familiar touch. A calming one.

She left him there to walk over to her brother's grave. Nora knelt down in the grass like he had seen her do many times before and Charles thought for a moment that he should kneel as well, that it was the right way to do this, but there was no right way.

The right way, Charles realized, was to do what was best for him so he stepped forward and set down the flowers he brought–daisies. His mother's favorite.

Charles rested a hand on the headstone and said, "I'm so sorry I've been so angry with you, mom." An admission that was as much for her as it was for him. Whether he admitted it or not, he had been angry everyday since she died, he just pushed it far away enough to pretend it wasn't there.

"I couldn't understand why you left me. I couldn't understand why you would give yourself up for me, just to leave me all alone. But more than anything, I miss you. I miss the way you used to make me laugh. I miss you reading to me at night. Your book is not the same without your voice."

A tear fell down his face and he let it. "I want you to know I'm happy." Charles's eyes drifted up to where Nora knelt on the other side of the cemetery. As if she could feel him staring, she returned his gaze, flashing him an encouraging smile as blonde-pink hair drifted around her face in the breeze. "You would have never believed the last year I've had, but I think you would have been proud of me, or at least I hope you'd be. I think you would like Nora too. She is brilliant and strong and kind." Charles smiled softly.

"I have been idling for so long, mom, not realizing how stuck I was in not feeling. Not realizing how much I was missing. Your death took a lot from me and I am still learning to get it back, but I want you to know I'll get there. I promise. I love you. Keep Death company for me." Charles patted the headstone and reluctantly stepped away. With each step he took towards Nora, he felt lighter, like a weight was lifting off his chest he hadn't known was there.

Nora stood up when she saw him coming towards her and me him in the gravel pathway. As soon as she reached him, he wrapped her in his arms and buried his face in her hair. The sweetness of her pear scent filled his lungs and soothed the tension in his muscles. Charles would never get used to the feel of her. He let her warmth wash over him, absolve him of his faults, heal his soul.

"How was she?" Nora asked into his chest.

"She was really good," he murmured into her hair.

Charles let Nora go just enough to see her face, to see the life there.

"I love you," he whispered.

"I love you," she beamed.

He pressed his lips to her forehead. "Let's get home, we have usy day ahead of us."

ora groaned, "Don't remind me, please."

Don't pretend you aren't excited."

She scowled up at him, making him laugh. The girl was almost always angry, but there was nothing funnier than when she pretended. Charles draped his arm across her shoulders and led her out of the cemetery, back to the estate.

It had been weeks of planning and working with Mr. Blake who, to both Nora and Charles's delight, was retiring soon. Nora had worked hard for this day and Charles was incredibly proud of her—she was finally finishing the dedication of the wing. Her and Noah's rooms wouldn't have individual cere-monies, but the wing as a whole would be put to good use.

Charles was just happy she would be able to move on, to not feel beholden to a tradition that made her so uncomfortable.

A week after they shipped out the paintings, several news articles dropped around the world about how the paintings had been returned to their homes after decades of being missing. Each article and museum praised their's for their generosity, rendering Mr. Blake's claim with the police insignificant.

The curator back tracked, stating he forgot the paintings were being sent out, that he made his complaint in haste. The following week, he announced his retirement as curator.

As for the private collector's paintings, they were still being "held up" with customs and were unlikely to be released anytime soon.

The ceremony was set up in the long, wide hallway of the Kramer Wing dedicated to Nora's grandmother Roxanne. A riser was positioned at the end of the hall and the mass of chairs in front of it were filling quickly with people.

Members of the city council lingered close together. Sam offered him a curt nod, Lily waved enthusiastically. Charles had come to like Lily over his short time knowing her. She was kind and sat on the council because she genuinely wanted to help people. On the other hand, Charles was all too happy to be rid of Sam's recurring presence.

Nora was atop the riser already, talking with other members of the museum board. Charles made his way to the front row Nora had reserved for the lot of them. Charlotte followed, her arm looped through Vincent's, with Andrew and Dylan close behind.

His friends had been coming to the estate more often at an open invitation from Nora. Dylan was happy to spend time with Charles and get to know Nora more. She was growing on him, but Dylan had always been overprotective of his friends, Charles wasn't worried.

However, Andrew was eager to come over on the off chance he'd run into a particularly bubbly individual. Charlotte talked circles around Andrew, but he seemed content to just sit and listen.

Charles was thrilled to have his friends around more often, for whatever the reason.

The only person they were missing was Death. The immortal's absence was odd and Charles wasn't sure he'd get used to it, but he was surrounded by good people to help him through it. Nora missed Death too, but as always, she kept herself busy.

She had enlisted Vincent to have lunch with Charles every so often and Charles was grateful for her meddling. Grateful to get to know the caretaker a bit more and to keep to a routine, even if his company was no longer Death.

Charles had all but moved into the estate. His flat still existed, but the majority of his things now lived in Carter's old room. He hadn't changed anything in the room, despite Nora's insistence he do so. It didn't feel right to alter Carter's room, especially when he spent every night in Nora's room anyway.

He wasn't sure he'd ever get over Nora being alive. Charles had spent an entire year preparing to lose her. Now every time he saw her, he was convinced he was dreaming. Touching her, being near her, hearing her laugh, were the only things capable of reminding him of his reality.

Once everyone settled in their seats, Nora steadied herself in front of the microphone, taking a deep breath. She had opted for a black blazer over a white shirt, black jeans and white sneakers. Nora had re dyed the ends pink only a few days prior, making them a bright contrast to her dark clothing.

Her eyes found Charles where he sat in the front row, he nodded, flashing her an encouraging smile. Charlotte looped her arm through his from her seat next to him. To his left, Vincent remained his relaxed self in a light, blush pink sweater. The caretaker told Charles before they left the estate that the color choice had been requested by Nora or else he'd be in his typical gray.

"I want to start by thanking everyone for coming out today to celebrate the final dedication of the Kramer Wing. We have met here a lot over the years and I am happy to say, this will be the last time," Nora said, followed by a quiet laugh from the crowd. "My grandfather was a great many things in his life–an artist, a collector, a philanthropist–but most of all, he was just him. A grandfather, a father, a husband. And This wing was built on the foundation of everything he held most dear–his family.

"Norman was a flawed man, as we all are. He had his faults and his regrets, but he never let that stop him from teaching us everything he could in the short time we had with him. He encouraged us in everything, despite our reluctance, and we did not grow up short for anything. Any question, any need, any concern–he was there.

"It pains me that my brother is not here with us today, but he would agree with me when I say that we were all better off having had Norman in our lives. On behalf of the Kramer family, I want to thank you for the support of this community and make sure you all feel welcome here at the museum. It brings me great pleasure to share with you all, one of the greatest loves of my grandfather's life. Art."

Charles blinked back the tears stinging in his eyes as Charlotte held tighter to his arm.

Nora took a deep breath again. "In the wake of Mr. Blake's upcoming retirement, it is my pleasure to announce our new curator, Vincent Mueller. I have all the confidence that Mr. Mueller will excel in his new role and am excited for the direction of the museum under his care."

Applause rippled through the room as Nora beamed at Vincent.

"Next I would like to announce that I will be stepping into the position as President of the Board. This was my grandfather's position for many years until he died and I am thrilled to finally continue the good work he brought to this community. I know that with the help of the rest of the board, we will continue to see this museum grow."

The crowd erupted again. Next to him, Vincent's eyes were lined with tears as he watched Nora up on stage.

"Lastly, we will be providing free, monthly art classes to anyone in the community who wishes to participate. Art is made to be enjoyed. To be looked at. To be felt. The more people we can reach, the better. Thank you all for your time this morning, please stay and peruse at your leisure."

Nora stepped back from the microphone and exited the stage as the crowd of people applauded her off. Charles and Vincent clapped and Charlotte cheered loudly. The second Nora stepped off the platform, Charlotte jumped on her. She picked Nora up and spun her around, laughing the entire way.

Vincent was next when Charlotte reluctantly let Nora go. The old caretaker, now curator, hugged Nora tightly and whispered something in her ear that made her squeeze her eyes shut. When he released her, she turned toward Charles. Her gray eyes shining like a billion stars.

Charles took Nora's face in his hands and kissed her deeply.

He savored the moment without a care for the people around them. She was alive and whole and smiling and he wouldn't waste a moment pretending she wasn't his or that he wasn't hers. They were made of the same matter–the matter that made the stars–and Charles would never let her go.

He couldn't.

They were both okay with death, whenever he came for them, but he wouldn't leave this life without living it completely. Without living it with her.

"You are brilliant," Charles muttered against her mouth. Nora laughed, laying her head on his chest.

Sam wandered over for a moment to congratulate Nora, reminding her the council was there if she ever needed them. '*I don't,*' was her only response. The Hell Hound accepted her derision with a smile before shaking Charles's hand.

When Sam left, the six of them walked through the wing, starting with her room. She explained everything to Dylan and Andrew as they went through each one. Charlotte remarked on the family members she had met, Vincent helped fill in details of the others.

Charles merely followed along, listening, feeling truly at peace for the first time in a long time. Accepting the negative parts of himself hadn't been easy, but there were people around to help him through it, to remind him that they didn't make him any less worthy of happiness. Charles had people he loved, who loved him and he was grateful for this life, for the people who gave him purpose.

The group of them finished up in Carter's room before filtering into the final room of the wing–Noah's. Nora stopped before the door, staring at the sunny room beyond it. Her face was blank, but Charles knew she was fighting the urge to fall apart, to crumble to the floor.

Nora had been avoiding Noah's room since they arrived earlier that afternoon and it pulled at Charles's heart to see her struggling with it. He walked over to join her in front of the doorway, shoving his hands deep into his pockets.

"Going in?" Charles asked, despite knowing her answer.

Nora nodded frantically. "Of course." Her words lacked any sort of conviction, but they both knew that she was strong, she was brave, and she could do this. Charles would be there every step of the way if she needed him to.

"Hey Nora?"

"Yeah, Chuck?"

Charles smirked, looked at her sidelong and said, "Are you with me?"

A brilliant smile stretched over Nora's face showing her dimple at long last.

"Until Death comes for me."

# ACKNOWLEDGEMENTS

I first want to thank everyone who made it here to the end, holding this in your hands. I am so grateful for your time and am happy I got to share this story with you. Morbid Anniversaries was written as a way to get through my own grief, as a need to process frustrating loss. It has been a journey to get this to you. I appreciate you being here.

Next is the biggest thank you to my family, my parents and my sister, who listen to all my interests and new projects and crazy ideas and still support me endlessly. She might be good at what she does, but she doesn't do any of it without you.

And thank you to my beta readers—you all have been here from very early on in this adventure and truly helped this book get to where it needed to be. Your comments and feedback helped me to see this story from a different perspective which only made it better.

# ABOUT THE AUTHOR

Kenzie "K.C." Brooks is an emerging fantasy author. This is K.C.'s debut novel. When she isn't writing, she's taking photos, and when she isn't taking photos, she's reading. You are likely to find her in the DMV (if she's home).

Milton Keynes UK
Ingram Content Group UK Ltd.
UKHW030707021124
450460UK00014B/126/J